THE TICKET
OF FATE

THE TICKET OF FATE

NADINTAVSAN

ISBN: 978-1-0686166-4-8

First Edition

April, 2024

To the woman who is my everything,

Mom, this book is gently wrapped in the gratitude and love I hold for you. In the pages of my life, you are the most vibrant and comforting chapter, the one that gives meaning to my story. Your strength has been my shelter, your laughter my melody, and your love my unwavering light. Each day, I strive to be a reflection of the goodness and resilience you embody.

Your lessons are my treasures, teaching me to reach with steady hands for my dreams, to savor the path with its every rise and fall, and to stand tall, not for the victories, but for the courage to persist. My successes are echoes of your faith in me—a faith so profound that it transforms into a guiding star when I am adrift.

You are deserving of the world's wonders, of every slice of beauty and joy. This book is but a simple offering, a silent whisper of the profound impact you've made on me. Every accolade that comes my way is because you showed me what it means to dream, to fight, and to love.

With every beat of my heart, for all of time, this is for you.

Preface

Every life is a canvas, every decision a stroke of paint that marks the grand design of destiny. But what happens when one chance event—a twist of fate—alters the entire landscape? This book is born from such musings, a tale spun from the threads of 'what if,' and the power of serendipity.

Elena's story, while a work of fiction, echoes the realities many of us grapple with: the tug-of-war between who we are and who we're meant to be, the seductive pull of old habits, and the relentless pursuit of a life painted with our deepest desires and dreams.

As you journey through these pages, I invite you to contemplate the dance of fate and free will, the lottery of life that bestows its gifts in unexpected ways, and the resilience of the human spirit. May you find a piece of yourself within this narrative and be reminded that sometimes, the most significant gambles are those we take on ourselves.

Chapter One

The shrill cry of my alarm sliced through the stillness of dawn, wrenching me from the depths of a restless sleep. I groped in the dark, fingers fumbling over the cracked surface of the nightstand until they found the snooze button. The room fell silent again, but the echo of that piercing sound lingered, a stark reminder of another day begun.

I lay there for a moment, staring at the ceiling where shadows danced in the dim light, cast by the lone streetlamp outside the window. My room felt like a physical manifestation of my stagnation—a collection of faded posters peeling at the corners, a laundry pile that never seemed to diminish, and an array of trinkets that once held meaning now dulled by the thick dust of neglect.

With a sigh, I forced myself upright, the bedcovers pooling around my waist. I swung my legs over the side, toes recoiling from the cold touch of the hardwood floor. It was as though even my bedroom was urging me to wake up, to move, to feel something other than this pervasive numbness.

I padded toward the kitchenette, the familiar creaks of the floorboards accompanying each step. In the harsh fluorescence of the overhead light, I poured stale cereal into a chipped bowl, the flakes clattering loudly in the quiet. There was no milk left—just a sour scent wafting from the carton as I tilted it optimistically. I tossed it with a grimace and reached for the faucet, drowning the cereal in tap water. The first soggy bite tasted like resignation.

Back in my bedroom, I opened the closet and scanned the row of weary garments hanging limply on hangers. They were relics of a woman who had surrendered to the mundane, each piece a uniform of defeat. I selected a blouse—the color drained from it by countless washes and a skirt that hung off my hips just so, hinting at a figure that could be called attractive if anyone cared to look closely enough.

As I dressed, my reflection in the mirror watched me—a ghost of the woman I once hoped to be. Today, she looked particularly hollow, her hazel eyes lacking their usual spark. Her curly hair was tied back mechanically, restraining any hint of personality or flair.

"Is this it?" I whispered to her, my voice barely carrying in the silence of the room.

The woman in the mirror didn't respond, just continued to gaze back at me with those expressionless eyes. She'd heard it all before—the doubts, the dreams, the silent pleas for change. But today, something shifted within me, an ember of rebellion against the life I'd accepted.

"Is this really it?" I asked again, stronger this time.

My own voice startled me, ringing with a clarity that had been absent for far too long. It was the sound of a woman who knew she was meant for more than this, a woman tired of being smothered by the weight of unfulfilled potential.

For a fleeting second, hope flared in my chest, bright and hot, before reality doused it with the cold truth of my existence. But it left behind a trace, a tiny spark that refused to die.

Today was just another day. But maybe, just maybe, it didn't have to be.

"Morning," I muttered, the word hanging lifeless between Alex and me as he shuffled past me in our cramped kitchen. He grunted something that might be a greeting if it had any real human inflection.

"Sleep okay?" I asked, more out of habit than concern, my fingers mechanically curling around the handle of a coffee mug stained with traces of yesterday's lipstick—a reminder of attempted normalcy.

"Fine," he replied, his voice flat, eyes not meeting mine but fixed on the chipped countertop. There was no follow-up, no "and you?" lingering in the air. I took a sip of the bitter coffee, each gulp an effort to wash down the lump of unspoken words lodged in my throat.

"Got a long day ahead?" I tried again, attempting to bridge the widening gap with small talk that echoed hollowly in our tiny space.

"Like always," he said, and the finality in his tone was a closed door. I stared at the back of his head, at the hair I once ran my fingers through, now just another part of the scenery.

With a sigh that felt like it was dredging up years of sediment from the bottom of my chest, I turned away. The warmth from the coffee did nothing to thaw the chill that had settled inside me.

The bell above the shop door jingled, a sound that was meant to be cheerful but had become just another note in the monotonous soundtrack of my days. I plastered on the customer service smile that had been worn thin by time, greeting the shoppers with well-rehearsed lines.

"Welcome to Marigold's. Let me know if you need any help," I said for what must have been the hundredth time that day, my voice never wavering from its trained cheerfulness. But my mind was already elsewhere, drifting to those glossy images in travel magazines tucked under the counter.

"Thank you, dear," an elderly woman responded, her eyes crinkling kindly at the corners. She didn't see the dullness in my gaze, the way my attention was focused on the clock above her head, ticking away seconds, minutes, hours—time that seemed both endless and slipping through my fingers.

I folded another stack of clothes, the fabric whispering softly under my touch. It was a familiar dance, my hands moving of their own accord while my thoughts skated over the surface of dreams I had yet to taste—the tang of ocean salt, the sizzle of foreign sunsets, the symphony of bustling city streets.

"Can you check the stock for this in a size 8?" a customer asked, pulling me back, ever so briefly, into the present.

"Of course," I replied, my smile never reaching my eyes as I retreated to the storeroom, where the silence wrapped around me like an old blanket—comforting but threadbare.

As I climbed the ladder to reach the higher shelves, I allowed myself a moment to imagine it was not a ladder but a plane's gangway, leading me towards an adventure, a chance to feel alive. But then my hand closed around a shoebox, and I was grounded once more, the weight of reality settling onto my shoulders like a yoke.

"Here you go," I said upon returning, handing the box over, feeling the exchange like a transaction of my own vitality for the mundane. The store's fluorescent lights buzzed overhead, casting everything in a harsh glow that left no room for shadows or secrets.

Tick, tick, tick. The clock was relentless, and as much as I wanted to rip it from the wall, to shatter its face and the passage of time it dictated, I could only watch it, counting down the moments until I could leave, until I could return to my solitary contemplation of what could be.

The turn of the key in the lock signaled my return to the familiar. The door creaked open, a monotonous greeting to the same four walls that encased my stifling existence.

I stepped inside, shrugging off the chill of the evening air and the cloak of indifference that seemed to have settled around my shoulders.

"Hey," Alex's voice drifted from the couch, as lifeless as the flickering images on the television screen before him. He didn't look up.

"Hi," I responded, just as dispassionate, my toes curling against the threadbare carpet. My gaze flitted over the cluttered landscape of our shared space, each item a silent testament to the boredom that had crept into our lives.

"Did you eat?" His inquiry was absentminded, void of any real curiosity.

"Grabbed something at work," I lied, avoiding the truth that I had wanted to spare myself from another meal devoid of flavor or conversation. Instead, I reached for a glass, filling it with some wine that tasted faintly of rust and resignation.

"Okay." That was all he said, and I was grateful for the absence of further questions, for the silence that allowed me to slip away unnoticed.

With my glass cradled in hand, I found refuge on the edge of an armchair, my eyes drawn to the travel show flickering on the small screen in the corner of the room. The vibrant images spilled forth—a tapestry of azure seas, golden sands, and the lush green of distant hills. My heart swelled with a longing so sharp it carved out a hollow space within me.

"Look at that," I murmured, the words escaping like a secret prayer. "It's beautiful."

"Uh-huh," Alex grunted, his attention never wavering from his own electronic window to the world.

I sipped some wine, feeling its coolness slide down my throat, wishing it could wash away the yearning that clung to me like a second skin. On-screen, adventurers laughed with abandon, their smiles wide and genuine, a stark contrast to the strained exchanges that now passed for communication in this house.

"Wouldn't it be amazing to go somewhere like that?" I breathed out the question, not expecting an answer, but still hoping for some spark of connection, some indication that we were still alive in this relationship.

"Travel's expensive," came the flat reply, a verbal shrug that extinguished the flicker of hope.

"Right," I said quietly, turning back to the moving pictures that promised escape. In my mind, I was already there; I could feel the warmth of the sun on my skin, taste the exotic spices dancing on my tongue, hear the laughter mingling with the call of the sea. It was a brief respite, a fleeting flight of fancy before reality's gravity pulled me back down.

As the show painted dreams of far-off lands, I let myself indulge in the fantasy, in the belief that one day, I might break free from this cycle of sameness. I imagined stepping onto a plane, not just in my daydreams, but actually doing it—leaving behind the dimness of my bedroom, the stale cereal, the worn-out clothes, and the lifeless dinners.

"More wine?" I asked Alex, already rising to refill my glass. It had become a ritual, this numbing of senses, this liquid courage that whispered lies of bravery into my ear.

Maybe tonight, it would help me believe that change was possible, that I was not destined to fade into the background of someone else's story.

"Sure," he said, and for a moment, just a moment, I wondered if he too sought solace at the bottom of a bottle, if he too felt trapped in the confines of our dwindling love.

But then the moment passed, and we were strangers again, sharing space but not lives, while the TV continued to murmur promises of a world beyond our reach.

I curled my toes against the cold, bare floor, feeling the grit of dust that I had grown too weary to clean. The clock ticked away, a relentless reminder of how time can both stand still and race without mercy. A sigh escaped me as I glanced at Alex, his eyes glued to the late-night flicker of some mindless sitcom, the laughter track a cruel mockery of our silence.

"Did you ever think about us... traveling?" My voice was soft, almost lost in the distance that had wedged itself between us.

"Traveling?" he echoed without shifting his gaze from the screen, the remote clutched like a lifeline in his hand.

"Like them," I said, nodding towards the TV, where actors played out adventures in places we had never been. "Seeing the world together."

"Told you, sounds expensive," he muttered, and it wasn't the words but the indifference in his tone that tightened my chest, a knot of something akin to grief.

"Alex, are you even happy?" The question slipped out, raw and trembling with vulnerability.

"Happy enough." His response came too quickly, a reflex devoid of thought, and I knew then that we were past the point of pretense.

"Happy enough" wasn't enough for me; it was a resignation, an acceptance of defeat. I wanted to scream, to shatter the oppressive normalcy of our existence, but my rebellion was a silent one. It lived in the depths of my heart, where dreams of cobblestone streets and open skies still burned with an intensity that scared me.

"Wouldn't you like to try? To find something more?" I pressed on, willing him to understand, to see the desperation behind my eyes.

"More what?" He finally looked at me, brow furrowed, as if I were speaking in riddles.

"Passion, excitement... life, Alex!" The words poured out, a dam breaking within me, unleashing all that I had held back.

He shrugged, a gesture so casual it felt like a slap. "This is life, Elena. Not everyone gets to have a fairytale."

"Is this how it ends, then?" I whispered, feeling the sting of tears. "We just exist, side by side, until we don't?"

"God, Elena, why do you always do this? Why can't you just be content?" His voice rose, laced with frustration and something darker that I couldn't—or wouldn't—name.

"Because 'content' feels like suffocating!" I shouted back, the sound foreign in our usually quiet space.

"Then maybe you should go find whatever the hell it is you're looking for," he said coldly, turning away from me, back to the artificial glow that offers him comfort.

A hollow laugh escaped me, humorless and sharp. "Maybe I will," I retorted, though we both knew I was anchored here by chains of fear and doubt.

The room fell silent again, save for the television's incessant chatter. There was nothing left to say, nothing that would bridge the chasm between us. In this moment, I was more alone than I had ever been, sitting next to the man who once promised me forever.

It was in the quiet of the night, as I watched the blue light dance across his unchanging expression, that the wave of dissatisfaction crashed over me. I longed for something more, something different—a life vibrant with color and possibility, not this grayscale existence I'd come to accept.

"Goodnight, Alex," I murmured, though he was already lost to the screen's seductive pull.

"Night," he replied, absentmindedly.

I slipped under the covers, feeling the cool sheets against my skin, a stark contrast to the warmth I craved. The travel show had ended, the illusion of escape fading with it. But deep down, beneath the resignation, there was a spark, a defiant ember that refused to be extinguished. Someday, I swore to myself, someday I'd find the courage to fan it into flame.

In the shadowed cocoon of my bedroom, I traced the patterns of the ceiling with my eyes, each crack a roadmap of the life I'd been leading. My body was motionless, but my mind raced through the years, skidding over decisions like stones across a still pond.

"Is this it?" I whispered to the silence, the darkness swallowing my words as if they were never spoken. The question wasn't new; it was a nightly ritual, a litany of doubt that lingered long after the light faded. Yet tonight, it felt like a boulder in my chest, heavy and immovable.

I turned to my side, facing the wall, away from Alex's rhythmic breathing—the only proof of life in our shared space. The emptiness beside me was cavernous, a chasm stretching wider with every breath he took, unconcerned and unaware.

"Where did I go wrong?" I murmured into my pillow, tracing the frayed edges where the seam had come undone. It was a mirror of myself—unraveling slowly, thread by thread. A cascade of moments, choices made in fear rather than hope, had led me here: entombed in the mundane, in a relationship that was more habit than heart.

As I sat on the edge of my bed, the gray light of dawn barely filtering through the curtains, memories of my childhood crept into my mind uninvited.

The house I grew up in was more a prison than a home, each room haunted by the specter of my mother's addiction. I remembered the walls, stained with the scent of her struggle, the silence that hung heavy, filled with a desperation I felt in my bones. It was a desperation I was determined to flee from, to find a life where the echoes of addiction didn't reach.

Alex had appeared like a beacon of hope in that dim life of mine. I saw in him a promise of escape, a passage to a world free from the chains of my mother's afflictions.

At first, his love seemed like a choice—a choice that was mine to make, a love that felt like freedom. He came to me with promises that glowed bright, vows that he would stand by me, support me, be the unwavering pillar I so desperately sought. And I believed him, with a belief that was both naïve and fierce.

In those early days, his affection was a balm to the scars left by years of coping with a parent battling demons. He made me feel wanted, cherished, as though I had finally turned a page to a happier chapter. But as time wore on, those promises slowly eroded beneath the tide of his true nature. His presence, once my solace, became just another false haven. The support he pledged wavered, then faltered, leaving me to face my fears alone.

The man who had sworn to be my rock was now a source of disappointment, his promises empty, as insubstantial as shadows at dusk. I was left grappling with the realization that what I thought to be a refuge was just a mirage, and the love that had seemed so full of potential was nothing more than a beautifully wrapped lie. The happy relationship I had envisioned turned into a tableau of broken vows and unmet needs. I had sought escape, but found myself entrapped once again, this time by my own choices, in a love that was as hollow as the life I had tried so hard to leave behind.

The scent of his cologne, once comforting, now felt like an assault—a reminder of what we've lost or perhaps never had. The ghostly touch of his hand in mine, the echo of laughter that used to fill these walls—where did they go? Were they ever real?

Tears threatened at the corner of my eyes, not enough to fall, just enough to sting. I fought them back; there was no point in crying over a life half-lived.

"Maybe tomorrow," I told myself, "maybe tomorrow I'll change everything." But the words were hollow, a promise made on the precipice of sleep, where truth and lies blur indistinctly.

And yet, as I hovered in the limbo between waking and dreaming, a spark ignited within me. It was faint, almost imperceptible, like the first flicker of dawn against a starless sky. It was the part of me that yearned to break free, to seize the life I dream of when the world falls silent.

"Tomorrow," I vowed, the word a prayer, a curse, a possibility. Tomorrow might be the day I find the strength to shatter the chains I've forged link by link. Or it might be another day just like today.

But that spark—it glimmered with defiance, refusing to be snuffed out by resignation. And for tonight, that faint glow was enough to carry me into sleep, a lifeline thrown into the turbulent sea of my existence.

Chapter Two

The clock above my cubicle wall loomed like a silent jailer, its hands ticking away the minutes with indifferent precision. Each second was a tiny needle, stitching me tighter into the fabric of a life that had grown too small, too tight around the chest.

I used to count down the moments until freedom, but that day, as I shoved another stack of papers into an already overstuffed folder, I couldn't help but feel trapped in an endless loop of monotony. My once reliable indifference had abandoned me, leaving in its place a restive hunger for something—anything—different.

"Another thrilling day at the office," I muttered to myself, powering down my computer with a jab of my finger that felt more aggressive than necessary.

"Something wrong, Elena?" the voice of my coworker, Tammy, lilts from over the partition, tinged with that habitual note of idle curiosity.

"Same old," I replied, forcing a smile into my voice as I gathered my things. "Just ready to call it a day."

"Cheers to that!" she agreed, and I could hear the rustle of her own departure preparations.

The cool evening air greeted me like a half-hearted apology as I stepped out of the sterile chill of office air conditioning. I walked through the parking lot on autopilot, the familiar path to my car offering no solace that day. As I slid behind the wheel, a rogue impulse seized my chest—a reckless whisper urging me to drive anywhere but home.

"God, what am I doing?" I asked the empty passenger seat, my reflection in the rearview mirror offering no answers, just the sight of hazel eyes searching for a spark of something lost or perhaps never found.

I let my mind wander back to the little girl I once was, full of dreams bigger than the small, cramped world I lived in. I would lie on the grass, staring at the sky, spinning tales about the woman I'd become—strong, successful, free. I clung to those dreams, believing they were my ticket out. But here I was now, years later, my dreams gathering dust in the corners of my life, untouched and fading.

Every day, I told myself I'd reach for them, but as the sun set again, I realized I was stuck in the same place, still just dreaming and not doing. I'd become a bystander in my own story, watching life drift by, my childhood hopes still just that—hopes, not the reality I once fiercely believed they'd be.

Then, without conscious decision, I found myself pulling into the convenience store two blocks from my apartment. My heart hammered against my ribs as I stepped inside, the fluorescent lights overhead casting everything in stark relief. The smell of burnt coffee and the low hum of a refrigerated case filled with sodas and beer accompanied me to the counter where a tower of colorful lottery tickets beckoned.

"Can I help you?" the cashier asked, his bored gaze flicking up from a magazine.

"Um, a lottery ticket, please," I said, surprising even myself. The words felt alien on my tongue, a rebellion against every sensible bone in my body. I felt almost embarrassed, as if they'd mock me for saying such a thing.

"Which one?" he prompted, gesturing to the assortment.

"I don't know, the golden one?" I answered with a shrug, an attempt at nonchalance that didn't quite mask the tremor in my voice. I handed over the cash, my fingers brushing his as he gave me the ticket—a quicksilver slip of paper that seemed to pulse with potential within my grasp.

"Good luck," he said, already losing interest as I turned away, clutching my unexpected purchase.

"Thanks," I whispered, though I wasn't sure if it was to him, to fate, or to the wild flutter in my chest that felt like the first breath of a new life. Luck was the one thing I'd never had.

In the sanctuary of my car, I stared at the numbers printed in neat rows on the ticket, each one a doorway to an impossible future. For a moment, I let myself indulge in the fantasy, the allure of change so potent it left me momentarily breathless. The thought of Alex's likely scorn made my stomach twist, but I pushed it aside. This wasn't about him; it was about me and the uncharted waters I suddenly yearned to navigate.

"Let's see where this goes," I said to my reflection, a determined edge sharpening my voice.

With a last look at the ticket, I started the car and drove home, the weight of the paper in my purse both insignificant and monumental, like a key to a door I never knew I wanted to open.

I slid the key into my apartment door, the familiar click of the lock disengaging mirroring something within me. The small rectangle of the lottery ticket pressed against my palm through the fabric of my purse. I'd never imagined that such a tiny act could feel like a coup against my own life's narrative.

"Change," I murmured to myself as I stepped into the dim hallway, slipping off my shoes and padding toward the kitchen, "even the smallest kind."

The air was still, heavy with the scent of last night's takeout, a silent testament to the routine of my existence. But that night, it carried a different weight—an electric charge of what if. I flicked on the light, the ticket now resting on the table as I poured myself a glass of wine, its presence turning the mundane into an altar of potential. I couldn't take my eyes off it; it carried every wish, every possibility of my life.

"Ridiculous," I scoffed, my laugh coming out more breathy than I intended. It was one ticket, one chance in millions, yet it anchored me to this spot. I traced a finger over the numbers, each digit a brushstroke in an abstract painting of tomorrow. The thrill that had sparked in my chest earlier, in the fluorescent glow of the convenience store, now bloomed into a full-blown firework display, illuminating the caverns of my restlessness.

"Who are you right now, Elena?" I asked my reflection in the window, the darkness outside throwing back my image. The woman staring back seemed infused with a strange, new vitality. Her hazel eyes gleamed with secrets and silent promises. I almost didn't recognize her—the version of myself that dared to embrace spontaneity, who flirted with destiny on a whim.

"God, listen to you," I chastised myself, but I couldn't ignore the shift in my veins, a restless current urging me away from the shore of my well-charted life.

The wine swirled in my glass, casting ruby shadows across the white expanse of the table. I thought of Alex, his likely practical words already echoing in my mind, but that night, they couldn't reach me here. This small, quiet rebellion belonged to me alone—a private dance with chance that no one could step on or diminish.

"Let them call it foolish," I whispered to the ticket, a smile curling my lips. For once, the skepticism didn't win. In its place, there was a burgeoning sense of wonder, a tender shoot emerging from the soil of my discontent.

I finished my wine and moved to sit on the couch, leaving the ticket on the table like a beacon in the night. My thoughts churned with images of freedom, of adventure—of a life unfettered by the 'shoulds' and 'musts' that had long held sway. It was dizzying, this liberation, even if it was only in my head. Maybe especially because it was only in my head.

"Tomorrow," I said to the quiet apartment, "everything could be different."

I let the possibility wash over me, sinking into the fibers of my being, rooting itself deep within. Tomorrow, I might wake up to the same life, the same routines. But that night, in the soft glow of my living room, with the heady aroma of possibility hanging thick in the air, I allowed myself the luxury of dreaming.

The clatter of keys on the kitchen counter punctuated the silence as Alex walked in, his gaze flitting briefly over the lottery ticket before settling on me with a mixture of amusement and scorn. "Really, Elena?" he said, his voice dripping with condescension. "A lottery ticket?"

I felt the muscles in my jaw tighten, the weight of the tiny paper rectangle suddenly heavy with significance. "Yes, a lottery ticket," I shot back, my tone defiant. "It's just for fun, Alex."

"Fun," he scoffed, discarding his jacket onto a chair with careless ease. "You're always so sensible, so logical, and now this? What's next, betting on horse races?"

"Maybe I'm tired of being sensible all the time," I retorted, feeling the sting of his words like a slap. We were always so careful, so measured in everything we did. But that day, the boundaries chafed. That day, I wanted to feel something other than the numbing predictability of our well-orchestrated life. This ticket symbolized a rebellion against every single thing that's predictable, boring, and routine.

"Come on, Elena. You know that's not you," he replied, his voice edged with frustration as he approached the fridge. The soft hum of its motor filled the space between us, a reminder of the static comfort of our routine.

"Maybe I don't want to be 'me' anymore," I whispered, almost to myself. It was a confession, an admission of the restlessness that had been gnawing at my insides.

Alex turned to me then, his expression a mix of disbelief and irritation. "And what's that supposed to mean? You're just going to throw away everything we've built over some midlife crisis?"

"Is it so wrong to want more from life?" My question hung in the air, a plea for understanding that I already knew would go unanswered.

"More?" He snorted, crossing the room to stand before me, his presence oppressive in its familiarity. "What more could you possibly need, Elena? We have a good life."

"Good doesn't mean fulfilling, Alex." I could hear the bitterness creeping into my voice, each word laced with years of silent compromises and unspoken dreams.

"Christ, you sound like one of those self-help books!" His laugh was hollow, dismissive. "What do you want? A thrill? An adventure?"

"Maybe I do." The words tumbled out, raw and unfiltered.

"Then go find it," Alex spat, turning away from me, his hands gripping the edge of the sink as if to hold himself steady against the tide of my discontent. "Go chase your damn fantasy."

With that, he stormed out of the kitchen, leaving me alone with the echo of our argument and the ghost of our closeness that seemed to dissipate more with each passing day.

I sank into a chair, my eyes fixed on the small piece of paper lying innocently on the table. The numbers printed on it were meaningless, yet they held a promise of something different, something unpredictable. In the quiet aftermath of our clash, the lottery ticket beckoned to me, whispering of possibility.

I reached out and touched it tentatively, allowing myself to indulge in the thought that somewhere within those digits lay the key to a new existence. A life where change wasn't feared but embraced. A life where my hidden desires didn't have to stay hidden.

The room around me was still, the only movement the gentle flutter of the curtains in the evening breeze. The outside world seemed to recede, leaving me in a bubble of introspection. Here, with my fingertips grazing the crisp paper, I found a sliver of hope. It was fragile, fleeting, but it was mine.

"Maybe this is the start," I murmured to the empty room, daring to believe that chance could lead to choice—that this small act of rebellion could unravel the tightly wound fabric of my existence and weave it anew.

"Maybe," I continued, a bittersweet smile playing on my lips as I picked up the ticket, feeling its potential pulse against my skin, "just maybe, this could change everything."

The soft glow of the bedside lamp cast a warm light across the room as I unbuttoned my blouse, the fabric whispering against my skin. A sigh escaped my lips, laden with the weight of longing and uncertainty. The mirror on the dresser reflected back an image of a woman caught at the crossroads of dissatisfaction and yearning.

"Change," I whispered to my reflection, watching the word shape my mouth, a silent vow hanging in the air like a promise yet to be fulfilled. I turned away from my own gaze, feeling the pull of my thoughts toward the unknown and what could be.

My fingers lingered on the hem of my skirt before it joined my blouse in a pile of discarded routine on the floor. Clad in my simple cotton nightgown, I approached the table where the lottery ticket lay innocently, its presence a stark anomaly amid the usual clutter of bills and mundane paperwork.

The air was heavy with the scent of jasmine from the open window, nature's own perfume mingling with the charged atmosphere of my silent rebellion. With each step closer, my heart paced a little quicker, a symphony for the stirrings of a life less ordinary that could be just within reach.

"Freedom," I breathed out, closing my eyes as I picked up the ticket, letting its texture impress upon my fingertips. Images cascaded through my mind—exotic landscapes, the vibrant thrum of a city at night, the exhilaration of embracing the unfamiliar. My pulse quickened at the thought of adventure, a sense of liberation swelling within me, seeking an outlet, a release.

"Adventure," I continued, my voice stronger now, infused with a daring I hadn't allowed myself before. I envisioned stepping off a plane into a new world, the rush of adrenaline as I navigated streets I'd never walked, conversations in languages I barely understood. The thrill of change beckoned, seducing me with whispers of a life unscripted, free from the confines of expectation and predictability.

I clutched the ticket to my chest, feeling its edges press into my flesh, a talisman against the stagnation that sought to claim me. The room spun with the dizzying array of potential futures, each one more vivid than the last. Visions of who I could become danced tantalizingly before my closed eyelids, a possibilities set against the backdrop of my current reality.

"Could this be it?" the question hanging in the quiet room, echoing off walls that seemed too close, too familiar. "Could this slip of paper be the key to unlocking everything I've been too scared to even dream?"

My thoughts suddenly growing bolder, more certain. "Enough playing it safe, enough waiting for the right moment.

It's time to seize the chances we're given, no matter how small they seem."

The silence of the room enveloped me, a stark canvas for the riot of emotions clamoring within. The excitement that had surged through my veins earlier now warred with a creeping skepticism. Whispered taunts of reality nipped at the heels of my hope, each 'what if' shadowed by a lurking 'but what about'.

"Change," I whispered into the stillness, the word tasting like a promise on my tongue, yet it trembled, vulnerable to the onslaught of doubt. My gaze drifted over to the innocuous piece of paper lying just inches away—so small, so unassuming. Could such an insignificant act truly be the catalyst for the upheaval I craved?

"Stop it, Elena," I scolded myself softly, feeling the tightrope of my resolve waver. "Don't drown in cynicism before you even begin."

I reached out, my fingers brushing against the ticket's edges—a tactile anchor to a fleet of desires that threatened to capsize under the weight of practicality. It was just paper, and yet, it thrummed with potential beneath my touch, an electric current of 'might-be's and 'could-be's.

"Let yourself dream," I urged, and as though the words were a spell, the room around me seemed to expand, the walls retreating from their suffocating closeness. In the quiet, I could almost hear the breathless whispers of adventure, the silent promises of freedom.

"Damn the odds," I muttered, defiance blooming warm in my chest, banishing the chill of skepticism. My fingers curled around the ticket, cradling the possibility like a precious stone.

"Maybe this is foolishness," I conceded to the shadows, "but isn't there a thrill in the folly?" I allowed myself to imagine a life unfettered by the mundane, a tapestry of experiences woven with threads of risk and reward. The thought sent a shiver down my spine, not of cold, but of anticipation.

"Escape," the word was soft, a secret shared between me and the night. It echoed back, not as a hollow reverberation, but as a clarion call to something deep within—a yearning for transformation that hungered for nourishment.

With care, as one might handle the fragile wings of a butterfly, I placed the lottery ticket under my pillow. It was a talisman now, a keeper of wishes and a guardian of the dreams I dared not voice aloud. The linen whispered against the paper, a lullaby of change, a gentle reminder of the precipice upon which I stood.

"Tomorrow," I vowed, my voice steady, resolute, "begins the metamorphosis." And with that, I closed my eyes, surrendering to the embrace of sleep. The contours of the ticket pressed faintly against my temple—a beacon in the darkness, guiding me toward a dawn filled with the iridescent hues of possibility.

Chapter Three

The first tendrils of dawn caressed my face, and I was slowly drawn out from under the veil of sleep. Dreams, vivid and wild with the taste of adventure and liberation, dissipated like mist as the chill of the morning seeped into my bones. My eyelids fluttered open, hazel eyes adjusting to the muted glow spilling through the half-drawn curtains. The room—my room—suddenly felt like a prison, its walls too close, holding me captive in a life too small for the sprawling dreams that haunted me.

I sat up, the blanket falling away from my shoulders, and shivered. There was a stiffness in my joints that echoed the rigidity of my daily existence. I could almost hear the monotonous tick of the clock, counting down another day of sameness. But beneath the surface of this well-worn routine, something stirred—a flicker of hope, a spark of what-if.

My hand slid beneath the pillow, seeking the crumpled slip of paper that had spent the night pressed against my skull. I could feel the creases etched into its surface as my fingers wrapped around it. Pulling it out felt like drawing a breath after being submerged too long underwater. The ticket lay limp in my palm, its numbers a prayer whispered into the void.

"Let this be it," I murmured to the empty room, to the stillness of a new day not yet marred by disappointment.

The paper was both nothing and everything, a talisman carrying the weight of my dreams. My thumb brushed over the printed numbers, each one a key to a door I'd only ever peeked through in fantasies. It was funny how something so small, so innocuous, could hold the power to unravel the fabric of my world.

"Change," the word tasted unfamiliar on my tongue, rich with possibility. But there was fear there, too, lurking beneath the layers of longing. The addiction to what's known, however stifling, was a hard habit to break. I'd grown comfortable in my chains.

I tucked the lottery ticket into the pocket of my robe, feeling its presence against my thigh like a burning secret. I stood, stretching limbs that craved more than just physical release. My reflection in the mirror caught my eye—curly brunette hair framing a face not quite awake, not quite alive.

"Today could be different," I told the woman staring back at me. Her eyes, wide and expectant, dared to dream. But they were also haunted by the specter of Alex, his absence a chasm in this small space we once shared. Would he even rejoice in my potential fortune, or would he see it as the final wedge, the thing that undid us completely? His complacency, like a silent contagion, had already infected too much between us.

I turned away from my reflection, from the questions reflected in those hazel depths. For now, I'd wear the mask of normalcy, let routine carry me forward until I was ready to embrace—or be crushed by—the enormity of what might come.

The ticket burned against my skin, a promise and a threat, as I began the day that could end the life I knew.

The clink of my spoon against the ceramic bowl had played a monotonous soundtrack to a breakfast that failed to interest me. I couldn't help it; the blandness of my morning oatmeal paled in comparison to the electric possibility buzzing through my veins, threatening to override every sense with its silent promise. The numbers—I couldn't shake them from my head, six little digits scribbled on a scrap of paper that might as well have been a detonator for all the power it had to explode my reality into fragments of before and after.

I glanced down at my watch, feeling the pulse of anticipation quicken within me; it was almost time. With sudden urgency, I dashed toward the television, fingers fumbling with the remote until the news broadcast flickered to life. Standing there, in the stillness of my living room, I sent a silent challenge to the universe, a plea wrapped in defiance.

"Let this be the moment," I whispered against the soft hum of anticipation that filled the air, "Let this be the turn of the tide, the shift in my stars." I held my breath, the numbers about to be drawn—a sequence that could unfurl the future I'd longed for, the life I'd dared to dream of.

"Twenty-seven," the announcer's voice sliced through the humdrum of the local news broadcast, each syllable a sledgehammer to the quietude of my kitchen. My grip on the ticket tightened, crinkling the edges as if trying to hold onto the moment before everything changed or didn't.

"Forty-three," another number tolled, and it was like the air grew thicker, resistant to each shallow breath I took. I was caught between the desperation to believe and the compulsion to guard against hope, a tug-of-war that stretched taut across my chest.

"Sixteen." The sound reverberated, a haunting echo bouncing off the faded wallpaper and the half-empty cup of coffee growing cold beside me. I glanced at the ticket again, my hazel eyes tracing the lines of ink that suddenly seemed so profound, etched with fate or folly—I couldn't decide which.

"Thirty-nine…" It was almost surreal how time could morph, stretching out like a languid river or snapping back with the ferocity of a rubber band. Right now, it was doing both, each tick of the clock a lifetime and an instant wrapped up in a paradox that made my head swim.

"Four…" A shiver coursed through me, unbidden and uncontrollable, as my mind reeled from the gravity of this dance with chance. I'd always been one to weigh decisions, to live within the safe confines of calculated risks, but this—this was akin to standing on the edge of an abyss, peering into the thrilling and terrifying unknown.

"Seventeen..." My breath caught, held hostage by the weight of implications bundled within that innocuous number. I was teetering on the brink, suspended between who I was and who I could become if the universe tilted in my favor just this once.

The finality of the last number hung in the air, a specter of change looming over the familiar landscape of my small-town existence. What does one do when life offers a crossroads disguised as a gamble? Do you take the leap, embracing the chaos of transformation, or do you shrink back, choosing the devil you know over the angel you don't?

My fingers curled around the ticket, its texture suddenly too significant, a portent of upheavals and revelations. I was mindful of its potential, aware that beneath the veneer of numbers lay a catalyst that could either liberate or ensnare, gifting freedom or forging new chains from the twin shackles of wealth and desire.

My heart was a drumbeat too rapid, a symphony of possibilities crescendoing to a deafening roar. The room seemed brighter, the air charged with the static of change. The crushing weight of years spent dreaming, yearning for more, dissipated in the span of seconds.

And then, it crashed down. A deluge of anxiety flooded through me, the enormity of what lay ahead daunting in its vastness. My hands, traitorous things, shook as they clutched the now priceless paper, the harbinger of upheaval.

"Congratulations to our lucky winner," the announcer's voice echoed hollowly through the suddenly claustrophobic kitchen. They didn't know. They couldn't feel the seismic shift beneath my feet, the terrifying precipice on which I teetered between elation and dread.

In a daze, I moved, hiding the ticket away in a book—a token of dreams within a repository of stories. It felt almost sacrilegious to tuck such power among pages that spoke of fictional lives and imagined worlds.

My fingers lingered on the spine as I slid the book back onto the shelf. The act felt like sealing a pact with destiny, the click of the bookend a soft sentence to the life I'd known.

The walls pressed close, peeling wallpaper witnesses to my seismic secret. My small, mundane world, once a comforting cocoon, now suffocated me with its proximity. Every corner of this kitchen whispered of a past self, a version of me unacquainted with the intoxicating, terrifying freedom that money promises.

I stood amidst my old life, a specter haunted by the future. The specter of addiction loomed, a siren call to the human frailty for excess and escape. How easily could this windfall become a tempest, sweeping me into a vortex of pleasure and pain?

"Fuck," I whispered, the expletive a prayer, a plea for strength. My gaze drifted to the window, the view unchanged despite the cataclysmic shift within me. The world outside remained ignorant of the earthquake that had just rearranged my very soul.

The clock ticked, indifferent to my internal tumult. Time, it seemed, would march on, regardless of the numbers that aligned like stars to chart a new destiny. But for now, I was frozen, caught between the before and the after, grappling with the magnitude of a secret that could either liberate or ensnare.

The silence of the room was deafening, my heartbeat echoing like thunder against the walls. I sat paralyzed on the edge of an unmade bed, the morning sun casting a mocking glow over what should have been just another day.

"Alex..." His name was heavy on my tongue, laden with secrets and the weight of a decision I had never imagined needing to make. He was out there, lost in a world that didn't include lottery tickets or life-changing secrets.

I knew him—his rational mind, his love for structure, and his dismissal of whims like the lottery as mere foolishness. No, he wouldn't understand the storm brewing inside me, how a single piece of paper had become the axis on which my entire universe now tilted.

"Would you even see me," I whispered to the empty room, "if you knew?" The gap between us widened with the question, a chasm filled with unspoken dreams and desires that had long outgrown the confines of our shared life.

I rose, feeling the gravity of change pull at my feet. My reflection in the mirror stared back at me—a woman on the brink, her eyes brimming with a mix of elation and terror. This blend of emotions was both a lover's touch and the edge of a knife.

Stepping into the shower, I let the hot water wash over me, each drop attempting to cleanse away my doubts. Yet, they clung to me like a second skin. The steam rose, carrying with it memories of simpler times when Alex and I were everything to each other. Those days were now fading memories, sepia-toned snapshots in an album I could no longer open without pain.

"Fuck," I cursed, my voice breaking through the mist. My hands traced the familiar tiles, seeking comfort in their coolness. "What am I going to do?"

The initial thrill of victory, the rush of joy—it was now tainted, infected with fear of the unknown. For years, I had drifted in a sea of 'what ifs,' and now, the shore of 'what now' appeared before me, rugged and unwelcoming.

I turned off the water, its sudden absence a stark contrast. Wrapping a towel around myself, I felt vulnerable, exposed by fortune's capricious hand.

"Today's just another day," I lied to my reflection. But the truth was a bitter pill in my throat. With every step, every routine act, I sensed the tremor of impending transformation. It wasn't just about the money; it was about desire, the craving for dreams that had fermented in my heart, threatening to intoxicate my reality with their potent allure.

I dressed mechanically, choosing clothes that felt like a costume, a uniform for a life that was slipping through my fingers. The fabric whispered against my skin, a reminder that everything had changed, yet nothing had.

"Keep it together," I told myself, staring into a closet that held more than just clothes—it held the remnants of who I used to be. I closed the door, its sound final in a world where everything else felt uncertain.

"Nothing will change today," I promised the silence. But the words were empty, a chant devoid of belief. Today, I stood on the threshold of a new existence, balanced between rebirth and oblivion, utterly and irrevocably alone.

The hiss of the espresso machine blended with the morning chatter of the café, a mundane symphony I heard a thousand times before. Yet that day, each note struck me as alien, sounds from a world I no longer belonged to. The steaming brew in my cup smelled of routine, but as it scalded my tongue, I was reminded that everything had changed, even though nothing appeared to have.

"Same old latte, Elena?" Joanne, the barista with a flair for remembering regulars' orders, asked, her smile a fixture behind the counter.

"Yep, same old," I replied, my voice steady despite the tempest brewing within me. I paid with crumpled bills, not the promise nestled securely in my lockbox at home.

As the day unfolded, every tick of the clock, every ring of the phone, every casual conversation was filtered through a veil of unreality. The clack of my keyboard sounded like distant thunder, presaging the storm of change on my horizon. My co-workers laughed and gossiped, their words floating towards me like leaves on a breeze, but I was rooted, incapable of drifting with them.

"Hey, Elena, you joining us for happy hour tonight?" Mark's invitation, innocent and habitual, was a siren call to a ship that had already set sail for new shores.

"Maybe next time," I murmured, my gaze fixed on the spreadsheet before me, a mosaic of numbers that paled in comparison to the digits seared in my memory.

The life I known, predictable in its monotony, could be discarded, a snake shedding its old, worn skin. I stood at a crossroads, with the power to redefine my existence. The temptation to walk away from it all, to be the benefactor of some grand, philanthropic gesture, was there. It was safe, expected, noble.

But another part of me, a part that had been dormant for too long, stirred by the adrenaline of change, wanted to take the leap. To risk the comfort of the known for the thrill of the unknown. This money, this sudden, immense power—it was not just a chance; it was a challenge. Could I step out of the shadows and really live? Could I harness this opportunity to sculpt a life rich with experiences, one where every day was a canvas of possibility? It was a gamble, but for the first time, I was ready to bet on myself.

The sun dipped below the city skyline, painting the clouds in hues of escape. The office emptied, laughter and footsteps fading into the evening, leaving me in the quiet aftermath of another day.

I returned to the sanctuary of my apartment, the walls whispering secrets of the life I had lived within them—a life now too small for the dreams that swelled inside me. My reflection in the mirror was a ghost, a specter of normalcy I struggled to maintain.

"Nothing's different," I told the woman staring back at me, but the quiver in my voice betrayed the lie.

Alex wasn't there, and honestly, that was for the best. As I stood in the quiet of our shared space, the weight of the decision before me felt both liberating and daunting. The question of whether to bring him into this whirlwind of change lingered heavily in the air. It wasn't the money that was making me doubt—it was the clarity it brought with it. For so long, I felt tethered, caught in a cycle of monotony and dissatisfaction that I had mistaken for comfort, for stability.

But now, with the promise of a new beginning just on the horizon, I realized the power I held. The power to reshape my destiny, to finally break free from the shadows of discontent that had lingered for too long. This wasn't just about leaving something old behind; it was about stepping into the life I had always imagined for myself, one brimming with positivity and purpose.

And as I pondered my next steps, I was faced with the undeniable truth that I wasn't sure if Alex fit into that vision anymore. Not because of the wealth that was suddenly within my grasp, but because I had had enough of settling, enough of not choosing myself. For once, the choice was mine to make, and it was a chance to embrace the change I had always yearned for.

Night fell, and I was alone with the glow of streetlights filtering through the blinds. In the silence, I opened the small lockbox, its contents a beacon in the darkness. The ticket lay there, unassuming, yet it held the power to illuminate or consume my future.

In bed, the sheets were cool against my skin, a stark contrast to the fevered thoughts racing through my mind. Scenes of what could be flickered behind my eyelids—travel, luxury, freedom—all tinged with an undercurrent of fear. What if this newfound wealth became an addiction, a craving for more that could never be sated?

"Who will I become?" I whispered to the shadows.

The choices loomed, daunting in their vastness. Would I succumb to the seduction of excess, or find the strength to forge a path true to the woman I wanted to be?

Sleep eluded me, chased away by visions both fantastical and frightening. I hovered at the edge of tomorrow, my heart yearning for the leap, even as my mind recoiled.

"Ready or not," I breathed into the stillness, confronting the precipice of my new existence.

I was Elena, and my life was a question mark, punctuated by the heartbeat of chance.

Chapter Four

Waking up felt like a déjà vu, a relentless echo of the same, unvaried day. For a moment, the reality of my lottery win had slipped my mind, buried under the weight of routine. Then, like a sunrise after a long night, the memory of it all rushed back, illuminating every corner of possibility that lay ahead.

With this resurgence of hope, I decided to tell Alex about the win. A part of me wondered if our dull existence, the broken promises, were merely byproducts of circumstances, of financial strains we couldn't escape. Perhaps, with this newfound fortune, we could rewrite our story.

Lost in thought, the sharp whisper of an envelope sliding under the door had snapped me back to reality. It was addressed to me, "For Elena." My mind raced—was this about the lottery? Could it be the promised check, or something far less welcome? Rumors spread fast, and not all intentions are kind.

My heart hammered against my chest, a mix of fear and anticipation making it hard to even breathe. I stared at the envelope, torn between wanting to know its contents and fearing what truths it might unveil.

Finally, curiosity overpowered fear. I tore it open, and what I found inside sent a chill down my spine. It was not what I expected, not a check, nor a threat, but something far more personal, something that stirred a whirlwind of emotions within me. It was a revelation, one I wished I could unsee, yet one that I needed to face. It shed light on truths I had ignored, about Alex, about us.

I decided to wait for Alex to come home. This envelope, its contents, it changed everything. It was not just about the money anymore—it was about us, what we had been, and what we might never be.

As I sat there, the envelope in hand, I realized that no amount of fortune could dictate the course of the heart. Tonight, there would be confrontations, revelations, and decisions that would define the path of our lives. "Alex," my voice had sliced through the quiet, steadier than the tremor I felt in my core. He stirred beside me, groggy eyes blinking open in confusion.

"What's wrong, Elena?" His words were slurred with sleep, but the sharp undercurrent of guilt was already audible.

I thrust the photo towards him, unable to bear its weight any longer. "This. Explain this."

He took the picture, his eyes widening as he registered the embrace between him and the woman who was not me. The silence swelled as he searched for words, but none came. It was as if he was forcing his mind to come up with the best lie for me to believe.

"Deny it," I challenged, a strange detachment creeping over me, shielding me from the full force of my emotions. It was like watching a scene play out on a screen—disconnected, the pain muffled by a thick blanket of shock from last night's lottery win.

"Jesus, Elena..." Alex began, his voice a blend of fear and resignation.

"Was it worth it? Her?" I demanded, feeling the sting of tears threatening to breach my defenses.

"It... it didn't mean anything," he stumbled over the confession, the lie so blatant it barely needed calling out.

"Didn't it?" I pressed, standing now, the distance between us filled with the chasm of his deceit.

"Look, we can get past this. We can..." He reached out for me, but I recoiled.

"Can we?" The thought of the money that was suddenly mine flickered through my mind, a twisted lifeline offering escape. How naïve I was even to thing we could share this new life?

"Please, Elena," he pleaded, desperation seeping into his tone.

"Save it, Alex." My voice was ice, cutting him off. "I've heard enough."

My heart thundered against my ribs, a cacophony amidst the silence. I couldn't reconcile the man before me with the one I had loved, trusted. The revelation of his infidelity clashed violently with the surreal knowledge of my win—a win that should have been ours, a future that was no longer shared.

"Get out," I said, my voice low, brooking no argument.

"El..."

"Out!" The word exploded from me, a surge of pent-up fury and disbelief.

Instead of explanations or apologies, he simply left. There he was, walking out the door, leaving me with a turmoil of thoughts and emotions. It felt surreal, like watching a scene from someone else's life play out in front of me.

Shouldn't this be more difficult? I found myself wondering. In the stories, this is where the impassioned pleas and promises come into play, where efforts to mend what's broken are made. Yet, there was none of that—just silence and a rapidly closing door. It seemed too easy, too simple for something that felt so significant, so life-altering.

But then, a harsher truth dawned on me—would I have listened even if he had tried? My trust in him had been hanging by a thread, worn down by unmet promises and unfulfilled dreams. Maybe this was just the final cut, the one that severed what little hope remained for us. In this moment of stark realization, I understood that perhaps the ease of his departure wasn't a reflection of his feelings but a mirror of our reality—of a bond too fragile, too weary to withstand the weight of yet another trial.

The room was silent once more, save for the harsh breaths escaping my lips. The early morning light began to creep in, casting long shadows across the walls, but the darkness inside me remained untouched. The lottery ticket lay there, innocuous yet life-changing. I reached for it, fingers trembling.

"Fuck you, Alex," I whispered to the empty room, a vow etched in sorrow and rage. And with that, I began to contemplate the vast, uncharted expanse of my new reality.

Woken by the sound of Alex's footsteps, my heart sank. He wasn't supposed to return before I had the chance to leave. The nerve of him coming back after everything felt like a slap in the face. We needed to talk, yes, but the mere thought of seeing him, confronting the remnants of our broken promises, was unbearable. I couldn't stand to face the man who turned our dreams into dust.

"Look, I never meant for it to happen," Alex's voice was a blade attempting to slice through the tension, but I could feel the weight of my newfound fortune anchoring me with an unexpected fortitude.

"Didn't mean for it to happen?" The incredulity sharpened my tone as I turned away from him, the bitter taste of betrayal coating my tongue. "That's your justification?"

He paced, the familiar creak of the floorboards underfoot, but now each step echoed the widening chasm between us. "Elena, you know we've been drifting apart. It wasn't anything serious. She doesn't mean—"

"Stop!" The command burst from me, a dam breaking under pressure. "Just stop lying to yourself, to me. We both know the truth." My hands clenched into fists, nails digging into palms. The pain was grounding, a reminder that I was still here amidst the whirling chaos.

The room seemed to constrict around us, walls closing in, suffocating with the scent of his cologne and his deceit. How had I not seen it? The signs had been there, woven into the fabric of our languishing relationship, frayed edges I'd chosen to ignore.

"Was any of it real, Alex? Or was I just convenient?" The question hung heavy in the air, charged with years of complacency mistaken for contentment.

"Of course, it was real. You know I love—"

"Love?" I laughed, hollow and mirthless. "Your kind of love is a poison, slowly leeching away at me." With every word spoken, clarity pierced the fog of my thoughts like sunlight through overcast skies.

He reached for me, desperation contorting his features, but I stepped back, repulsed by the touch I once craved. "Don't," I warned, my voice laced with an edge he'd never heard before. "This is over, Alex."

His face crumpled, the mask of confidence slipping to reveal a man I no longer recognized. "Elena, please—"

"Please what?" My words were daggers now, sharp and unrelenting. "Please forget how you've shattered everything? Please pretend we can go back to the way things were?" I shook my head, the ghost of a smile playing on my lips. Not out of amusement, but liberation. "I'm done."

Turning my back to him, I could feel his gaze burning into me, but it no longer had any power. The realization washed over me like a cleansing tide, leaving behind only the stark truth of my existence. The comfortable life I had built with him had been nothing more than a gilded cage.

"Where will you go? What will you do without—"

"Without you?" I spun around, eyes alight with the fire of indignation and the glow of potential. "I have a whole world waiting for me, possibilities you can't even begin to fathom."

He faltered, understanding dawning in his eyes as he saw the resolve etched into every line of my face. This was not the Elena he knew, the one who forgave and clung to the hope of change. This was someone new, someone forged in the crucible of betrayal and unexpected fortune.

"Goodbye, Alex." The words were final, a period at the end of a long, convoluted sentence. "Just, go."

As he left, his footsteps heavy with the gravity of our severed ties, I allowed myself to feel the full brunt of the pain. It seared through me, raw and all-consuming, yet beneath it, there was something else—an ember of excitement, a spark of freedom.

I had won so much more than money; I had won the chance to rediscover myself.

The suitcase snapped shut, a crisp echo in the stillness of our—no, his—bedroom. I scanned the room, ensuring I left no traces of myself behind, no fragments of the woman I once was for him to cling to. My hands were steady as they gripped the handle, but my heart thrummed an erratic beat. It was done. I was leaving.

I tucked the lottery ticket into the inner pocket of my purse, its weight insignificant yet monumental. Each step towards the front door was heavy with the years spent walking these floors, each creak of the floorboards a whisper of memories best left behind.

With a final glance over my shoulder, I closed the door. The click of the lock severing ties that had bound me, the sound strangely loud in the morning hush. The chapter of Elena and Alex concluded with that soft, finite noise.

My studio apartment welcomed me with open arms and the faint smell of acrylic paint, a testament to the nights I'd lost myself in canvas and color. Here, there were no shadows of shared laughter or whispered promises. Here, I could breathe.

The sunlight streaming through the window bathed the sparsely furnished space in a warm glow. It touched upon the worn-out couch, the small kitchenette, and the easel standing proudly by the corner—a sentinel guarding my most vulnerable expressions.

I perched on the edge of the bed, the springs protesting under my weight. A laugh, tinged with both sadness and relief, bubbled up from my chest. I was free. Free from the man who had sought solace in the arms of another, free from the town that felt more like a well-worn blanket—comforting but stifling.

"Okay, Elena," I murmured to myself, fingering the edges of the ticket that held my future. "What now?"

The world outside seemed vast, an expanse of unknowns that stretched beyond the confines of this town, beyond the life I had meticulously built around a love that was as fragile as it was consuming. Despite the fear that nipped at my heels, anticipation coursed through me, wild and uncharted.

"Small steps," I decided, my voice stronger than I expected. "You've always wanted to see Paris, to taste real Italian gelato. To live."

Images of cobblestone streets, vibrant paintings, and bustling cafes danced in my vision. There was a whole world out there waiting to be savored, experiences ripe for the taking. And I was ready. Ready to indulge in pleasures that were mine alone to claim, to find connections deeper than anything I'd known before.

"First things first," I declared, standing and moving to the window. The reflection that stared back at me was a stranger's— brave, bold, a woman on the precipice of something grand. "Celebrate your win, Elena. Celebrate your freedom."

I grinned at my reflection, the excitement building within me a heady rush. The possibilities were endless, and for the first time in a long time, I was in control of which thread of fate I chose to follow.

"Here's to new beginnings," I toasted the quiet room, my heart swelling with the promise of tomorrow.

I sat at the edge of my bed, the lottery ticket between my fingers as if it were a delicate butterfly that might flutter away. The numbers printed there were more than just digits; they were the keys to an entirely new existence. I had never felt so powerful and so powerless all at once.

"Where do I even begin?" I whispered to myself, tracing the embossed edges of the ticket. A future I had only ever dreamt of was now a mere decision away. But choices can paralyze, and I felt the weight of each one bearing down on me.

With tentative resolve, I tucked the ticket into my purse. The leather felt cool and foreign against my skin—a symbol of the life I was about to claim. I stepped outside, the morning sun casting long shadows on the pavement, as if pointing me towards my destiny.

The lottery office was nondescript, a sharp contrast to the enormity of what it represented. As I handed over the ticket, a breath I didn't realize I'd been holding escaped my lips.

"Congratulations," the clerk said, his voice tinged with routine. "Two hundred and seventy-five million dollars is quite the windfall."

"Two hundred and seventy-five million," I repeated, the number sounding alien and yet intoxicating. A wave of giddiness swept over me, chased by a pang of something darker—an addictive thrill of control and possibility.

"Would you like to say anything for our press release?" the clerk asked, pushing a form across the counter.

Words failed me. What could I possibly say? That this money was freedom, yes, but also a gateway to temptations I had never before encountered?

"Um, just that... I'm grateful. And looking forward to new beginnings." It sounded hollow, but the truth was too raw, too private for public consumption.

"Very good," he replied, stamping the form. "Your account will be credited within twenty-four hours."

"Thank you," I said, a polite mask over the churning emotions inside.

As I left the building, the reality of my wealth settled around me like a cloak woven from threads of exhilaration and dread. I knew then that I must celebrate—not just the fortune, but the woman who had survived betrayal and emerged unbowed.

"Tonight," I decided, speaking aloud to the universe, "I toast to the life I'm leaving and the one I'm about to embrace." I took a deep breath, and it felt like a fresh start. I had never felt this way before - excited but also a bit scared. It was like I was waking up to a new me, ready to face whatever comes next.

And with that, I turned my face toward the sky, letting the warmth of the sun mingle with the tears that slid down my cheeks—tears of mourning, of joy, and of an unspoken pledge to navigate the treacherous, beautiful waters of change.

Stepping back into the studio apartment, the door clicked shut behind me with a sound that echoed off the bare walls. The place was smaller than I remembered, or perhaps I had already begun to outgrow it, filled as I was with the enormity of change. I flicked on the light and the bulbs buzzed before casting their harsh glow over the familiar chaos.

"Time to find something to wear," I muttered to myself, surveying the room.

The closet door groaned in protest as I yanked it open, revealing the modest collection of clothes that had always been good enough. But tonight, they seemed dull and threadbare—a wardrobe of necessities, not celebrations. I rifled through hangers, my fingertips grazing polyester blends and cotton, searching for a piece that might feel right for this new chapter.

There was nothing; even my best felt unworthy of the occasion. I could buy anything now, but that thought overwhelmed more than excited me. What did a wealthy woman wear? How did she carry herself?

"Later," I decided, pushing the thought away like an unwanted advance. "I'll learn to be that woman another day."

With a resigned sigh, I picked out a plain black dress that had served me well at past office parties and slid it over my head. It hugged my body in familiar places, a comforting embrace from a life I was leaving behind. A swipe of lipstick— bright red, a silent act of defiance—and I was ready, as much as one could be for stepping into the unknown.

In that moment, the weight of my choices hit me hard. I realized I had no one left; I had pushed away every friend for

Alex. And for what? It all seemed for nothing now. They were gone, just like Alex, and there I was, completely alone.

I locked the door behind me, taking a deep breath as I descended the stairs. My mind raced with memories, each step a reminder of the countless times I'd walked this path. Alex's face flickered in my thoughts, his charm that had once captivated me now tainted by the sharp sting of betrayal. We had struggled together, our love a fortress against hardship, until it wasn't. His deceit hadn't just broken my heart; it had shattered my understanding of what we were, of what I had endured.

"Fuck him," I whispered fiercely into the night air as I hailed a taxi. "Fuck all of it."

Raising my hand, I called a taxi, marveling a little at the simplicity of the action, now loaded with new significance. The truth was, I could afford this – afford to go anywhere, really. But more than the luxury, I sought the thrill of feeling vibrant, of being acknowledged in the world's eye, a sensation I hadn't experienced in ages.

The driver glanced at me in the rearview mirror, his eyes meeting mine briefly before he pulled away from the curb. I gave him the name of the most extravagant bar I knew—one I had never dared enter before.

"To the Jasmine bar please" I said, excited.

"Nice choice," he said, his voice tinged with approval.

"Is it?" I replied, my gaze fixed on the city lights that blurred past. "I wouldn't know."

He hummed a response, and we lapsed into silence. The city seemed different, like I was seeing it for the first time through a lens of opportunity and loss. The ache of Alex's infidelity throbbed within me, a cruel reminder of how undeserving his touch had been. I had loved with everything, fought for us, while he had carelessly indulged in someone else's bed.

"Here we are, ma'am." The driver's voice cut through my reverie as the taxi pulled up to the bar. Its facade was imposing, gleaming with an opulence that made my stomach knot.

"Thank you," I said, handing him a bill and waving away the change.

I hesitated at the entrance, feeling a pang of anxiety. The threshold before me was more than just a doorway to a bar; it was a portal to a life where I wasn't someone who got cheated on, wasn't the woman scraping by. Yet, despite the tumult of emotions—the hurt, the anger, the excitement for what lay ahead—I knew I needed to step inside, to claim this moment for myself.

"Here we go," I breathed, squaring my shoulders as I pushed open the door.

The interior enveloped me in a warm, golden glow, the clink of glasses and the murmur of conversation wrapping around me like a cashmere shawl. I was here alone, solo in a sea of faces, but I was also free. Free to explore, to indulge, to become whoever I wanted to be. And tonight, I was a woman with a fortune in her bank account and a heart ripe for mending.

"Champagne, please," I told the bartender, my voice steady, belying the storm of emotions within. "The best you have."

As I waited, I allowed myself to truly feel it all—the weight of the past, the thrill of the future—as I stood on the precipice of a life reborn.

Chapter Five

The bubbles danced on my tongue, a luxurious tickle that spread into a smile I couldn't contain. I had never tasted champagne so decadently crisp, nor felt the silken caress of such an atmosphere—plush and alive with the murmurs of clandestine rendezvous and laughter cloaked in velvet shadows. I reached for another appetizer, the taste of smoked salmon mingling with cream cheese and dill, a symphony of flavor I savored without guilt.

But as I indulged, a strange impulse tugged at the hem of my consciousness. My gaze drifted, almost of its own accord, across the room. Couples entwined in intimate whispers, groups laughing over shared secrets—but it was the solitary figures that caught my eye. The single men, their glances tentative or boldly assessing, each one a story untold, a possibility unexplored.

I had been loyal to Alex. To everyone. A good girl, reliable, predictable Elena. Yet here, amidst the heady thrill of newfound freedom, something within me craved... more. It was an itch beneath my skin, a curiosity that demanded attention. I didn't know why I was doing this, scanning for the telltale signs of availability, but the urge was undeniable, irresistible.

"Excuse me," I heard myself say, my voice steady despite the tumultuous storm of emotions brewing inside. The stranger turned, his eyes locking onto mine with an intensity that felt like a physical touch.

"Hi," he replied, his smile cautious yet inviting. Was this what I wanted? This fleeting connection, this temporary salve for a wound I couldn't yet name?

"Enjoying the evening?" My own flirtation surprised me, the words rolling off my tongue laced with a seductive promise I'd never made before.

"Much better now," he quipped, and I could feel the undercurrent of desire in our banter. His gaze held mine, a silent question hanging between us.

I knew then that this wasn't about him, not really. It was about me—proving to myself that the ties binding me to a past life were severed, that I could be someone else, someone free. With each heartbeat, I felt the foundation of my old self crumbling, making way for a new Elena who was fearless, who dared to seize control of her destiny, even if only for one night.

"Want to get out of here?" I asked, my voice laced with a boldness born from the deepest recesses of my being. There was no going back now, the decision made as much by the clench of my heart as by the whisper of yearning that had taken root within me.

"Lead the way," he said, standing up and offering his hand. I took it, feeling the warmth of his skin against mine, the electric charge of contact that signaled the beginning of something. Something reckless, perhaps, something dangerous—but undeniably, irrevocably liberating.

As we left the chatter and clinking glasses behind, I didn't look back. The seeds of addiction, of a hunger for the carnal and the immediate, nestled silently in the dark soil of my soul, waiting to bloom forth in the heat of our impending encounter.

The door to his apartment creaked open, a silent admission to a space that would bear witness to our unnamed desires. There were no introductions, no pretense of getting to know each other; our intentions needed no articulation. The air between us was thick with anticipation, the walls already echoing with the whispers of what was to come.

His hands found me in the darkness, and I welcomed them, every touch dismantling another brick from the fortress I had built around myself. With each piece removed, I felt lighter, more combustible. He pressed me against the wall, and I gasped at the cold bite against my skin, a stark contrast to the heat emanating from his body.

We moved together—a dance guided not by rhythm but by instinct. His lips traced a path down my neck, marking territory with each kiss, claiming me in ways that Alex never had. I realized then how starved I had been for this raw, unapologetic hunger. Alex's tenderness, once a solace, now seemed a cage.

My clothes fell away like shedded skins, remnants of the woman I had been before this moment. Bare and unadorned, we sought out the truths hidden within flesh and bone. He laid me down with a reverence that belied our anonymity, his gaze igniting fires along every nerve ending.

The act itself was an awakening, each thrust a revelation that painted pleasure in strokes of ecstasy across the canvas of my body. This man, whose name I didn't know, played me like an instrument finely tuned to his touch. The world outside faded, leaving only the symphony of our coupling—a crescendo that built relentlessly, demanding release.

In those moments, I found freedom from Alex's lingering shadow, freedom from the expectations that had tethered me. The void left by our finished love was filled with a carnal fulfillment that whispered promises of endless appetites awaiting satiation.

When morning draped its light over the city, I slipped from beneath the sheets, careful not to disturb the stranger still sleeping—the architect of my liberation. My steps were light as I closed his door behind me, the click of the lock an echo of finality.

Back in my studio apartment, the familiar confines greeted me like an old friend. But I was not the same woman who had left these walls the night before. I powered up my laptop, and there it was—an email confirmation, a figure with enough zeros to redraw the map of my life. The lottery win was no longer a dream; it was reality, and with it came a wealth that extended beyond money.

I felt alive, more than I ever had, the pulse of independence coursing through me. The wind outside sang a chorus of new beginnings, and I knew that whatever path I walked, it would be one of my own making. Alex had become a chapter closed, his memory packed away with yesterday's doubts.

Freedom tasted like champagne, felt like silk against my skin, and promised an exhilarating adventure just on the horizon. For the first time in forever, I was the author of my story, and I intended to write an epic.

The cursor blinked on the screen, a rhythmic heartbeat against the backdrop of luxury apartments that scrolled past my eyes. Each one was more breathtaking than the last, high ceilings with exposed beams, panoramic windows that held the city in their glassy embrace, and kitchens gleaming with promise. I felt the thrill of potential with every click, my heart syncing with the possibilities that sprawled across the digital landscape.

"Are you looking for something specific, or just browsing?" The voice of the real estate agent crackled through the phone, punctuating the silence of my studio apartment.

"Something with a view," I found myself saying to the real estate agent, my voice carrying a yearning I hadn't realized was there until now. "I'm looking for sunrises that promise fresh starts every day." I paused, feeling the weight of my own desires, then added, "A walk-in closet is essential," with a bit more conviction.

"And a large bathroom with vanity mirrors," I continued, each request unfolding like chapters of a dream I'd held close my entire life. To others, these wishes might seem trivial, perhaps even indulgent, but for me, they symbolized more than just luxury; they represented a fulfillment of long-held aspirations. A realization of dreams that, until now, felt out of reach.

"Of course," she said, a note of understanding in her tone. "I have some properties that might interest you. Shall we set up some viewings?"

"Let's do it," I said, the words an incantation summoning the life I was daring myself to embrace.

With appointments penciled into tomorrow's once-empty calendar, I closed my laptop, the screen's glow fading like a sunset on my old self. I was left alone, surrounded by the quiet of a night untouched by another's breath, uncluttered by the expectations of those who thought they knew me.

The bed seemed vast—an ocean of sheets undisturbed by any shore. I sank into it, the cool fabric kissing my bare skin, whispering secrets of solitude. My fingers traced patterns on the pillow next to me, finding comfort in the absence rather than the presence. I was alone, truly alone, for the first time in years, and the magnitude of it wrapped around me like a shroud.

I should have felt small, but instead, I expanded—filling the space with the depth of my breaths, the breadth of my thoughts, the height of my newfound freedom. There were no shadows here, only the soft luminescence of streetlights filtering through my window, casting a gentle glow on my emancipated existence.

In the stillness, I tasted the bitter tang of decisions made, actions taken—a cocktail of exhilaration and regret that lingered on my tongue. But there was sweetness there too, in the form of independence that promised no chains, no anchors, just the open sea of choice.

As sleep tugged at my consciousness, offering dreams tinted with the colors of my burgeoning reality, I understood that this solitary night was both a fortress and a bridge—my refuge from the world and the path leading toward a dawn of my own design.

The cardboard seemed to swallow the contents of my life, each object a surrender to change. I wrapped frames in newspaper, the faces of friends and family blurring beneath ink-smudged headlines. My fingertips lingered on the glass of a photo where Alex and I were frozen in an eternal embrace. The smiles we wore now seemed as distant as the stars that had watched over us that night.

I realized I needed to say goodbye to my old life first. There were things from my past that still held me back. Saying goodbye to them felt important, like I was making room for all the new and exciting things waiting for me. It was time to let go and move on.

"Goodbye," I whispered, tucking the memory into the depths of the box. It wasn't just a farewell to a photograph; it was the severing of a tether, the first step along a path paved with shards of my former self.

I pulled out the dress I'd worn on our last anniversary, the fabric still carrying the ghost of that evening's laughter and whispered promises. I let it slither through my fingers like liquid regret, pooling at my feet before being cast into another box marked 'Donation.' With every piece of my past that I exorcised, the air in my tiny studio grew lighter, almost effervescent, as if charged with the ions of potential futures.

A pile of journals stacked against the wall caught my eye, their pages crammed with dreams penned in the hopeful ink of a girl who believed love was a fortress against the mundane. I opened one, its spine cracking like the ice of a frozen lake giving way to spring. And there, in my own looping handwriting, was the confession of a heart that yearned for more—a mantra repeated page after page, "There must be more than this."

My chest tightened, a sob clawing its way up my throat. These books were the archives of my soul, yet they spoke of a life half-lived, a narrative punctuated by ellipses where there should have been exclamation points. I couldn't take them with me; they belonged to a woman I no longer recognized.

"More," I commanded myself, feeling the weight of the word on my tongue. I closed the journal with a snap, the sound echoing off bare walls stripped of their memories.

"Enough," I said, the word a whip that split the air, severing the chains of complacency. I would no longer be a vessel of unfulfilled desires, a reliquary of someone else's dreams.

The mirror called to me then, a silent witness to my transformation. I stood before it, naked in the truth of my reflection. The woman staring back was both known and mysterious, her hazel eyes burning with the fires of reinvention. There were lines of laughter and sorrow etched upon her face, each a testament to the life she had lived and the lives she had yet to claim.

"Who are you?" I asked her, a challenge laid bare.

She didn't answer with words but with a slow smile that crept across her lips, a knowing curve that spoke of secrets yet to be told. Her gaze held mine, unwavering, as if daring me to live up to the promise reflected in those depths.

"Let's find out," I murmured, turning from the mirror with a resolve that felt like the first true step. My past packed away, my body alive with the thrill of the unknown, I was ready to chart the course of the woman I was becoming.

As I stepped out of the door, the chapter of my old life shut behind me with a soft click, leaving nothing but the echo of possibility and the whisper of a name that tasted like freedom on my lips: Elena.

Chapter Six

The city breathed a different kind of air, thick with possibility and the musk of uncharted paths. I sat at a corner table in a bustling cafe, the hum of conversation and clinking cups creating a cocoon for my burgeoning plans. My fingers traced the rim of my coffee mug, its warmth seeping into my skin, as I scribbled down lists on a crisp white notepad – furniture, neighborhoods, business strategies. Each item was a stepping stone away from the Elena who had been too scared to dream big.

"Can I get you anything else?" The waitress's voice jolted me from my reverie.

"Another coffee, please," I said, offering a smile that didn't quite reach my eyes. I needed the caffeine; every decision felt weighty, charged with the potential of becoming the woman I envisioned.

This coffee shop might have been the last piece of my past I still clung to, yet I genuinely enjoyed it. As I sat there, lost in thought, it struck me—my boss hadn't even reached out, despite my absence from work for two days. And on my part, I hadn't felt the need to explain or declare that I quit. It was a silent goodbye to another chapter of my life, one that seemed to close itself without any drama.

I ventured out into the afternoon light, the city's pulse guiding me through streets that once seemed like pages from someone else's fairytale. Now they were open to me, real estate listings in hand, each address a whisper of a life that could be mine. I connected with one of the city's top real estate agents, who introduced me to some of the most extravagant properties available.

"Top floor, great view, natural light floods the living space," the agent gushed as we entered yet another apartment. It was beautiful, the kind of place Alex would've dismissed as impractical, too indulgent for our small-town sensibilities. She guided me through each room meticulously, unveiling a house that seemed to be pulled straight from my dreams. Every corner, every space, held the very details I had longed for.

"Plenty of room for entertaining," she continued, her words painting pictures of laughter-filled evenings and clinking glasses.

"Or just for one," I murmured, the image flickering and fading. The rooms loomed, filled more with silence than potential.

"Of course, a sanctuary for yourself," she corrected, her smile unfaltering. I wondered if she ever doubted her life's choices or if uncertainty was a luxury she couldn't afford.

As we left the building, a pang of something familiar – fear? regret? – twisted in my gut. Could I really sever the ties to the girl who had been content with porch swings and shared beers at the local dive bar? Each step echoed with the temptation to run back to that simplicity.

I paused at a street corner, watching the people around me, each absorbed in their own narratives. They moved with a purpose I both envied and feared. My phone buzzed with a reminder of the next apartment viewing, but I hesitated. Was I chasing a fantasy, draping myself in a life that wasn't truly mine?

"Excuse me, are you alright?" A passerby's concern broke my trance.

"Fine, just... deciding which way to go," I replied, forcing a laugh that sounded more hollow than hearty.

"Always the hardest part, isn't it?" he said with an understanding nod before moving on, disappearing into the crowd.

"Which way to go..." I repeated under my breath, the weight of my choices pressing down like the summer heat against my skin. This journey was mine alone, each selection of marble countertops or leather couches a declaration of independence, a signature on my new identity.

"Next viewing?" the agent prodded gently, sensing my hesitation.

"Let's go," I asserted, my voice firmer than I felt. But with each affirmation, the foundation of my future self seemed to solidify, crafting a person who could embrace her desires without shame, who could conquer addiction with the same tenacity she applied to her ambitions.

This was more than a hunt for living spaces; it was a quest for transformation. And I was determined to rise above every doubt, every echo of the past that dared to call me back.

Once again, the aroma of fresh espresso and the murmur of early morning conversations surrounded me as I sat in the corner of Café Lumière, my notebook sprawled open with lists that seemed to grow like tendrils across the pages. I penned down 'sleek sectional' followed by 'abstract art,' each item a stepping stone towards a life meticulously curated and entirely mine. The outside world bustled, but within these walls, I commanded a moment of stillness, marshaling my thoughts against the tide of change.

"Another coffee?" the waitress asked, her smile warm and familiar.

"Please," I nodded, grateful for the liquid clarity it promised.

"Coming right up."

I felt the day stretching before me, pregnant with potential. Yet there was an undertow of restlessness, a thrumming beneath my skin that no list could silence. It was an insatiable hunger that gnawed at the edges of my newfound discipline.

By evening, the sun had slipped below the horizon, and I found myself pushing through the doors of the Jasmine Bar once more. The dim lighting wrapped around me like a shroud, the pulsating music resonating with the beat of my own desires. My addiction wasn't just a shadow trailing behind me; it was a living entity, coiled and ready to spring.

"Can I get you a drink?" A voice cut through the thrum, low and inviting.

"Whiskey, neat," I replied without missing a beat, turning to face the source—a man leaning casually against the bar, his dark hair slicked back, eyes piercing in their intensity.

"Make that two," he said to the bartender, his gaze never leaving mine.

We didn't bother with pleasantries or pretenses. Our conversation was terse, charged with the unspoken agreement of what was to come. Within the hour, we were entangled in his apartment, a space as unfamiliar as the contours of his body against mine.

"God, you're incredible," he groaned as our movements became frenzied, a symphony of flesh and desire.

"More," I gasped, lost in the carnal dance, the raw energy that consumed us both. This was the fire I craved, the blinding passion that made me feel inexorably alive.

It was hardcore—intense and primal. With each touch, each kiss, I shed another layer of the woman who had been too scared to dream beyond the boundaries of a small town.

Sated and spent, I watched his chest rise and fall with a post-coital rhythm. I slid from under the tangle of sheets, dressing silently, the need to preserve this new domain compelling me to leave before dawn's light could lay claim to the night's anonymity.

As I walked out into the cool air, the city's pulse was a backdrop to my solitary departure. The streets beckoned, whispering promises of reinvention with every step. I headed towards the luxurious shops, where the glow of luxury boutiques began to replace the stars fading in the sky.

In a parade of luxury, each store I entered was a shrine dedicated to the finest in fashion and luxury, and I, its fervent devotee, was on a pilgrimage for transformation. My fingers traced the contours of opulent materials and designs, each piece a testament to craftsmanship and desire. I caressed the buttery leather of a Saint Laurent tote, its price tag of $2,990 a mere number for the promise it held—a sophisticated companion to carry the dreams and plans of my burgeoning empire.

Next, I draped myself in the iconic embrace of a Burberry trench coat, priced at $2,250. It settled on my shoulders with a weight that felt like destiny, transforming me into a vision of power and determination. This wasn't just a garment; it was my declaration to the world of my newfound status and intent.

As I moved through the polished interiors of these high temples of fashion, I paused before a display of Chanel No. 5, $200 for a bottle that promised an aura of timeless elegance.

With each spritz, I imagined it as the scent of success, a fragrance that would announce my arrival in any room.

"Will that be all?" The sales associate's voice was silk-smooth, laced with the sweet anticipation of commission.

"Add the Louboutin pumps—the black patent ones," I said, pointing to the $695 heels that promised to elevate more than just my height.

"Of course." She smiled, approving of my choices, oblivious to the tremors of doubt that vibrated beneath my calm exterior.

My journey continued to the sleek minimalism of an Apple store, where the latest MacBook Pro sat with a price tag of $2,399. It wasn't just a laptop; it was the key to unlocking my potential, a tool that would bridge my ambition with reality.

Lastly, I found myself drawn to the sparkling allure of Tiffany & Co., where a diamond bracelet glistened under the soft lighting—$5,000 of pure, unadulterated beauty. It was more than an accessory; it was a symbol of my achievements and the tangible rewards of my courage to dream.

With each purchase, I wasn't just acquiring items of luxury and utility; I was building the foundation of my new life. These brands, these prices, they were all milestones on my journey of self-discovery and reinvention, each adding a layer to the persona I was eager to embrace and present to the world.

"Thank you for shopping with us, Ms. ..."

"Callahan," I filled in swiftly, claiming the name as though it were a talisman against the past.

"Ms. Callahan," she repeated, sealing my identity with her parting words.

I stepped back outside, the morning now fully awake, and turned my face to the rising sun. Today, I was the architect of an existence far removed from the confines of yesterday. Yet as I glanced at my reflection in a passing window, adorned in the trappings of wealth, I knew the most profound metamorphosis would have to come from within.

The sharp scent of roasted coffee beans mingled with the mustiness of old books as I pushed open the door to the quiet café. It was my attempt at normalcy, a ritual to anchor myself in the tidal wave of change that had swept through my life. I chose a secluded corner, one where the morning light filtered through stained-glass windows and danced upon the mahogany table.

"Your usual, Elena?" The barista's voice cut through the hum of distant conversations and the gentle clink of porcelain.

"Make it a double shot today," I replied, my voice steadier than I felt.

He nodded, his eyes briefly meeting mine—a silent acknowledgment of the shadows beneath my eyes, no doubt darker from last night's escapade.

As I waited, I pulled out my notebook, its leather cover worn from constant use. My hand trembled slightly as I uncapped the pen and pressed its tip against the clean page. The first bullet point etched into the paper—a tangible mark of progress.

"New apartment essentials," I whispered to myself, trying to corral my thoughts. A list, any list, was a life raft in the churning sea of independence I had thrown myself into.

"Here you go, extra strong," the barista said, placing the steaming cup beside me. His smile was kind, but I could feel the loneliness nipping at my heels, a persistent reminder that no amount of caffeine could stave off the emptiness within.

"Thanks," I murmured, returning the smile with a shadow of my own.

I sipped the bitter liquid, letting its heat scald away the remnants of last night's passion. Yet, as the caffeine hit my bloodstream, a pang of solitude gripped me. No number of silk sheets or designer dresses could fill the hollow space that craved something more—something real.

"Friends." The word slipped out unintentionally—a whisper of desire for connections that ran deeper than cashmere-deep. It was a luxury I hadn't allowed myself to consider until now.

"Business partners," I added, scribbling down another item on my list. Partners implied equality, a shared vision, and maybe, just maybe, a shared laugh over a cup of coffee that wasn't laced with underlying needs.

But it was the next line that made my heart skip a beat, "Personal assistant." The words carved out a new possibility in the landscape of my existence. Someone who could navigate both the gloss of success and the grit of reality. A companion in this labyrinth of self-reinvention.

"Someone who gets it," I muttered, chewing on the end of my pen. An impulsive energy surged through me, over the edge of caution, and I reached for my phone. In a flurry of keystrokes, the ad took shape.

"Seeking personal assistant. Knowledge of fashion and business essential. Must be discreet, intuitive, and ready to dive into a world of high stakes and higher standards."

It was done. I hit 'post' before doubt could claw its way back in. The ad was my beacon, a call across the vast expanse of my new life, hoping to find someone who could help me stitch together the frayed edges of my ambition with the delicate threads of companionship.

"Anything else, Elena?" the barista asked, his question snapping me back to the present.

"Just the check, thanks," I said, feeling the weight of the day ahead.

I glanced once more at my phone, at the ad pulsating with potential, and tucked away my notebook. As I stood to leave, the sunlight caught my reflection in the window. There I was— dressed in newfound opulence, yet searching for something money couldn't buy.

The path I was embarking on demanded a version of myself that was refined, knowledgeable, and polished. It wasn't just about changing my wardrobe or my address; it was about embodying the persona of someone who belonged in this new world I was stepping into. I needed to dress with elegance and purpose, selecting outfits that spoke of sophistication and confidence. My behavior had to match the circles I aspired to join, adopting manners that reflected grace and poise.

I was committed to learning—to expanding my knowledge on culture, art, business, and the myriad of subjects that would allow me to converse fluently in any gathering. Saying the right things, engaging in conversations that were both meaningful and enlightening, became as important as the air I breathed. I had to do more than just show up; I needed to contribute, to add value, to make my presence noteworthy.

Networking had to become an art form, a strategic endeavor to connect with individuals who could open doors, offer insights, and become allies on my journey. Being seen in the right places would no longer be a matter of chance; it was a carefully curated plan, ensuring I was a familiar face at gallery openings, charity events, and cultural gatherings that defined the societal landscape of my new life.

Leaving behind my old self wasn't merely about shedding a past life; it was about embracing the potential to become my best self. This new version of me had to excel, not just fit in. She was someone who was not only adapting to a world of opulence and opportunity but was also determined to make her mark within it. The transition was challenging, filled with moments of doubt and introspection, but it was a journey I embarked on with determination. The future I envisioned was bright, but to reach it, I had to be the best version of myself—educated, eloquent, and exemplary in every aspect.

The clink of porcelain and the bitter scent of coffee pulled me from a haze of restless thoughts. I had perched myself in a corner of the café, a fortress built of espresso and ambition. My phone, now an extension of my hand, buzzed incessantly, each vibration a testament to the ad's reach.

The significance of this role couldn't be overstated; this person would be my right hand, my bridge to the life I was meticulously crafting. Each call was an opportunity, a chance to find someone who not only understood the logistical demands but also grasped the nuances of the world I was stepping into.

The first candidate, while impressively organized, lacked the warmth I knew was essential for navigating the social intricacies of my new circles. Their responses, though competent, echoed with a formality that felt too rigid for the fluidity my lifestyle demanded. I thanked them, promising a follow-up I wasn't sure would come.

The next call was with someone whose enthusiasm bubbled through the phone line, their excitement palpable. Yet, as we delved deeper into the conversation, it became clear their fascination was more with the glamour associated with the job than the job itself. I needed someone grounded, someone who saw beyond the veneer of luxury to the hard work underneath.

As the afternoon sun began to wane, casting long shadows across my paperwork, I dialed the number of the next candidate. From the moment they answered, I sensed a different energy. They spoke with a confidence that was neither overbearing nor submissive. Their experience was impressive, not just in the tasks they had managed but in their understanding of discretion, tact, and the importance of privacy. They asked questions that cut to the heart of what I needed—an ally, a confidante, someone who could navigate both boardrooms and ballrooms with ease.

We spoke of schedules, of travel arrangements, of managing correspondence and liaising with contacts whose names carried weight in art, business, and society. But we also touched on the less tangible aspects—the ethos of the life I was building, the balance of maintaining authenticity in a world that often prized appearance over substance.

By the time we concluded our conversation, the room was bathed in the soft glow of the evening. I leaned back in my chair, feeling a flicker of excitement at the prospect of having found my assistant. This wasn't just about filling a position; it was about choosing a partner for the journey ahead. As I stared out the window, considering the possibilities, I realized this was more than a step towards organizing my new life—it was a leap towards realizing my dreams.

I then received a call from a candidate named David. There was something immediately comforting about his voice, a familiarity that eased the slight tension I hadn't noticed I was carrying. Talking to him was effortless, like conversing with an old friend. His qualifications were solid, his experience impressive, but it was his demeanor that truly caught my attention. He listened attentively, responded thoughtfully, and even in our brief interaction, I sensed a kindness and sincerity that was rare.

"David speaking, am I talking to Elena?" A voice, confident yet unassuming, filtered through the speaker.

"Speaking," I said, trying to mask the tremor in my words.

"Your ad caught my eye. I have a background in fashion merchandising, and I've worked with several startups. I believe I can provide the guidance you seek."

As we spoke, I found myself opening up more than I had intended, discussing not just the job specifics but my aspirations, my hopes for this new phase of my life. David's responses were not just professional but personal, showing a level of empathy and understanding that went beyond the call of duty. It was then, in the midst of our conversation, that something clicked within me. I realized that what I needed in this whirlwind of change wasn't just an assistant. I needed someone who could also be a friend, someone who saw me, not just the job or the lifestyle that came with it.

David, with his easy manner and genuine warmth, seemed to offer the best of both worlds. As we concluded our call, I found myself smiling, a sense of peace settling over me. The decision suddenly seemed clear. In David, I felt I would have not just the professional support I needed but also a companion for the journey ahead. His familiarity, his kindness, it was what I had been seeking without even realizing it. In that moment, choosing David felt like choosing a path that was aligned not just with my professional goals but with my personal well-being too.

"Meet me tomorrow at Café Rosetta, 10 AM. We'll talk more then." I hung up feeling a spark of hope ignite within me.

My coffee grew cold as I scribbled down notes, plans, and aspirations. Lists became my lifeline, a way to tether my soaring dreams to the tangible world. A new apartment, minimalistic yet chic; a business model that shimmered with promise. The urgency to escape my former self was palpable, squeezing around my chest like a corset laced with the steel threads of anticipation.

But beneath the veneer of excitement lay an undercurrent of fear—a silent whisper questioning whether I was constructing a new life or simply dressing up old insecurities in designer labels. Each decision felt like walking a tightrope between who I was and who I wanted to be.

"Are you all right, miss? You seem... intense," the barista remarked, his eyes reflecting genuine concern.

"I'm fine," I lied, plastering on a smile that didn't quite reach my eyes. "Just planning my future."

"Let it not just be a plan," he said softly before retreating behind the counter.

I stared at the screen, watching messages pour in. Each caller vying to become the Virgil to my Dante in this modern-day inferno where desires burned hot and bright, threatening to consume me if I lost my way. And yet, amidst the cacophony of voices, it was David's assured tone that echoed in my mind.

"Help me transform," I whispered to my reflection in the window, a plea to the universe—or at least to a stranger named David—to guide me through this labyrinth of change. But as the fervor of new beginnings settled into a quiet lull, I was left with a stark realization.

The rush of breaking free, the thrill of anonymous flesh, the allure of crisp banknotes—they were all ephemeral highs, leaving behind an emptiness that echoed through my newfound palace of solitude. The lists in front of me, once brimming with potential, now seemed like little more than thinly veiled distractions from the hollow echo of my heart's deeper chambers.

"More than this," I murmured, folding the paper away, a silent vow that tomorrow, with David or without him, I would begin to weave the fabric of a life filled with more than just the fleeting satisfaction of surface-level indulgences. It was time to unravel the complexities of Elena, to discover the worth beyond the reflection, beyond the social status.

As I rose from my seat, my legs felt unsteady, but my resolve was iron-clad. This was more than a search for assistance; it was a journey to the core of my being, a venture into uncharted territories of the soul. And I knew, with both trepidation and exhilaration, that there was no turning back.

Exiting into the bustling street, the weight of solitude settled over me like a shroud. I walked without direction until I found myself outside the familiar neon glow of Jasmine Bar. The pull was magnetic, an ache within that demanded attention.

Inside, the thrum of music and chatter swirled around me, a maelstrom of escape. Bodies pressed close in the dim light, each seeking their own solace in the anonymity of touch. It wasn't long before I felt the heat of a gaze, turning to meet eyes that promised to momentarily fill the void.

"Care for a drink?" His voice slid over me, smooth and enticing.

"Lead the way," I replied, my mouth curving into a semblance of desire.

Our conversation was superfluous, our intentions clear. Drinks turned to fevered kisses, hands roaming with urgency as we stumbled into the night, toward his place—an address I wouldn't remember come morning.

In the impassioned haze, I surrendered to sensation, to the raw, primal need clawing beneath my skin. Our bodies collided with a ferocity that bordered on desperation, each movement a mutual grasping for a lifeline in the tempest of our own making.

But as dawn crept through the blinds, casting stripes of light across tangled sheets and sweat-slicked skin, the hollowness returned with a vengeance. Silently, I dressed, stepping softly over the discarded remnants of our encounter.

The door clicked shut behind me, sealing away the echo of passion that already felt like a distant memory. I walked, the cool air sobering, as reflections danced across my mind's surface.

"Is this freedom?" I whispered to no one, my voice barely there.

The city stretched out before me, gleaming with promises and pitfalls. I had leaped, but the landing was nowhere in sight. The dizzying changes—the money, the sex, the luxury—they were but gossamer threads in the tapestry of who I was becoming.

"More than this," I repeated, the words now a mantra. The external world had shifted dramatically, my metamorphosis visible to any onlooker. Yet, the internal journey—fraught with shadows and longing—was just beginning.

I acknowledged the yearning that material wealth or fleeting pleasures could never satiate. There was a void within, profound and persistent, begging to be filled with something more substantial, more enduring.

"More than this," I vowed, stepping forward into the burgeoning light of a new day.

Chapter Seven

Morning light spilled across the expanse of my new bedroom, teasing me awake. I blinked against the brightness, my eyes tracing the contours of a ceiling far more ornate than any I had known. The silk sheets, a whisper against my skin, felt like an indulgence too sumptuous for someone like me. My heart hammered with a mixture of adrenaline and anxiety as I sat up, letting the reality of my surroundings sink in.

"Is this really mine?" The question escaped my lips, a tiny sound swallowed by the enormity of the apartment. I slid out of bed, the plush carpet comforting my bare feet. Every step was a reminder of the distance between who I was and who I could become.

The reflection that greeted me in the full-length mirror was one I barely recognized—sleek black hair cascading over shoulders clad in high-fashion sleepwear, a stark contrast to the thrift-store finds I used to don. Yet, beneath the surface, the same hunger lingered—a craving for something more profound than what material luxury could offer.

I needed guidance, someone who could help me navigate the treacherous waters of this new world without losing myself. Determination set my resolve as I perused the stack of resumes on the marble kitchen island, each more impressive than the last.

"Experience isn't everything," I murmured, sipping my coffee. It was strong and rich, another novelty. I wanted someone who understood the game but wasn't consumed by it. As the interviews commenced, candidates paraded through the living room, their rehearsed poise and polished words blurring together.

Then he walked in—David. There was an ease to his demeanor, a genuine smile that reached his eyes. He wasn't just familiar with high society; he moved through it with a quiet confidence that spoke volumes.

"Ms. Elena," he began, extending a hand, "it's a pleasure to meet you."

"Call me Elena, please," I corrected, shaking his hand. His grip was firm, reassuring. "Tell me, David, what makes you different from the rest?"

He considered the question, not rushing to fill the silence. "I believe one can embrace the splendor of this world without becoming lost in it. It's about balance—finding the line between enjoying the fruits of your labor and remembering where you planted the seeds."

His answer resonated within me, echoing the very fears and hopes that kept me awake at night. It was as if he saw through the facade, recognizing the void I was desperate to fill.

"Can you help me stay true to that? To not lose sight of who I am?" The vulnerability in my voice surprised even me.

"Absolutely," he said with a certainty that wrapped around me like a blanket. "It's not just about managing schedules and events. It's about ensuring you remain authentically Elena, no matter the setting."

That was it—that was what I was looking for. Someone who didn't just fit the role but understood the importance of maintaining my core amidst this opulent new existence. I offered him the position, and as he accepted, I felt a small piece of the puzzle click into place.

"Welcome aboard, David." My words were a mix of relief and anticipation. For the first time since stepping into this lavish life, I sensed a glimmer of hope that perhaps I could find my way without losing myself entirely.

"Thank you, Elena. I won't let you down." His assurance was a promise, one I intended to hold onto tightly.

As he left, I wandered to the balcony, overlooking the city that was now mine to conquer. The chapter of my life that began today felt weighty with potential, fraught with challenges, but I was ready. With David's help, I would carve out a path that was uniquely mine—opulent, yes, but also authentic, filled with growth from pleasures more meaningful than ephemeral delights.

"David, are these forks just for decoration, or am I actually expected to use all of them?" My voice carried a playful note, but beneath it lay a genuine current of bewilderment. I was seated at the dining table, an array of polished silverware spread before me like a metallic garden.

"Each fork has its purpose, Elena," David explained with the patience of a seasoned teacher. "This one, for instance..." He pointed to a slender, menacing piece of cutlery. "...is for seafood."

I picked it up, turning it over in my hands, feeling its cool weight. It was ridiculous, really, how something as simple as utensils could symbolize my foray into a world where opulence was the norm and excess went unnoticed.

"Alright, let's try this again," I said, straightening my back and squaring my shoulders in determination. "Soup first, then the fish, followed by the entree, and so on?"

"Exactly," David assured me, his eyes reflecting a pride that bolstered my waning confidence. "You're getting the hang of it far quicker than you realize."

For the next hour, we danced through lessons in finance—spreadsheets and projections that made my head spin, but were essential to mastering my new life as an entrepreneur with wealth that still felt alien in my bank account.

"Compound interest, diversified portfolios, trusts, and estates," David recited, tapping on the tablet that contained my financial future. "These aren't just terms, Elena; they're tools. And with them, you'll build empires."

As evening descended and David left, I found myself alone, surrounded by the grandeur of my apartment. The soft hum of the city below filtered through the balcony doors, a reminder of the pulse of life that surged on, oblivious to my internal tumult.

I poured myself a glass of wine, the rich aroma promising a temporary reprieve from doubts that clung to me like shadows. With each sip, I tried to drown the whispers that told me I didn't belong—that girl from the wrong side of the tracks, playing dress-up in a world that wasn't hers.

"Who the hell am I kidding?" The words escaped my lips, laced with both derision and despair. The reflection in the window showed a woman with sleek black hair, clad in high fashion, yet her eyes betrayed the turmoil within.

Each lesson, each step toward assimilation into this new reality was a battle against the imposter syndrome that gnawed at my sense of self-worth. How could I ever reconcile the Elena who fought tooth and nail for every scrap of success with this... stranger living a life of luxury?

"From survival to splendor," I whispered, tracing the rim of my glass. "But at what cost?"

The wine left a bitter aftertaste, mirroring the realization that knowledge and comfort in high society couldn't fill the void of authenticity I feared losing. As the night deepened, the loneliness settled in, heavy and unyielding.

"Maybe the price of this crown is more than I can afford," I mused, looking out at the twinkling city lights. They held promises and perils alike—temptations of the flesh that called to me, seductive and dangerous, offering a reprieve from the solitude, if only for a night.

But tomorrow would come, and with it, the daunting task of finding purpose beyond the allure of empty pleasures. For now, though, I allowed myself to succumb to the silence, letting the darkness embrace me, a reluctant queen in a kingdom of gold and ghosts.

David's entrance into my life heralded a period of profound transformation, one that touched every aspect of my daily existence and fundamentally altered how I engaged with the world around me. His arrival was the catalyst for a journey of personal evolution, a path that led me to discover not just the intricacies of social etiquette but also the deeper layers of my own identity within this new existence I was carving out for myself.

He began by focusing on the basics, the foundational elements of presence and presentation. "Your posture speaks before you do," he reminded me gently, guiding me to adopt a stance that radiated confidence and grace. This wasn't just about correcting how I sat or stood; it was about embodying a persona that commanded respect and attention. Practicing in front of mirrors, observing my reflection as I made small adjustments, I gradually began to see a transformation—not just in my posture but in the way I started to perceive myself.

Our sessions delved into the art of conversation, an area I hadn't realized was ripe for improvement until David shed light on its complexities. "It's not merely about the words you choose, but the intention behind them," he explained. He coached me on the dynamics of engaging dialogue, teaching me to listen actively and speak with purpose. Each lesson was a step towards mastering the delicate dance of interaction, ensuring I could hold my own in the sophisticated circles I aspired to join.

Introductions became a craft under David's tutelage. "Think of it as your personal signature," he said, helping me refine the way I presented myself to the world. We worked on creating an introduction that was authentic yet polished, striking the perfect balance between humility and confidence. This wasn't just about making a good first impression; it was about laying the groundwork for meaningful connections.

But David's influence extended far beyond these initial lessons. He introduced me to the language of fashion, showing me how to curate a wardrobe that was not just stylish but spoke volumes about my personality and ambitions. Together, we navigated the world of high-end brands, each piece a building block in the persona I was constructing. Chanel, Alexander McQueen, The Row—these names became part of my vocabulary, each chosen garment a declaration of my new-found status and sense of self.

He also illuminated the social landscape for me, mapping out a strategy for navigating the myriad events and gatherings that dotted the social calendar. "Every occasion is an opportunity," he would say, emphasizing the importance of being seen in the right places, with the right people. But it wasn't just about attendance; David taught me how to make each appearance count, from the subtleties of networking to the art of leaving a lasting impression.

Perhaps the most significant lesson David imparted was the understanding that true elegance and sophistication lie in the nuances—the perfect pairing of an outfit, the timely contribution to a conversation, the grace with which one navigates the complexities of high society. It was about finding harmony between standing out and blending in, ensuring that my presence was both noticed and appreciated for all the right reasons.

As I reflect on the journey I've undertaken under David's guidance, I realize he did more than just prepare me for a life of prominence and luxury. He equipped me with the tools to build a life that was authentically mine, one that resonated with my deepest values and aspirations. With each lesson, I grew not just in knowledge but in confidence, ready to embrace this new chapter with openness and determination.

David's mentorship transformed me from an outsider looking in to a woman firmly rooted in her new reality, poised to make her mark. He showed me that the essence of thriving in this glittering world wasn't in mere adaptation but in the bold assertion of one's individuality, armed with elegance, wit, and a clear sense of purpose. Through his eyes, I came to see not just the life I was stepping into but the person I was becoming—complex, capable, and ready to embrace the future with grace and dignity.

The clink of ice against glass was the only sound in the dimly lit bar. I took another sip, the sharp tang of the whiskey mingling with the restless throb of music pulsing through the room. With each swallow, the heat spread through me, a counterfeit warmth that couldn't chase away the cold gnawing at my insides.

"Can I buy you another?" His voice sliced through the haze, smooth and expectant.

I turned to face him, a stranger with a crooked smile and eyes that promised oblivion. "Sure," I replied, my voice barely above the thrum of bass.

His place was stark, monochromatic—a contrast to the opulence I'd come to know. In the confines of his shower, steam veiled the world beyond as we collided with an urgency that bordered on desperation. Water cascaded over us, mixing with the salt of our skin as our movements became a language of their own—craving, seeking, demanding release from the shackles of loneliness.

"More," I gasped, fingers digging into his shoulders, the need to feel something other than emptiness driving me to the brink of madness.

"Yours," he breathed against my neck, his hands tracing paths of fire across my flesh, guiding me toward a fleeting pinnacle where nothing existed but the raw pulse of life.

But when dawn's light crept through the blinds, the afterglow faded, leaving me hollow, the void within unfulfilled. I slipped away, the whisper of fabric the only goodbye, and stepped out into the crisp morning air.

Back in the sanctuary of my apartment, the mirror reflected a woman I scarcely recognized—one who sought solace in the arms of strangers. It wasn't enough. It would never be enough. The wealth, the sex, the distractions—they were just gilded cages, keeping me from facing the truth.

I had to find meaning. Purpose.

"Make a difference, Elena," I murmured to myself. "Do something real."

Picking up the phone to call David felt like reaching out to a beacon of knowledge in the sea of my new life. As the call connected, I dove straight into the purpose of my call, bypassing the usual pleasantries. "David, I've been thinking a lot about how I can use this opportunity to give back. I need your insight on reputable charity organizations. What do you think I could do for them? How can I make a real impact?"

David's response was immediate and thoughtful. He began listing several well-respected organizations, each dedicated to causes ranging from education for underprivileged children to environmental conservation. He detailed the missions of each, helping me understand where my contributions could be most effective.

"For starters," he suggested, "you could organize a fundraiser or donate a portion of your winnings. But beyond financial support, consider offering your time. Many of these organizations need hands-on help or expertise in various fields. You could make a significant difference by getting involved directly."

Taking David's advice to heart, I embarked on a journey of philanthropy. It wasn't just about writing checks; I found myself organizing charity galas, participating in community outreach programs, and even lending my voice to raise awareness for these causes. Each step I took in this direction filled me with a sense of purpose and fulfillment that money alone had never provided.

Giving back became a pillar of my new identity, a way to anchor my newfound wealth in the reality of the world's needs. It was through David's guidance that I discovered the joy of philanthropy, not just as a means of assistance but as a form of personal growth and connection to the community around me. My efforts in supporting these organizations not only helped those in need but also offered me a deeper understanding of the power of generosity and the impact one individual can have.

I shook hands with organizers, listened to stories of struggle and resilience, each tale a thread weaving into the tapestry of my awakening conscience.

"Education, children, the environment—what speaks to you?" one organizer asked, her eyes alight with passion.

"Something... tangible," I replied, searching for a connection that could anchor me to this new existence. "A cause that needs more than just money thrown at it."

"Then let's find where your heart lies," she smiled, offering a bridge to a world where perhaps my wealth could pave the way for change—where my past and present could converge to create a future worth embracing.

As the city lights flickered beneath my balcony that night, I stood alone yet not defeated. The vast expanse whispered of both promise and peril, a siren song of what could be. And somewhere between the shadows and the stars, I began to understand that true fulfillment lay not in the escape but in the journey itself.

Under the resplendent glow of crystal chandeliers, the grand ballroom unfolded before me like a scene from a fairy tale, albeit one set in the heart of the city's elite. Adorned in a gown chosen by David, its fabric whispering secrets of newfound confidence with every step, I clutched my champagne flute, a lifeline in a sea of opulence and whispered deals.

"David," I whispered, clutching the champagne flute with a nervous hand as we stood at the edge of the gilded ballroom. "Everyone seems to know everyone else."

He leaned in, his breath carrying a hint of mint, "That's because they do, Elena. But trust me, just be yourself and you'll stand out in the best possible way."

I scanned the room, taking in the sea of sleek black tuxedos and shimmering gowns. Laughter tinkled like crystal, the air was perfumed with wealth and sophistication, and my heart beat an erratic rhythm against the confines of my designer dress. David had been invaluable these past weeks, a beacon guiding me through the tempest of high society. His introductions were smooth, each one opening doors to circles I had never imagined I'd enter.

"Mrs. Van Der Luydens, may I present Ms. Elena Callahan," he said, leading me toward a regal woman whose diamonds caught the light with every poised nod. Her smile was warm, but her eyes appraised me with cool calculation.

"Delighted," she murmured, her grip on my hand both frail and commanding. There was an art to this, a dance of words and glances that I was learning step by precarious step. We spoke of charity galas and upcoming auctions, her interest piqued at the mention of my recent forays into philanthropy.

As the night progressed, I met more faces, received more smiles that didn't reach eyes, and exchanged pleasantries that skimmed the surface like pebbles over still water. David was right beside me, always watchful, always ready to steer me clear of conversational reefs.

"Remember, it's not just about what you can gain from these connections. It's about what feels genuine, who you want in your corner," he reminded me in a hushed tone during a brief respite.

"Authenticity," I mused. "It's rarer than the jewels in this room."

The evening wore on and the orchestra swelled in a crescendo of violins and cellos. I allowed myself to be pulled into a waltz, the practiced steps a metaphor for the life I was stepping into. One-two-three, one-two-three... The rhythm was soothing until a laugh—too loud, too sharp—shattered the melody.

Abruptly, the facade of grandeur crumbled, revealing a poignant hollowness beneath the laughter and the clinking glasses. These opulent figures, moving through their expensive motions, seemed suddenly like marionettes—strings pulled by duty, by appearances, by a relentless pursuit of something more. They were like me, I realized, searching for a fulfillment that silk and diamonds couldn't provide.

"Are you alright?" David asked, his hand gently on my back as we stepped away from the dance floor.

"Have you ever felt," I started, my voice barely above the music, "like we're all just chasing shadows?"

He didn't answer immediately, but his silence spoke volumes. And in that moment, surrounded by the splendor and the emptiness it masked, I found a sobering clarity. My resolve hardened like a diamond under pressure.

"Let's go," I said firmly, pulling away from the crowd. "I need air."

"Of course." David followed, his presence a reminder of the few genuine bonds I had begun to form.

Outside, the chill of the night wrapped around me like a shawl. Above, the stars blinked indifferently at the follies of man.

"Thank you, David," I said, feeling the weight of the day's mask slip away. "I think I've had enough of chasing shadows. It's time to start building something real."

"Anytime, Elena," he replied, the corners of his eyes crinkling in a sincere smile. "Anytime."

The night air was a cold kiss on my flushed skin as I left the event, the lingering scent of expensive perfume and false promises mingling in my wake. I had left behind the cacophony of clinking glasses and hollow laughter, but I couldn't shake off the loneliness that clung to me like a second skin.

I met him outside the Jasmine Bar, which somehow became my destination for one night pleasures, which was wrong and I knew it but no matter how much I wanted to stop this act of emptiness, I just couldn't. I had it all now, the money that could buy everythin, and I could be anyone, but the emptiness inside, the void, I just couldn't fill it.

A figure leaning against the lamppost, his smile a beacon in the murky sea of my discontent. His name was lost to the night, yet our eyes spoke of mutual understanding, a silent agreement that we needed no more than this fleeting connection.

"Want to get out of here?" His voice was smooth, a soothing balm to the raw edges of my psyche.

"Lead the way," I replied, my response automatic, driven by an aching void that demanded to be filled.

His apartment was a stark contrast to the opulence I'd grown accustomed to. Bare floors, unadorned walls—it was a space unpretentious and real. Without words, we came together, two strangers seeking solace in the storm of life. Our movements were urgent, bodies entwined on the cool hardness of the floor, a passion fueled by desperation rather than desire.

"God, you're incredible," he gasped between fervent kisses, his hands tracing the contours of my body with a hunger that mirrored my own.

"More," I urged, the word torn from my lips as the intensity of our encounter crescendoed. For a moment, I was lost in the sensation, the heat, the pulse of life that seemed to thrum beneath my skin.

But as quickly as the fire had ignited, it dwindled to embers, leaving me colder than before. Lying there, on the unforgiving floor, the ghost of our passion dissipating into the air, I felt hollow—a shell discarded by the tide of temporary pleasure.

"Stay the night?" he offered, a note of hope threading his words.

"I can't," I whispered, the lie sitting heavy on my tongue. I couldn't stay because there was nothing left to stay for.

Dressing quietly, I left him in his apartment, a stranger once more. The door closed with a soft click, sealing away the echoes of what could never fill the cavernous spaces inside me.

Back in my apartment, the silence was a stark reminder of the emptiness I carried within. I stepped onto the balcony, the city sprawling before me like a canvas of light and shadow. The hum of life rose up to greet me, a symphony of the lost and the found, the dreamers and the disillusioned.

Standing there, high above it all, I felt the weight of solitude pressing down on me. Yet, amidst the ache, there was a glimmer of something else—clarity. It cut through the fog of my thoughts, sharp and unyielding. I needed more than these empty encounters, more than the superficial trappings of wealth.

The lights below twinkled with promise and peril, a reflection of the journey I was on. A journey that was mine alone to navigate, fraught with pitfalls and peaks, darkness and dazzling brilliance.

"Find what fulfills you," I murmured to the night, a vow etched into the marrow of my bones. "Find purpose beyond the pleasure, meaning beyond the material."

My eyes traced the skyline, each building a testament to human endeavor, each light a soul searching for its place in the vast tapestry of existence. And as I stood there, a solitary figure amid the grandeur and the grit, I knew that my search was just beginning.

Ever since my life transformed overnight with the lottery win, the incessant ringing of an unknown number had become a curious constant. Initially dismissed as telemarketers or a wrong number, it was a minor nuisance overshadowed by the whirlwind of changes. But one evening, against the backdrop of the city's transition from day to night, my curiosity got the better of me. I answered.

"Elena?" The voice was unmistakably Alex's, tinged with a familiarity that now felt foreign.

"Why are you calling?" I asked, my tone colder than intended, a reflex against the unexpected flood of emotions.

"I've been thinking about us," he started, his voice a mix of desperation and something else I couldn't quite pinpoint. "I know I messed up, but I believe we deserve another chance."

"There's no 'us' to think about, Alex. It's over," I replied, trying to keep the conversation short.

"But I love you, Elena. Can't we just meet and talk about it?" His voice carried a plea that almost sounded sincere.

"No, Alex. There's nothing left to discuss," I insisted, feeling a mix of annoyance and sadness.

But Alex was persistent. His calls continued, each one more insistent than the last, until the day he decided to confront me directly, standing at my doorstep uninvited.

I reluctantly opened the door, and there he was, looking determined yet visibly agitated. "Elena, we need to talk. I know about your win. I just... I think I deserve a part of that."

"Deserve?" I echoed, disbelief coloring my tone. "Alex, you walked out. Whatever I won, it's mine. Not ours."

"But if it weren't for me, you wouldn't have bought that ticket. It's only fair," he argued, his voice rising.

"That's not how fairness works. You need to leave," I said, firm yet shaken by his audacity.

Alex's frustration boiled over. "You owe me this, Elena. After everything we've been through..."

I was appalled. "Owe you? I owe you nothing. Security will see you out."

As security escorted him away, his protests filled the air, a painful reminder of the distance between the past we shared and the present. Watching him leave, I felt a mix of relief and a profound sadness. This confrontation was a harsh awakening to the realities my new life entailed.

In the aftermath, I stood in the quiet of my apartment, the echoes of our exchange lingering. It was a somber realization that some ties, once cut, reveal truths about people we thought we knew. This encounter with Alex, though fraught with tension, cemented my resolve to move forward, leaving behind those who valued wealth over genuine connections. It was a stark lesson in discerning who deserves a place in my new life and who does not.

Chapter Eight

Morning light spilled across the duvet, its warmth stirring me from sleep. I stretched languidly, the softness of the sheets a tactile reminder of newfound luxury. Yet, as I lay in the quiet comfort of my bedroom, a solitary ache wound its way through the threads of opulence.

After the unsettling encounter with Alex, I made a conscious decision to brush off the discomfort and move forward, rather than dwell on the negativity. The episode, though jarring, was a stark reminder of the strength I'd garnered through my recent changes. With a renewed sense of purpose, I resolved to immerse myself in the day's activities, allowing no room for the shadows of yesterday to cloud the possibilities of today.

"Today," I murmured to the empty room, "I find something real."

Pushing back the covers, I padded barefoot to the window, hazel eyes scanning the cityscape that sprawled before me. The high-rise view was once a symbol of my ascension from small-town obscurity to this dizzying urban life. But the reflection staring back at me from the glass was searching for more than just a skyline—the craving for authentic connection was palpable.

Showered and dressed in an outfit that straddled the line between elegance and comfort—a cashmere sweater hugging my frame and tailored pants skimming my legs—I made my way to the kitchen. The rich aroma of coffee filled the air, a balm to my restless spirit. Each sip grounded me, emboldening my resolve.

"Enough with the surface-level chit-chat that fades with the evening's last toast," I told David, "I want friendships that thrive in the sobering light of day."

"Real friendships," David mused one afternoon, "are built on shared experiences and genuine affection, not just social obligations or mutual benefits." His words struck a chord with me, highlighting a truth I had nearly overlooked in my rapid ascent into wealth.

With that philosophy in mind, we hatched a plan to cultivate a circle of true companionship. "Let's host a gathering at your place," David proposed. "Nothing too grand or formal, just a warm, cozy event. We'll invite the people you've met at other functions—the ones you felt a genuine spark with."

I warmed to the idea immediately. It seemed like the perfect opportunity to peel back the layers of formality and really connect with people on a deeper level. Together, we crafted a guest list, intentionally small, focusing on those individuals whose interactions had left me feeling uplifted, intrigued, or simply happy.

David's expertise shone through in planning the event. He suggested a theme that resonated with my interests, ensuring the evening would offer more than just idle chitchat. "How about an evening of art and music?" he offered. "You could showcase some of your favorite pieces, maybe even include a small musical performance. It'll give everyone something to talk about, something more meaningful than the usual small talk."

With the caffeine sharpening my intentions, I unfurled my laptop.As David outlined the concept for the evening, his vision clear and his advice invaluable, I sat down to craft the invitation email, translating our plans into words. The cursor blinked patiently on the screen, waiting for me to begin. With a deep breath, I started typing, each word infused with the warmth and anticipation I felt for the upcoming event.

"Dear friends," I typed, fingers dancing with a nervous energy, "I would be delighted if you could join me for an intimate gathering at my place this Friday evening. Let's enjoy good food, fine wine, and even better company."

I hesitated over the 'send' button, a pulse of vulnerability coursing through me. This was more than a mere soirée; it was an unveiling of sorts, the beginning of a journey toward the depth I yearned for. With a deep breath that felt like a leap, I clicked 'send'.

The day unfolded with anticipation weaving through each task. I selected music that resonated with my mood—melodies that promised kinship and whispered of shared confessions. I arranged flowers, their colors bold yet warm, an unspoken welcome to those who would step through my door.

As the day of the event approached, I found myself looking forward to it with a mix of excitement and nervous anticipation. This gathering would be a far cry from the lavish, impersonal events I had grown accustomed to. This was about laying the groundwork for friendships that could thrive outside the glitzy confines of high society—a crucial step in building the fulfilling life I yearned for.

As the sun dipped below the skyline, casting a golden hue over the apartment, a soft knock signaled the first arrival. My heart quickened as I opened the door, greeting each guest with a smile that reached my eyes.

"Come in," I said, my voice laced with sincerity. "I'm so glad you're here."

Laughter soon filled the space, a symphony of burgeoning connections. We shared stories and sipped wine, the barriers of our varied worlds dissolving with each candid exchange. I reveled in the authenticity of the moment, feeling the layers of my guarded heart peel away.

The evening itself was a revelation. The relaxed, inviting atmosphere of my home allowed everyone's guard to come down. Conversations flowed freely, laughter filled the air, and I could see the beginnings of genuine connections forming.

Looking around at the smiling faces, engaged in animated discussions about art, music, and life, I felt a profound sense of contentment. For the first time since my windfall, I wasn't just surrounded by people—I was among friends.

"Here's to new friendships," I toasted, raising my glass. The clink of crystal was like a vow, an agreement to journey into the unknown terrain of true companionship.

The laughter subsided as the conversation took an unexpected dive into deeper waters. I found myself swept along by a current of confessions, my own words surprising me as they spilled out with raw honesty.

"Back in my hometown, life was...predictable," I began, the group's attention anchoring on me. "I remember staring at the same stars each night, wishing for something different. When fortune came knocking, it was like waking up in someone else's story."

I paused, feeling the weight of their gazes, a blend of curiosity and understanding knitting the space between us. My fingers traced the stem of my wine glass, the cool touch grounding me.

"Money changed everything and nothing at the same time. Yes, I escaped the monotony, but the reflection in the mirror started to feel like a stranger. There's this constant noise—the parties, the shopping, the... men. It's intoxicating and empty all at once."

A collective exhale filled the room, shared empathy painted in soft shadows against the walls. Clara leaned forward, her eyes mirroring a sea of storms weathered and survived.

"I get it, Elena. My life flipped upside down when my marriage ended," Clara revealed, her voice steady yet tinged with the residue of battles fought. "Suddenly, you're thrust into this new existence, expected to navigate without a compass. The loneliness—it can be overwhelming."

Her admission was like a lifeline thrown across the chasm of my own experiences. Our connection deepened, tethered by the threads of upheaval and rebirth.

"Exactly," I affirmed, feeling a kinship with Clara that transcended the evening's pleasantries. "It's as if you're walking through a crowd, screaming inside, but no one hears you."

"Until someone does," she said softly, a knowing smile touching her lips.

Our conversation flowed like a river breaking free from its dam, sweeping away debris of pretense and superficiality. We delved into the chaos of change, the addiction to adrenaline highs, and the craving for something more substantial than the ephemeral high of a credit card swipe or a fleeting caress.

The evening stretched on, the air thick with revelations and the scent of vulnerability. As the candles burnt low, casting dancing shadows upon our faces, I felt a solidarity with Clara and the others that had been foreign to me in this new cityscape of glamour and guise.

In that moment, I realized that perhaps the most valuable currency wasn't found in my bank account, but in the heartfelt exchanges between souls stripped bare, willing to share the messy, beautiful tapestry of their lives.

"Alright, Elena, let's create some magic," my assistant, David, exclaimed the next morning, his hands poised over racks of clothing like a conductor ready to orchestrate a symphony. He had transformed my living room into a boutique-style frenzy, with designer labels vying for attention.

"Balenciaga or Burberry?" he queried, holding up two exquisite jackets, one a fusion of classic tweed and modern cut, the other a bold statement in sleek leather.

"Both," I replied, my heart skipping at the thought of enveloping myself in such luxury.

David's eyes sparkled with shared excitement as she meticulously selected pieces—a cascade of silk from a Saint Laurent dress, the structured elegance of a Chanel suit, a whimsical Gucci skirt that promised to twirl with every step.

"Try this on," he insisted, passing me a Valentino gown that shimmered like midnight. The fabric kissed my skin, a lover's caress, as I slipped into it. The price tag dangled, irrelevant in the face of such beauty—three thousand, maybe more?

"Divine," he breathed out, and I spun, the room blurring into a carousel of opulence and delight.

We laughed, high on the thrill of transformation, as I modeled each outfit, envisioning grand entrances and envious glances. A pair of Jimmy Choo heels clicked on the hardwood floor, a punctuation mark to my newfound confidence.

"Look at you," David cheered, "You're the queen."

An intoxicating happiness bubbled within me, a potent cocktail of adrenaline and allure. Each swipe of my credit card was a promise of pleasure, a guarantee of joy—or so I believed in the heady rush of possession.

As the sun dipped below the horizon, bags piled around us like trophies, a testament to a day spent chasing euphoria through the acquisition of threads and leather.

"Thank you," I said, my voice soft with genuine contentment. "Today was perfect."

"Anytime," David grinned, his eyes mirroring my own satisfaction.

But as the door closed behind him, leaving me surrounded by the spoils of our spree, a whisper of doubt crept in, unbidden yet persistent. Was this happiness or just a beautiful facade destined to crumble under the weight of longing for something beyond the tactile embrace of fabric and design?

I shook off the unease, choosing instead to bask in the glow of my treasures, unaware that the seeds of revelation were already taking root, preparing to bloom in the most unexpected of ways.

I slid a silk blouse from its hanger, the smooth fabric whispering secrets against my skin. It was beautiful, undoubtedly. Yet as I gazed at my reflection, adorned in yet another emblem of luxury, I felt a hollow twinge in the pit of my stomach—a void that no amount of opulent drapery seemed able to fill.

"Another beauty," I murmured, feigning a smile for the benefit of my own reflection. But the lie tasted bitter on my tongue.

"Hey," Clara's voice filtered through the room, a soft undercurrent of concern. "You okay?"

"Of course." The word was automatic, a shield raised against introspection. But Clara's gaze pierced through it effortlessly.

"Your eyes," she said gently, stepping closer. "They're not shining like they used to when you put on something new. What's going on?"

The dam broke with her words, and the truth spilled out, raw and unpolished. "I feel empty, Clara. Like I'm trying to fill spaces inside me with things... Things that don't matter."

She nodded, her expression a mirror of empathy. "I've been there," she confided. "It's like chasing a high, isn't it? The thrill of the hunt, the rush of the purchase. But then it fades, leaving you craving more."

"Exactly," I sighed, letting the blouse slip from my fingers, watching it pool on the floor like spilled ink. "It's an addiction."

"Then let's find something better to be addicted to," Clara proposed, her eyes alight with a challenge. "Experiences, Elena. Memories that don't lose their luster."

"Like what?" The skepticism in my voice couldn't mask the spark of hope that flickered within.

"Let's start small," Clara suggested, reaching for my hand. "A walk in the park, perhaps? No credit cards, just us and nature."

"Sounds terrifying," I joked, but took her hand all the same.

"Good," Clara smiled. "Terrifying means it's worth doing."

And so we walked. Beneath the dappled light of the setting sun, our footsteps were silent testimonies of our journey. The park unfolded around us, a tapestry of greens and golds, and I found myself breathing deeper, pulled into the moment.

As time went by, Clara and I grew really close. We talked about everything - our past, our fears, and our dreams. I found in her the kind of friend I'd always wanted but never really had. It was a deep and true friendship that made me feel understood and less alone.

"See that?" Clara pointed to an elderly couple sharing a picnic, laughter dancing between them like a tangible thing. "That's wealth, Elena. That right there."

Her words resonated deep within me, striking chords I had long forgotten. We sat by the pond, the air rich with the scent of damp earth and the symphony of city life humming in the distance.

"Tell me something real," Clara whispered, her eyes reflecting the twilight sky.

"Real?" A thousand definitions fluttered through my mind, elusive as shadows.

"Something you can't buy."

I closed my eyes, letting the world fall away until there was nothing left but the truth. "Love," I said at last. "Connection. Friendship."

"Exactly," she affirmed, squeezing my hand. "These are the cravings worth indulging in."

As night embraced the city, we spoke of dreams and fears, of past wounds and hopeful tomorrows. Clara listened, truly listened, and I saw myself reflected in her—a woman yearning for authenticity in a world draped in pretense.

"Thank you," I whispered, the city lights casting halos around us. "For seeing me."

"Always," Clara replied, her voice thick with sincerity. "I see you, Elena—the person, not the price tag."

A tear escaped, tracing a path down my cheek, a testament to the power of connection. In Clara's presence, I found a solace I hadn't known I'd lost.

"Let's make a pact," I said impulsively, energized by the rawness of the evening. "To seek experiences over possessions. To live fully, deeply."

"Deal," Clara agreed, her smile the most valuable thing I could ever hope to possess.

Together, we rose, our bond solidified under the canopy of stars. I knew the road ahead would be riddled with temptation, but with Clara by my side, I dared to believe I could traverse it—one genuine step at a time.

The clinking of my apartment door closing behind Clara echoed with a resonance of change. I stood alone in the silence, wrapped in a newfound clarity yet haunted by an insatiable craving that clawed beneath my skin—a longing not even the deepest of friendships could quell.

"Shit," I muttered, pacing the hardwood floors, my heels clicking in syncopation with my accelerating pulse. My reflection caught in the mirror, hazel eyes ablaze with a familiar, feral hunger. No shopping bag or silk dress could satiate this desire. It was carnal, visceral—a raw need threading through my veins.

I knew it was reckless, another addiction perhaps, but the emptiness begged to be filled, and only one thing promised temporary relief.

"Are you going to keep denying yourself what you want?" I challenged my reflection. A smirk played on my lips as I grabbed my purse and keys, already feeling the anticipation building within.

The city's nightlife pulsed around me, an electric current that fueled my daring strides. In the crowd, faces blurred until he emerged—dark hair, blue eyes that locked onto mine with an intensity that matched my own. He was a stranger, yet in that split-second exchange, we recognized something primal in each other.

"Hey," he said, his voice smooth and inviting.

"Hey," I replied, my breath hitching slightly as he stepped closer, the subtle scent of his cologne wrapping around me.

"Alone?" he asked, one corner of his mouth lifting in a half-smile that suggested he knew exactly what I was after.

"By choice," I answered, my voice steady despite the chaos raging inside me.

"Mind if I change that?" His question wasn't really a question; it was an offering, a mutual understanding of the transaction about to take place.

Without a word, I took his hand, leading him through the throngs of people. The night air was cool against our heated skin as we stumbled into the backseat of a cab, our lips crashing together in a frenzy of need. His hands roamed over my body, igniting flames wherever they touched, and I reciprocated with equal fervor.

"Your place or mine?" he gasped between kisses.

"Doesn't matter," I panted back, lost in the intoxicating blend of lust and liberation.

We ended up at his apartment, a place high above the city where the view was breathtaking. The dazzling lights below seemed to dim as he pulled me close, our kiss filled with a rush of feelings that left me gasping. My dress fell away, and his shirt was quickly discarded, revealing the strength and warmth of his embrace.

"You're incredible," he whispered, his gaze intense, capturing every part of me in that moment.

"Show me," I said, my voice a mix of eagerness and anticipation.

He picked me up effortlessly, taking me to where the moonlight softly lit the room. We came together with a passion that felt all-consuming, every movement a testament to the intensity of our connection. I was completely drawn into the moment, lost in the sensations that overwhelmed us both.

"Elena," he breathed out, his urgency matching mine as we reached the height of our shared frenzy.

"More," I urged, the world around us reduced to the electric charge of our closeness.

And then, in a rush, we reached a crescendo together, our cries a release of the buildup of passion. We held onto each other as the echoes of our connection slowly faded, our breathing the only sound in the quiet room.

As we lay there, the reality of the moment started to settle in. I traced the lines of his face quietly, the stillness around us filled with the complexity of what had just happened. It was a brief escape from everything else, yet it left me feeling more aware of the emptiness I couldn't shake.

"Thank you," I murmured, beginning to collect my clothes. The words felt inadequate for the moment, unable to fully bridge the gap I felt inside.

"Anytime," he replied softly, his smile gentle but his eyes looking away.

Leaving his apartment as the first light of dawn began to break, I felt a mix of emotions. The immediate thrill had passed, leaving a quiet introspection in its wake. I had sought something in his arms, but each step I took away from him reminded me of the void I was trying to fill.

I was struggling to understand why I kept seeking these moments that didn't really make me happy. What was I missing? I didn't even like the person I was becoming because of it. Yet, I couldn't stop myself from going back for more, hoping to find whatever it was I felt was lacking in my life. Each time left me more confused and less like the me I wanted to be.

"What am I doing?" I whispered to myself, the silent city offering no answers, only reflecting back my own solitude.

I sat at the mahogany desk, my fingers drumming an impatient rhythm on the polished surface. Morning light streamed in through the floor-to-ceiling windows, bathing the room in a soft, golden hue that belied the turmoil inside me. I had spent countless hours here, scheming and strategizing, building an empire on whims and indulgences. But as I flipped through the pages of my business plan, something felt different.

Feeling a mix of excitement and urgency about a sudden burst of inspiration, I knew I had to share it with someone who could understand its potential. Without hesitation, I reached out to David. "Can you come over as soon as you can?" I urged, barely containing the enthusiasm in my voice. "I've got this new idea, and I really need to bounce it off you." David, ever the anchor in the midst of my brainstorming storms, agreed immediately. His presence had always been a catalyst for turning my ideas from fleeting thoughts into tangible realities, and I couldn't wait to explore this latest concept with him.

"Time for a change," I whispered to myself, the words carrying more conviction than they had in years.

The sleek lines and cold numbers on paper no longer excited me. Instead, I envisioned a venture that pulsed with life, one rooted in passion rather than profit. A place where creativity wasn't just encouraged but celebrated—a gallery, maybe, or a boutique that showcased local artisans. My heart quickened at the thought, and for the first time in ages, I felt a spark of genuine excitement.

"Make it about connection, not just transactions," Clara's voice echoed in my head. Her influence was undeniable, her support like a lifeline pulling me from the depths of isolation. With each shared experience, each heartfelt conversation, she reminded me of who I could be—someone who found worth in authenticity, not accolades.

"Alright, let's do this." Empowered, I began to scribble down ideas, my hand moving with a fervor that matched the racing of my thoughts. It was messy and chaotic, but it was real—the raw blueprint of a dream taking shape.

When David arrived, the air was electric with creativity and potential. We dove straight into the heart of my new idea, spreading out notes and calculations across the living room table. With David's knack for seeing both the big picture and the minute details, we meticulously planned each step, considering every possibility and challenge.

As we exchanged ideas, it felt like pieces of a puzzle clicking into place. David's insights were invaluable, helping to refine and shape the concept into something both ambitious and achievable. Together, we mapped out the entire project, from initial concept to final execution, each decision and calculation bringing us closer to realizing the vision.

It was a session of intense collaboration, where time seemed to stand still, and the only thing that mattered was the work unfolding between us. By the end of it, we had not just a plan but a shared dream, ready to be brought to life, step by meticulous step.

Hours passed in what felt like minutes, and when I finally looked up, the sun had begun its descent, casting long shadows across the room. I leaned back, my eyes tracing the lines of ink that now covered the pages before me. There was a sense of accomplishment, a sense of purpose that filled the space where emptiness once reigned.

But old habits die hard.

A notification chimed on my phone, a siren call from one of my favorite luxury boutiques announcing an exclusive sale. My pulse quickened, a familiar itch spreading through my veins. Just a quick look, I told myself, standing up. I deserved a break, didn't I?

"Come on, David, we need to celebrate this," I exclaimed, the excitement bubbling over. Grabbing his hand, I pulled him up from the sea of papers and plans that covered the table. Sharing a laugh that spoke volumes of our shared relief and anticipation, we headed out to shop. It was more than just a shopping trip; it was a way to mark the moment, a tangible reminder of the milestone we had just reached together.

The stores were temples of temptation, every surface gleaming with promise. Sales associates greeted me by name, their smiles as polished as the displays they stood beside. They knew me—the regular who couldn't resist the lure of silk and suede, of diamonds and gold.

"Something caught your eye, Elena?" one purred, her gaze sharp beneath thick lashes.

"Everything," I confessed, my voice a breathless whisper.

Our celebration unfurled into a lavish quest for luxury, with David navigating each choice with a keen eye for style that matched my own. The day's expedition took us through iconic havens of opulence, each selection a marker of our collective achievements and my personal evolution.

Our first foray was into the elegant world of Hermès, where the storied ambiance was as captivating as the treasures it held. Here, David's expertise shone brightly as he chose the iconic Birkin bag in Togo leather, an artifact of unmatched craftsmanship. "This is far more than an accessory; it's a beacon of luxury," he noted, its $12,000 price tag a testament to its timeless allure and our venture's auspicious start.

Drifting next into the esteemed corridors of Tiffany & Co., we were greeted by the radiant sparkle of the Tiffany T1 Wide Diamond Hinged Bangle in 18k rose gold. Its luminous diamonds set against the soft rose gold spoke to me of elegance encased in strength. "It's a symbol of sophisticated resilience," David mused, the $28,000 bangle weaving another thread of luxe and grace into our day's narrative.

The journey led us onward to Alexander McQueen, a domain where innovation meets daring elegance. David selected a sculptural blazer, its design bold yet imbued with an undeniable elegance. "This piece won't just be remembered; it will be revered," he promised. Priced at $3,340, it stood as a bold declaration of my evolving style and confidence.

Our path then took us to the distinguished Rolex boutique, where time itself seemed to pause in admiration. We chose the Rolex Datejust 31, its white gold and diamond ensemble a harmonious blend of precision and splendor. "This celebrates not just the moments past but those awaiting us," David reflected, its $38,000 value a crowning jewel of our day's pursuits.

As dusk began to hint at its arrival, marking the end of our illustrious journey, my thoughts turned towards expressing my gratitude towards David. Our final destination was Louis Vuitton, a brand synonymous with enduring sophistication. There, I carefully selected gifts that spoke of my appreciation: a sleek Louis Vuitton briefcase, priced at $5,200, for his professional moments; chic Louis Vuitton Horizon wireless earphones, at $1,090, for times of leisure; and the Louis Vuitton Tambour Street Diver watch, a dive into luxury at $7,200, ensuring he'd always carry a token of our shared success and enduring bond.

This day transcended the mere acquisition of luxury; it was a celebration woven from the threads of hard work, friendship, and a shared journey. Each piece curated was not just a testament to personal style but a landmark of our collective achievements and the promise of the many adventures that still lay on the horizon.

Outside, night had fallen, the city's lights flickering like stars brought down to earth. I walked the streets with bags hanging heavy on my arms, their weight nothing compared to the burden in my chest. Guilt swirled within me, dark and relentless, as the façade of fulfillment crumbled.

The reflection in the shop windows revealed a stranger, a woman draped in finery but stripped of joy. In that moment, I saw the truth of my addiction laid bare—an endless cycle of desire and despair.

"Enough," I said, the word a vow. "This has to stop."

But even as I spoke, doubt lingered, a shadow I couldn't quite shake. Could I really break free from the chains I'd forged link by link, purchase by purchase? Or was I doomed to dance this dance forever, spinning in circles until I collapsed from exhaustion?

"Tomorrow," I promised the night, "I'll be better."

And with each step toward home, I tried to believe it.

After our big shopping spree, I felt a mix of happiness and a bit of emptiness. So, I said goodbye to David, grateful for his help, and went to see Clara, my new best friend. I was looking for some peace and real conversation, something to ground me after a day of focusing on fancy things.

Clara has become a really close friend to me, someone I can talk to about anything. We met up at our favorite little gallery, a place that felt like a cozy escape from the rest of the world.

"Art is the lie that enables us to realize the truth," Clara murmured as we entered the gallery, her voice a soft counterpoint to the hushed reverence that enveloped us. The quote, Picasso's, lingered in the air like an invocation as we stepped further into the embrace of creativity and color that unfolded around us.

I glanced at the canvases, each one a whisper of some artist's soul, a fingerprint left deliberately for others to feel. My fingers itched with the memory of textures—the smoothness of silk, the cool kiss of gold. But here, before these works of art, I hungered for a different kind of touch—a communion with spirits that spoke not of possession but of experience.

"Look at this one," Clara said, drawing me towards a painting where chaos reigned in splashes of crimson and midnight blue. It was raw, almost violent in its beauty, and it held me captive.

"Feels like a tempest," I breathed, feeling the colors swirl inside me, evoking emotions I'd tried to quell with the cold comfort of things that glittered but gave no warmth.

"Or maybe a revolution," she suggested, her hazel eyes reflecting the turmoil on the canvas. "Sometimes you need to tear everything down to start anew."

The words echoed my own unspoken thoughts, resonating with the struggle I housed within, between my old self and the person I was desperately trying to be. The woman who sought meaning beyond the price tags and the fleeting high of acquisition.

We moved through the exhibit, each piece a window into another's world, another's heart. Scenes of intimacy painted with bold strokes, fragile moments captured in delicate hues—all of them pulling at the threads of my being, unwinding the tightly wound spool of my former desires.

"Art doesn't ask for your money," I mused aloud, "it asks for your time. Your empathy."

"Exactly," Clara agreed, her arm brushing against mine, a gesture of solidarity in our shared revelation. "And isn't that what we're all searching for? Someone to share time with, someone who understands?"

The question hung between us, simple yet profound. I thought of the countless hours spent chasing shadows—luxuries that promised happiness but led only to emptiness. Now, those same hours were filled with conversations, laughter, and the pursuit of something infinitely more precious.

"Thank you for bringing me here," I told Clara, my voice a mix of gratitude and awe. "I didn't realize how much I needed this."

"Anytime," she replied, her smile genuine. "There's more to the world than what money can buy, Elena. And I think you're just starting to scratch the surface."

As we lingered before a final painting—a serene landscape bathed in the golden light of a setting sun—I felt a shift within me, subtle but undeniable. I wasn't just looking; I was seeing. Not just existing, but living.

"Beautiful, isn't it?" Clara whispered, her words matching my thoughts.

"More than beautiful," I answered. "It's real."

And as the chapter of my life marked by excess and artifice drew to a close, I stepped into a new narrative—one painted in authentic strokes, rich with possibility and vibrant with the true colors of connection and discovery.

Chapter Nine

The whiteboard loomed before me, an expanse of possibility that mirrored the restless churn of my thoughts. I uncapped a marker, its pungent aroma sharp and intoxicating, and approached the board with a sense of ceremony. My hand trembled slightly as I sketched the first lines of what would become my manifesto—a business model that wove the delicate threads of my values into a tapestry of practicality and impact.

"Think broader, Elena," I whispered to myself, the words a mantra to stave off the temptation of old habits. The lure of lavish spending, the seductive whisper of silk against skin from another unnecessary shopping spree—these were demons I had vowed to conquer.

In the heart of the loft, I'd gathered a mosaic of minds—a sculptor whose hands shaped the abstract into reality, a tech wizard who dreamed in code, and a social activist whose voice could set a room ablaze. They sat around the reclaimed wood table, their faces alight with the kind of fervor that fuels revolutions.

"Let's start with sustainability," I said, the word tasting like a promise on my tongue. "It's not just about being green. It's about creating something that lasts—both in business and in the community."

The sculptor, her salt-and-pepper hair framing her face in wisps of rebellion, leaned forward. "Sustainability is an art form. It's finding balance, harmony. Your business should be a reflection of that."

Her words struck a chord within me, resonating with the deeper connection I yearned for. I nodded, scribbling down her insight as the workshop hummed with the electricity of shared purpose.

"Okay, but how do we monetize that without losing the soul of what you're trying to build?" The tech guru challenged me, his sleek black hair falling into his eyes as he peered at me.

I considered his question, feeling the weight of it. "By being authentic. We don't sacrifice our integrity for profit. We innovate. We find new ways to bring value that aligns with our mission."

"Authenticity," he echoed, testing the word like it was a new flavor on his palate. "That's going to be your edge, Elena."

The intensity of the session grew with each passing hour, ideas sparking and igniting like a carefully curated chemical reaction. And in the midst of it all, I stood—no longer the woman shackled by small-town monotony or blinded by the gleam of gold and glitter. Here, I was a force, a visionary stoking the fire of change.

"Your determination is infectious, you know?" The social activist said, her gaze piercing through to my core. "You make me want to fight harder for what I believe in."

"Then let's channel that energy," I urged, my voice steady despite the chaos of emotions swirling within me. "Let's create something that isn't just profitable but profoundly transformative."

As dusk painted the sky in hues of fading light, I surveyed the fruits of our labor—the bones of a business plan that promised more than success; it hinted at redemption. In this space, with these people, I found the strength to resist the siren call of my addictions, replacing temporary highs with the enduring rush of creation and connection.

With every affirmation and challenge, my vision crystallized, no longer a nebulous dream but a clarion call to action. This was my path, paved with the jagged stones of my past and leading to a future where fulfillment didn't come from a price tag or an empty embrace.

"Thank you," I said as the workshop drew to a close, my heart thrumming with gratitude and resolve. "This is just the beginning.".

The air crackled with palpable tension as I stood at the head of the conference table, my hands planted firmly against its cool surface. The room was a battleground of ideas, and the latest salvo had been launched squarely at me.

"Social impact is a luxury, Elena," one of the collaborators said, skepticism etching his voice like acid. "It's a nice-to-have, not a cornerstone. You're running a business, not a charity."

I felt the weight of their gazes, expectant and probing, as if they could peel back my layers to find the insecurity that once would have crippled me. Only, it wasn't there anymore. In its place thrived a garden of conviction, blossoming from seeds of change I'd sown myself.

"Profit without purpose is an empty victory," I countered, my voice steady but ablaze with passion. "We have the resources, the minds, and the opportunity to make a difference. Why settle for less when we can elevate our mission and serve a greater good?"

The room fell silent, the hum of the fluorescent lights above serving as a subtle chorus to my declaration. I saw the flicker of understanding in their eyes, the slow nods that began to ripple around the table. It was more than agreement; it was respect—hard-earned and infinitely satisfying.

"Alright, Elena," another finally spoke up, his tone reflective of newfound commitment. "Show us how we integrate this into the business model. Let's make an actual impact."

The wave of relief and triumph that washed over me was potent, a heady concoction that made my heart swell within the confines of my chest. This was it—the moment where my vision took flight on the wings of collective will.

"Thank you," I said, a smile of genuine gratitude curving my lips. "Let's get to work."

Later, as Clara and I stepped into the sanctuary of the local art gallery, the tranquility of the space enveloped us like a soft shawl. Here, amidst the silent conversation of colors and forms, the relentless pace of planning and strategizing melted away.

"Look at this piece," Clara whispered, her voice hushed in reverence as she gestured toward an abstract painting that dominated the nearby wall. Its vibrant strokes pulsed with life, a chaotic yet harmonious blend that echoed the tumultuous journey of my own transformation.

"Isn't it remarkable?" I murmured, my eyes tracing the lines that seemed to dance before me, a visual symphony of struggle and triumph.

"It makes you feel something profound," Clara observed, her gaze lingering on the canvas. "Like it's speaking directly to your soul."

And it was. The artistry before me wasn't just color on canvas; it was a mirror reflecting the tumult of my inner world, the turmoil that had once pushed me toward the ephemeral comfort of material excess and reckless abandon.

"Clara," I started, turning to her with a fervor ignited by the artwork, "this is it. This is what our business needs—a commitment to culture, to society. We have to weave this kind of inspiration into our very fabric."

Her eyes lit up with understanding, and she nodded, her enthusiasm mirroring my own. "We'll do more than sell a product, Elena. We'll sell an experience, a connection to something greater."

Yes, that was the path I yearned to carve out, a venture imbued with the beauty and complexity of the human experience. The realization settled within me, a clarion call to press forward, to infuse every decision with the richness and depth that life—and art—had to offer.

The visit to the gallery was indeed a respite, a breath of fresh air in the stifling confines of commerce and calculation. But it was also a catalyst, propelling me toward a future where my business was an extension of my values, a testament to the power of shared humanity.

"Let's capture this essence, Clara," I said as we exited the gallery, the evening light spilling onto the sidewalk like molten gold. "Let's create something that resonates with every soul it touches."

"Let's make art," she agreed, and together, we stepped into the twilight, ready to mold my dreams into reality.

The hum of conversation and clinking glasses swirled around me, a symphony of affluence that both intimidated and intrigued. I stood at the fringe of the bustling room, my fingers tracing the stem of a wine glass, a prop that grounded me in the sea of wealth and power that filled the high-end social event. It was here I had hoped to find investors, allies—kindred spirits that saw the world not just as a marketplace, but as a canvas. My appearance was a carefully chosen armor, the Elie Saab gown a testament to the persona I wished to project: confident, visionary, undaunted by the grandeur that enveloped me. The dress, a masterpiece of design, draped over me, its deep emerald hue offsetting the room's opulence, making me a beacon of elegance in a sea of glittering attire.

"Quite the turnout, isn't it?" As his voice reached me, I turned to find this man, casually leaning against a marble column. The reality of him surpassed the image his voice had painted in my mind, his sharp suit perfectly accentuating his physique and the striking blue of his eyes even more piercing in the soft light, rendering him more handsome than I had envisioned.

"Overwhelming," I replied, betraying a hint of vulnerability I hadn't intended. "But necessary."

"Ah, the paradox of success," he mused, closing the distance between us with a few deliberate steps. "How it isolates us even as it draws crowds."

"You sound like a man who's familiar with the conundrum." I couldn't help but smile despite the ache in my chest, "Elena, Elena Callahan."

"Micheal Stevens," he smiled, offering a glass of champagne from a passing tray. "To the pursuit of dreams that keep us awake at night."

Our glasses clinked—a toast to ambition or perhaps to the façade we all donned like armor. I sipped the bubbly liquid, feeling the effervescence tickle my throat as Michael's gaze held mine, a challenge wrapped in a smirk.

"Tell me, Elena," he began, tilting his head slightly, "what keeps you awake?"

I hesitated, aware of the precipice before me. To reveal the truth would be to expose the chasm within—my craving for connection, my fear that every endeavor was just another lonely step on an endless ladder. But Michael's scrutiny felt more like an invitation than an inquisition, and the words tumbled out.

"Uncertainty," I confessed. "Wondering if what I'm building will matter, if it will touch anyone."

"Ah," he said, his voice dropping an octave, intimate and resonant. "You seek to leave a mark on the world, not just a footprint."

"Exactly." My pulse quickened as he stepped closer, his presence enveloping me like a warm shroud. The air between us crackled with an intensity that was as thrilling as it was dangerous.

"Perhaps," Michael murmured, his breath grazing my ear, "we can find solace in shared ambitions. After all, two dreamers are less alone, aren't they?"

His hand found the small of my back, guiding me away from the throng of people and into an alcove framed by heavy velvet curtains. The sudden privacy felt like stepping into another world—one where the rules of engagement were dictated by desire and the need to feel something genuine.

As Michael's words lingered in the air between us, we found a secluded spot away from the bustling crowd, where the dim lighting and the soft hum of distant conversations created an almost private world. Settling into this newfound intimacy, it felt as if the room, the event, even time itself had faded into the background, leaving just the two of us, wrapped in a bubble of shared understanding and curiosity.

"For someone who fears uncertainty," Michael continued, his gaze never wavering, "you seem to dive headfirst into the unknown. It's a fascinating contradiction."

I laughed, a genuine sound that surprised even me. "Maybe it's the thrill of the challenge," I admitted. "Or maybe it's just making peace with the chaos."

"Chaos can be a ladder," he quipped, his eyes twinkling with amusement. "But it's also a place where we find out what we're truly made of. It separates those who dream from those who achieve."

His observation sparked a fire within me, igniting a desire to share more, to delve deeper into the complexities that made us who we were. "Achievement without connection feels hollow," I found myself saying. "I'm looking for something... more. Something real amidst all the facades."

Michael nodded, understanding dawning in his eyes. "Real connections are rare in places like this," he said, gesturing vaguely to the surrounding opulence. "But not impossible to find. Sometimes, it's about taking the chance to reach out, to forge something genuine in the midst of pretense."

Our conversation meandered through a myriad of topics, from the philosophical to the trivial. We discussed art, our favorite books, the cities we dreamed of visiting, and the myriad ways the world could change in the next decade. Each topic revealed new layers to our characters, binding us in a tapestry of shared laughter, insights, and even disagreements that only served to enrich the connection blossoming between us.

Hours passed unnoticed, the event around us winding down as guests departed, leaving us enveloped in the quiet aftermath of the night. It was only when a staff member discreetly informed us that the venue was closing that we realized how long we'd been engrossed in our dialogue.

"Time flies when you're dissecting the universe," Michael remarked with a rueful smile, standing and offering his hand to help me up.

"Indeed, it does," I agreed, accepting his hand. As we made our way out into the cool night air, the early hours of the morning lending the city a serene, almost ethereal quality, I felt a sense of contentment and exhilaration I hadn't experienced in a long time.

"Thank you, Michael," I said as we paused outside, the night sky a canvas of stars above us. "For an unforgettable conversation... and for making me feel a little less alone in this vast, uncertain world."

"Anytime, Elena," he replied, his smile genuine. "Remember, two dreamers wandering under the same stars are bound to cross paths again."

And with that, we parted ways, the promise of future conversations and shared dreams lingering in the air, a beacon of hope in the pursuit of something real, something meaningful amidst the chaos of our lives.

As I continued to mingle with the other guests, every conversation felt increasingly hollow, the words slipping through my mind without leaving a mark. In the back of my thoughts, Michael's presence lingered, casting a shadow over every interaction. Each sentence spoken to me by others seemed devoid of meaning, my polite nods and smiles automatic as my thoughts wandered back to him.

When the event finally drew to a close and I stepped outside, the cool night air felt like a relief, a chance to breathe freely away from the pretense and noise. That's when I saw him again, waiting off to the side, as if he too sought an escape from the crowd. My heart skipped a beat, then began to race—a sensation so foreign yet exhilarating, it had been ages since anyone had stirred such feelings within me.

The sight of him under the soft glow of the streetlights, looking as captivating as he had in the midst of our earlier conversation, reignited the spark of anticipation that had been kindled inside me. It had been such a long time since I felt like this for anyone, and the realization that I was eager to explore whatever lay ahead with Michael was both thrilling and terrifying in equal measure.

When he saw me, Michael's face lit up with a recognition that felt like a warm embrace from afar. He started walking towards me, each step closing the distance between us, mirroring the quickening pace of my heart. It was as though he felt the same magnetic pull, a silent understanding passing through the space that separated us.

With every step he took closer, my anticipation grew, my heart skipping a beat, fluttering wildly like a captive bird eager for the freedom of the skies. This moment felt charged with possibility, each of us drawn to the other by an invisible thread woven from our earlier connection.

He guided me away from the remnants of the crowd, towards a secluded spot that was shrouded in darkness yet sparkled with its own kind of magic under the canopy of stars. As we moved together, the rest of the world seemed to fade away, leaving just the two of us in our own hidden corner of the universe.

I found myself trying to remember if anyone had ever stirred such intense feelings within me before—this blend of intrigue and fervent anticipation. Michael had an air of mystery about him, an enigmatic aura that was as compelling as it was passionate. Standing there, under the vast, starlit sky, with him so close, I realized the depth of the connection that was unfolding, mysterious and yet profoundly real.

"Would you be interested?" His question was a whisper, his lips hovering a breath away from mine.

In that moment, I realized that the line between networking and intimacy had blurred beyond recognition. The craving for a meaningful connection battled with the impulse to lose myself in the distraction of skin on skin. And there, beneath the weight of my own contradictions, I surrendered to the latter.

"More than anything right now," I breathed against his lips before they captured mine in a kiss that was both a promise and a reprieve. The rest of the evening faded into insignificance as we wove together a tapestry of passion and abandon, each touch a testament to our mutual escape from the solitude that dogged our days.

The encounter was spontaneous, raw—a collision of two souls seeking respite in the eye of the storm. It was everything I thought I needed and nothing I truly wanted, a temporary balm for the persistent ache of isolation that I had long since learned to mask with fleeting pleasures.

As our tangled embrace led us further from the glaring lights of the event and deeper into the shadows, I realized that this was yet another detour on my journey toward something deeper, something real. With every caress, with every gasp, I was both losing and finding parts of myself I had forgotten—or perhaps never truly known.

The dichotomy of the night was not lost on me; it mirrored the very essence of my existence—a constant tug-of-war between the professional facade I presented to the world and the private battles I faced when the curtain fell. Tonight, I indulged in the illusion of connection, all too aware that when dawn broke, I would once again don the mask and face the day with a renewed focus on the business, the vision that demanded everything of me.

But for now, I allowed myself to slip away, to drown in the depths of Michael's gaze and the promise of oblivion that awaited us in the dark.

The moon hung like a silent witness above the city as I stepped out of the opulent venue, the night air cool on my flushed skin. My heels clicked rhythmically against the pavement, an echo of the heartbeat throbbing through me. Each step was an effort to maintain composure, to hold onto the remnants of the poised businesswoman I needed to be.

"Leaving so soon?" The voice cut through the stillness, smoky and familiar. Michael leaned against the sleek body of his car, the streetlight casting a halo around his sleek black hair. His eyes were pools of something dark and indecipherable, pulling me into their depths.

"Shouldn't you be inside, charming investors?" I teased, but my voice betrayed my hunger—a hunger for him, for the oblivion he promised. He pushed away from the car and closed the space between us with predatory grace.

"Perhaps I've found something more captivating," he murmured, his breath warm against my cheek.

Hesitation fluttered in my chest, a bird trapped in a gilded cage. But desire beat stronger wings, and when his lips caught mine, I was lost. My body remembered him—every touch, every taste—and I surrendered to the urgency that consumed us both.

We went to his apartment which was a canvas of shadows and soft lights. Clothes became irrelevant as they fell away, our movements eager and unguarded. I reveled in the strength of his hands as they roamed over me, mapping the landscape of my flesh with authority and reverence. Our passion was a language only we spoke, each gasp and moan a wordless confession of need.

"Tell me what you want," he whispered against my ear, his voice a velvet command that sent shivers down my spine.

I couldn't form a coherent sentence, my mind was consumed with pleasure as we became one. We moved together in perfect harmony, bodies seeking fulfillment and completion. In that moment, nothing else existed - just the heat, the friction, and our mutual climb towards ecstasy.

When we finally reached the peak, it was an explosion of sensation that left us both breathless.

As our bodies melted into each other, our gasps and moans filled the room like a sweet symphony. We moved together, giving in to pleasure until we collapsed with heavy breaths. Then, as if assembling a puzzle, we carefully untangled ourselves and lay side by side, basking in the afterglow of shared passion.

The morning light peeked through the blinds, reminding us of the outside world and its demands. But here in Michael's bedroom, we had created our own sanctuary. Wrapped in his arms, I felt safe and content - yet a restlessness stirred within me as dawn brought new possibilities.

"Stay," he murmured, his voice thick with sleep.

I really wanted to stick around and see where things could go with Michael, but I was scared. I had been hurt before, and the thought of trusting someone again felt too risky. Everything with Michael was so new and so intense, and I wasn't sure how to deal with those feelings.

I also wasn't sure if Michael felt the same way about me. It seemed like he could have anyone he wanted, and I couldn't help wondering if I was just another girl to him. That idea made me feel really insecure. Deep down, I found it hard to believe that someone like him could actually have feelings for me. This mix of feelings made it really hard for me to just stay and let things happen.

But the call of the outside world was insistent, a siren song that whispered promises of a different kind of fulfillment. So, I untangled myself from the warmth of his bed and his embrace, dressing silently.

The city greeted me with its cacophony of sounds and the frenetic pulse of life rushing forward. Clara's words echoed in my mind, a reminder of the values I wanted to embody, the woman I longed to become. Yet, as I walked, an emptiness yawned wide within me—emptiness that the night's escapades had only briefly filled.

The storefronts beckoned, their windows a parade of luxury and excess. Without conscious thought, I found myself stepping into the cool interior of a boutique, the scent of leather and perfume enveloping me like an old friend.

"May I assist you?" The sales clerk at Chanel approached, her smile as polished and professional as the pristine layout of the boutique.

"Just browsing," I replied, my pulse quickening at the sight of silk dresses and jewel-toned handbags. I let my fingers glide over a Chanel Silk Crepe Dress, its fabric whispering promises of transformation. The price tag read $4,500, a testament to the luxury and allure of changing one's skin.

My eyes then caught the glimmer of a Saint Laurent Monogram Clutch in emerald green, priced at $1,250. The texture, the vibrancy of the color, spoke of nights filled with mystery and elegance.

I was drawn next to a Valentino Garavani Rockstud Spike Bag, its ruby red leather dotted with signature studs, a perfect blend of edginess and sophistication. At $2,800, it felt like holding a piece of the night sky, daring and limitless.

Slipping into a Versace Fitted Midi Dress that hugged my curves, I was transformed. Its bold red color screamed power and sensuality, making its $1,975 price feel like an investment in a new identity. In the mirror, I saw not Elena the entrepreneur, but Elena the enchantress, a woman of mystery and allure.

"Would you like to take this today?" The clerk's voice gently pulled me back from my reverie.

"Yes," I found myself saying, a mix of excitement and resolve in my voice. The transaction was swift—a swipe of a card, a signature, and the thrill of the purchase. Walking out with my bags, each bearing the name of the luxury it contained, the weight felt satisfying, grounding.

The euphoria of the purchase was temporary, much like the fleeting connections of the night. Yet, in that moment, it filled the void, a void that somehow Michael started to fill, a tangible reminder of the power of transformation, even if just for an evening.

The silk of the dress pooled at my feet, a molten pool of false promises. My reflection in the full-length mirror was a stranger, adorned in luxury that whispered lies of fulfillment. The weight of the bags around me felt like shackles, each item a monument to my moments of weakness. I sighed, casting a critical eye over the lavish spread.

"More?" I whispered to the silent room, the word a bitter taste on my tongue. "Is this really what you want, Elena?"

It wasn't. The rush of the purchase had vanished as quickly as it came, leaving behind only the stark reality of emptiness that no amount of spending could fill. There was no escaping the truth any longer — the euphoria of shopping was just another form of numbing, a way to avoid the deeper, gnawing hunger for something real, something lasting.

"Who are you trying to impress?" My voice broke the stillness, mockery and sadness lacing the question. The dresses, the shoes... they were all just a facade, an armor against the world, and against myself.

I collapsed onto the chaise, the cool leather against my skin grounding me as I considered the pattern of my life. Seeking validation from others, from things, I realized how I'd been sabotaging myself, mistaking indulgence for self-care, consumption for contentment.

"Enough," I decided, a newfound resolve hardening within me. I stood up, pushing the bags aside and made a promise to myself then and there. No more hiding, no more running.

Days passed, and with each one, the clarity of that moment sharpened. It was time for change, real change — not the superficial kind that came with a price tag. And so, I gathered a few people at my place, again, those who had begun to see past the gloss and glitter to the woman beneath.

"Isn't it fascinating," Clara mused, swirling her wine as she lounged on my new minimalist couch, "how art can capture the human condition so viscerally?"

"Entirely," I replied, feeling the warmth of genuine connection as we delved into the nuances of a piece we'd seen at the gallery. It wasn't the idle chatter of socialites; this was real dialogue, an exchange of ideas and dreams.

"Culture is our legacy," I found myself saying, "It's where we find meaning, where we connect with something greater than ourselves."

Heads nodded, and the conversation deepened, branching out into personal visions, aspirations for the future that were about contributing, not just taking.

As the evening waned, I looked around at these faces, no longer mere acquaintances but companions on a journey toward authenticity. There was laughter, there was debate — but most importantly, there was substance.

In the quiet that followed their departure, I lingered in the living room, the remnants of our discussions hanging in the air like music. This was it, the balance I had craved. Not the fleeting high of luxury, but the enduring richness of shared experience.

"Here's to finding worth beyond the wealth," I toasted to the empty room, knowing that the journey was far from over, but certain that the first step had been taken.

Chapter Ten

The morning light trickled in, too bright and yet not enough
to chase away the remnants of the dream. I blinked against the
sunlight, my eyelids heavy with images of Michael—those
intense blue eyes that seemed to cut through to the marrow of
my soul, leaving me bare and wanting. I exhaled, trying to shake
off the restlessness that had settled in my bones.

"Damn it," I murmured, rolling over to escape the
persistent gleam that mocked the darkness of my thoughts. The
sheets were twisted around my legs—a tangible reminder of the
night's turmoil as his face haunted my slumber, a ghostly imprint
on my consciousness. He was there in every dream, an echo of
desire that refused to be silenced.

Dragging myself out of bed felt like peeling away layers of a
vivid fantasy; each step away from the pillow where his image
lingered was a withdrawal from the drug that was Michael's

presence. My fingers brushed against the cool surface of the bedside table, pausing at my reflection in the mirror. Those expressive hazel eyes that stared back held a story untold—a woman on the precipice of something transformative, something terrifying.

"Focus, Elena," I chided myself, my voice sounding foreign in the silence of the room. It was just a man. Just a night. But even as I said the words, they rang hollow, a feeble attempt to deny the gravity of what had transpired between us.

I made my way to the shower, letting the hot water cascade over me in a vain effort to wash away the lingering touch of his hands, the memory of his lips tracing paths of fire across my skin. The sensation was maddening, addictive, a craving settled deep within my flesh that no amount of scrubbing could cleanse.

"Pull yourself together," I muttered, the sound drowned by the rush of water.

I emerged dressed in simplicity, choosing comfort over elegance—a soft sweater, jeans that hugged my curves without insistence. My hair fell in damp curls around my shoulders, a wildness I couldn't tame, much like the thoughts spiraling in my head.

Breakfast became a mechanical process, the fork lifting scrambled eggs to my mouth without taste or pleasure. Each bite was overshadowed by the memory of our conversations, the laughter we shared, and the undercurrent of something deeper—an intensity that threatened to sweep me away.

"Stop it," I snapped aloud, startling myself with the sharpness of my tone. The kitchen was silent, save for the ticking of the clock, marking the moments slipping by, each second a vast distance from the last time I felt his gaze upon me.

I left dishes in the sink, evidence of my disrupted routine, and gathered my things for the day ahead. Yet, as I stood by the door, keys in hand, I couldn't help but feel the pull of an invisible thread tethering me to the idea of him—the promise of another encounter, another chance to drink from the well of connection that had felt so unexpectedly profound.

"Michael," his name was a whisper, a secret spilling from my lips, a confession to the empty room. The mere utterance sent a shiver down my spine, a thrill mixed with dread.

Could I really afford to let him in? To indulge in this distraction when my very future—my dream—was at stake? But then, wasn't life about seizing moments of passion, about the risks that made one's heart race?

"God, what are you doing to me?" The question hung in the air, unanswered, as I stepped out into the world, the ghost of Michael's smile etched in the back of my mind, promising nothing but upheaval. And perhaps, just perhaps, that was exactly what I craved.

The blueprint rolled out before me, a canvas of potential and promise, yet the sketched lines and plotted points danced meaninglessly under my unfocused gaze. My colleagues discussed projections with fervor, their pens orchestrating futures on paper, but their voices faded into a muffled symphony as my mind slipped away from the boardroom.

"Michael," I sighed internally, a wayward thought breaking free. His smile crept into my vision, obliterating the numbers and margins. The warmth of his touch lingered on my skin, an electric current that buzzed through my veins, rendering the financial forecasts hollow echoes against the chamber of my heart.

"Are you with us, Elena?" My name snapped me back, a tether to reality. I nodded, feigning attention, scribbling irrelevant notes that were nothing more than coded pleas for focus. But this time it was more than random sex; it was an imprint on my soul, a craving that whispered seductively of depth and connection.

"Absolutely," I lied smoothly, my voice betraying none of the turmoil within, "Just considering the long-term implications."

My input was met with approving nods, but as the meeting droned on, every comment about client satisfaction and market shares felt insignificant compared to the conversations I'd shared with him. Michael's insights had cut through the superficial, reaching places in me that lay dormant, untouched by the daily grind of ambition and success.

As soon as decorum allowed, I excused myself, clutching at the excuse of another appointment while the truth was, I needed air—the kind untainted by corporate recirculation, free from the scent of wood polish and latent ambition.

The park greeted me with open arms, its lush greenery a stark contrast to the sterile office environment I had just fled. I walked aimlessly, attempting to clear the fog of infatuation clouding my judgment. Yet, nature's beauty only served as a reminder of his eyes—the blue of clear skies, deep and fathomless, holding storms and stories in their depths.

I paused by a bench, admiring the flowers that bloomed with abandon. Their vibrant colors and delicate forms should have offered solace, but they reminded me of the way he spoke about his passions—how his voice would soften with reverence when discussing art, or how his eyes lit up with the fire of someone who embraced life's intricacies fully.

"Dammit, Michael," I muttered, my attempt at solitude foiled by the persistent ghost of his presence. The breeze carried away my words, taking with it a petal that drifted downwards, a silent witness to the tumult raging within my chest.

"Focus, Elena. This is your dream job, your future," I chastised myself. Yet, what was a future if it didn't include the thunderclap of desire, the quietude of intimacy? If Michael was a distraction, then perhaps I'd been too focused all along, missing out on the very experiences that made life worth the chaos.

"Maybe the heart knows something the mind doesn't," I whispered, conceding to the possibility that surrendering to this feeling could be the most authentic decision I'd ever make. I stood there, amidst the whispers of leaves and the laughter of distant children, allowing myself to be swept up in the tide of an emotion I was only beginning to understand.

The park slowly emptied as the sun dipped lower, casting long shadows that stretched like fingers across the path. It was time to return, to face the world with a facade of composure. But beneath the surface, there was a current that pulled me towards an unknown horizon—a horizon painted in the hues of Michael's eyes.

I tapped the edge of my phone against my palm, each thump a metronome to the racing thoughts. My thumb hovered over the contact saved as 'Michael - Artist', a title too sterile for the man who had infiltrated the recesses of my mind with such fervor. It was ridiculous, this hesitation, when I knew full well that every fiber in my being ached to see him again.

"Take control, Elena," I murmured to myself. The words were a catalyst; I punched in a message with a feigned nonchalance I didn't feel. 'Hey Michael, fancy another artistic debate over coffee?' My finger trembled as I hit 'send'. The casual tone was a facade, a brittle veneer over the smoldering anticipation within.

The silence that followed stretched endlessly, punctuated only by the relentless ticking of the clock. To distract myself, I turned to the blueprints sprawled across my desk, plans for the future I was building—one where comfort and elegance would intertwine like the curls of my hair. Yet, they were just lines and contours on paper, void of warmth, devoid of life. They paled in comparison to the memory of his touch, which ignited fires along my skin.

I tried to focus on numbers and logistics, the backbone of my dream taking shape, but Michael's image loomed behind my eyelids. His intense blue eyes seemed to pierce through the veil of my concentration, questioning my resolve, challenging my desire for control. It was maddening how he occupied my thoughts, an addiction I was unprepared for, one that didn't involve substances but the intoxication of human connection.

"Damn it, Elena, get it together," I chided myself, pushing away from my desk to pace the length of my office. My reflection caught my eye in the window—a woman transformed, no longer fading into the background of her former small-town life. Yet, what did sophistication matter if my insides quivered like a schoolgirl's at the mere idea of a man?

"Focus on your work. Your empire," I whispered, attempting to anchor my drifting heart back to reality. But even the figures on the spreadsheet morphed into visions of his salt-and-pepper hair, the way it framed his face, the stark contrast to Alex's boyish charm. How could I plan for contingencies in business when my personal life felt like navigating without a compass?

I returned to my phone, its screen still void of a reply. A cocktail of emotions churned within me—longing, hope, frustration. The vulnerability was terrifying, a freefall from the tightrope of my carefully curated existence.

"Come on, Michael," I willed the words into the silence, a silent plea for him not to leave me suspended in this limbo. My heart beat a staccato rhythm, echoing the longing that refused to be quieted.

"Take control," I had said, but the truth was, in matters of the heart, control was often the first casualty. And so I waited, caught between the blueprint of my dreams and the pull of something far more intricate—the blueprint of desire.

The chirp of my phone sliced through the fog of concentration. One new message, and suddenly the room's air felt thin, as if every molecule had paused, waiting for me to swipe open the lock screen. It was him. Michael.

"Looking forward to seeing you again, Elena. When are you free?" His words, so simple, yet they sent a cascade of butterflies rioting in my stomach.

"This evening?" I typed back, my pulse thundering in my ears. The send button felt like a leap from a cliff's edge into unknown waters.

"Perfect. 7 PM?" His reply came quick, and with it a surge of something electric—excitement laced with a shot of pure apprehension. This wasn't just another date; it was a venture into uncharted depths, an exploration of a connection that seemed to transcend the physical. I was diving headfirst into vulnerability, and the thrill of it was intoxicating.

"See you then," I confirmed, sealing the pact. As soon as texting him, I called David. Told him to meeet me at home asap.

Standing before my open closet, I felt overwhelmed by the sea of choices, each piece a potential statement for tonight's encounter with Michael. Just then, the doorbell rang, and in walked David, my ever-reliable friend and now, fashion savior for the evening.

"Struggling?" David asked, a playful tone in his voice as he eyed the chaos of discarded outfits around me.

"I can't decide. I want to look confident, bold... but still me," I sighed, my frustration evident.

He picked up the silk blouse I had discarded earlier. "Not this," he agreed, setting it aside with a decisive motion. Then his eyes brightened as he pulled out a stunning, knee-length dress from the back of my closet. "How about this? It's chic, sophisticated, yet unmistakably Elena."

The dress was a deep, rich blue, almost matching his earlier description of an ocean calm but powerful. It had a simplicity that spoke volumes, paired with an elegance that didn't try too hard.

Slipping into the dress, I felt a transformation begin. The fabric hugged my frame just right, its hue accentuating my eyes. David nodded in approval, a grin spreading across his face. "Now, that's the Elena who's ready to take on the world—or at least, a certain someone."

I couldn't help but laugh, feeling a surge of excitement. "Do you think Michael will like it?" I asked, a hint of nervousness peeking through.

David walked over, placing a reassuring hand on my shoulder. "He'd be a fool not to. But remember, tonight is about how you feel in it. Confidence is your best accessory."

Together, we chose accessories—a simple, elegant necklace that spoke of understated class, and heels that were stylish yet practical, empowering me to walk with confidence.

As I looked at myself in the mirror, the reflection staring back was both exciting and reassuring. I felt like myself but elevated, ready for whatever the evening held.

"David, I don't know what I'd do without you," I said, gratitude filling my voice.

He smiled, his eyes meeting mine in the mirror. "You'd do just fine, but I'm glad I'm here to see you off. Now go, Elena. Go and show Michael exactly who you are."

With a final glance at my reflection, I felt a wave of bravery wash over me. Tonight wasn't just another evening; it was a step towards something more, a test of vulnerability and strength.

"Let's see what tonight brings," I said, more to myself than to David. With a deep breath and a final touch of lipstick for courage, I was ready. Stepping out into the evening, I felt a flutter of anticipation—the kind that heralded new beginnings. Tonight, I was not just meeting Michael; I was reintroducing myself to the world.

The restaurant's warmth embraced me as I stepped through its discreet entrance, a world away from the scrutinizing eyes of my usual circles. It was our chosen haven, a place where secrets could spill like sugar from a jar—sweet and unrefined.

Michael was already there, sitting by the window, his sleek black hair catching glimmers of the fading sunlight. He rose as I approached, his smile an open invitation to comfort, to be myself without the elaborate façades.

"Sorry, I'm late," I said, feeling the weight of every second I had spent changing outfits, chasing the elusive armor of perfection.

"Time is just a construct when I'm waiting for you," Michael replied, his voice laced with a patience that unwound my nerves. Michael stood up, gracefully closing the distance between us. He leaned in, placing a gentle kiss on my cheek, his presence carrying the fresh, enchanting scent of blooming flowers.

We ordered coffee—the rich aroma mingling with the undercurrents of anticipation. As we talked, the conversation undulated between playful banter and vulnerable confessions. My laugh, usually so carefully measured, tumbled out unrestrained, encouraged by the twinkle in his eye.

"I didn't realize you were this into art," Michael said, his voice tinged with surprise and curiosity as I shared a cherished memory from my college days—a time when my dreams were like bold strokes on a canvas yet to be muddied by life's more sober palette.

"It was more than just a hobby," I explained, feeling a warmth spread through me as I revisited those days. "Art was my sanctuary, my way of making sense of the world. There was this one project..." I paused, a smile playing on my lips at the recollection. "We had to create something that represented our deepest aspiration. I spent nights covered in paint, surrounded by canvases, lost in my own world."

Michael's eyes lit up, reflecting a genuine interest. "What did you create?" he asked, leaning closer, as if the space between us could dilute the essence of the story.

I laughed softly, the image vivid in my mind. "A chaotic mix of colors, with a single clear path cutting through the middle. It was...ambitious."

"Ambitious?" He echoed, a playful skepticism in his voice.

"Okay, maybe a bit pretentious," I conceded, rolling my eyes at my younger self's audacity. "But it was me—raw, unfiltered, dreaming of carving out my own path, no matter how tangled the rest of the canvas looked."

Michael's laughter mingled with mine, a sound that felt like coming home. "I wish I could've seen it," he said, his gaze holding mine.

"The painting or the mess I was during those all-nighters?" I teased, the ease between us growing with each shared laugh and look.

"Both," he admitted, his hand finding mine under the table, a touch that sparked a connection deeper than words. "It sounds like you poured your heart into it."

"I did," I whispered, allowing myself to get lost in the moment, in the understanding that flickered in his eyes. It was comforting to share a piece of my past, to reveal layers of myself I had kept hidden under the guise of practicality and restraint.

As our conversation continued, weaving through tales of dreams deferred and paths yet to be taken, I felt a sense of kinship with Michael that went beyond the here and now. Sharing that memory, exposing a sliver of my soul, had bridged a gap I hadn't even realized was there. It was as if, in recounting the passions of my youth, I had uncovered a forgotten truth about myself—one that Michael, with his gentle probing and genuine interest, had helped bring to light.

"Art was a passion before... before I let other things consume me," I admitted, the shadow of addiction briefly clouding the moment. But Michael's understanding gaze told me that here, shadows could exist alongside light.

"Show me?" His suggestion was unexpected, inviting.

"Show you?" I echoed, my curiosity piqued.

"Your art. The world through your eyes."

And so, we found ourselves wandering to a nearby gallery, the transition from coffee to culture as fluid as the brushstrokes adorning the walls. Each piece was a silent echo of human emotion, and we shared our interpretations, layers of meaning unfolding between us.

"Look at this one," Michael beckoned me over to a painting, its colors clashing yet somehow harmonious. "It reminds me of you—complex, vibrant, impossible to ignore."

"Because I clash?" I teased, though his words stirred something deep within me.

"Because you're real. You're not just one thing—you're a masterpiece of many stories, some hidden, some clear."

His insight took me by surprise, and I felt seen in a way that both exhilarated and intimidated me. This man, who I once thought was a mere chapter in my tale of recovery, might just be a pivotal verse in a song I'd forgotten how to sing.

"Thank you, Michael," I whispered, our fingers brushing against each other like tentative first strokes on a blank canvas.

"Thank you, Elena, for sharing this with me," he responded, his hand encasing mine, solid and sure—a lifeline amidst the swirling emotions that threatened to sweep me away.

As we left the gallery, the world outside seemed sharper, more alive, and I couldn't help but feel that in the grand tapestry of my life, new threads were being woven—threads of desire, of connection, of hope. And with each step, I walked a little closer toward the woman I was meant to be, my heart beating a rhythm of daring possibilities.

The chill of the evening air nipped at my skin as Michael and I paused outside the art gallery, our farewell lingering like the last note of a haunting melody. The intensity in his eyes held promises and secrets, an ocean I was both yearning to dive into and terrified to explore.

"Tonight was... it was more than I expected," I admitted, my voice barely above a whisper, trembling with the weight of unsaid words.

"Me too, Elena. It's rare to find someone who can walk through your thoughts so effortlessly," he replied, his hand lifting to brush a stray curl from my face, the contact sending shivers down my spine.

I nodded, my heart caught in a tangle of elation and ache. "Goodnight, Michael." My breath formed a misty cloud that mirrored the fog wrapping around my emotions.

"Goodnight, Elena," he said, stepping back reluctantly, the distance between us expanding with each second.

As he walked away, the parting was a physical pain, a sharp tug deep in my chest. I watched until he turned a corner and vanished, the echo of our connection throbbing in the empty space he left behind.

Back in the solitude of my apartment, the walls seemed to close in, reflecting the chaos of my heart. With trembling fingers, I pulled out my journal, the leather-bound confidant of my deepest thoughts. Pen poised over paper, I hesitated, then surrendered to the torrent within.

"Michael invades my thoughts, unbidden and persistent. There's a hunger, an addiction to the way he sees me—truly sees me. It terrifies me. This isn't just desire; it's a craving for validation, for a reflection in someone else's eyes that confirms I am more than my past mistakes, more than the sum of my fears..."

My words spilled across the pages, raw and uncensored, each sentence a revealing stroke of vulnerability. The ink bled my confusion, my longing, my silent plea for something tangible amidst the shifting sands of my new reality.

"His touch lingers on my skin, a phantom caress that whispers of what could be. But can I trust this? Can I trust him? Or is this another vice, a sweet poison dressed as salvation?"

I closed the journal, the clasp clicking like a door shutting on a room filled with whispered confessions. My thoughts swirled—a maelstrom of happiness, longing, and the addictive thrill of being understood.

"Damn you, Michael," I murmured into the silence. "For making me feel, for stirring this storm within me."

Lying in bed, I stared at the ceiling, the shadows there dancing like the echoes of our laughter, our shared moments. The darkness enveloped me, yet within its embrace, I felt an ember of warmth—the possibility of light in the form of a man whose words painted colors on my soul.

As sleep finally claimed me, I drifted into dreams where whispers of hope tangled with threads of fear, each one weaving a tapestry of what might be—a future with Michael at the center, a beacon in the haze of my life's complexities.

The cursor blinked on the laptop screen, a rhythmic pulse in the otherwise muted darkness of my home office. Restlessness fanned through me like an untamed fire, the heat of it chasing away any semblance of sleep that might have dared to creep upon me.

"Channel it, Elena," I whispered to myself, the words a talisman against the chaos of my emotions. "Turn this into something real."

I envisioned Michael's face, the way his eyes had looked at me with such intense clarity, as if he could see right through to the marrow of my being. It was his passion—a raw, infectious thing—that now fueled my own. With purposeful strokes, I began to outline a new project, one that would infuse my business with a vitality it had never known before.

The design concept unfolded before me, a fusion of form and function that mirrored the complexities of human connection we'd discussed. Each line I drew felt like a conversation with Michael, each curve an echo of his laughter. This project wasn't just a potential success; it was a coping mechanism, a way to harness the emotional turmoil that threatened to overwhelm me.

In those hours before dawn, my professional world expanded, taking shape in a way that felt intrinsically tied to the personal revelations I'd experienced. The restlessness within me settled, not extinguished but rather redirected into lines and figures that leapt from mind to screen with fervent urgency.

As the first light of morning filtered through the blinds, casting long shadows across my sketches, I finally allowed myself to retreat to the bedroom. Yet, as soon as my head hit the pillow, I was assaulted by a barrage of thoughts—vignettes of Michael and me, our conversations morphing into reveries of what might lay ahead.

"Be real, Elena," I chided myself, flipping the pillow to the cooler side, seeking some physical relief from the fever pitch of my internal struggle. "The future is a hazy mirage, tempting but treacherous."

The sheets tangled around me as I tossed and turned, a silent war raging between the thrill of newfound excitement and the specter of potential heartache. Michael had awakened a hunger, a deep yearning for a connection that went beyond the superficial trappings of my past life.

"Shit," I cursed under my breath, staring into the dark expanse above me, my body aching for rest, for peace, for him. His touch lingered on my skin, the ghost of our last encounter haunting me with promises of pleasure and pain intertwined.

"Dammit, Michael," I muttered, the words slipping out with a mix of desire and dread. He was the catalyst, the unforeseen variable in my carefully plotted existence that had thrown everything off-balance.

"Can I risk this?" I questioned the silence, my voice barely audible even to my own ears. "Can I dive into the depths with him and still come up for air?"

But there was no answer, just the steady thrum of my heartbeat and the encroaching day that demanded I face reality once again. The weight of my own longing pressed down upon me, a tangible force that refused to be ignored.

"Whatever this is... it's changing me," I admitted into the void, the truth of it resonating deep within the caverns of my soul. Michael, with every shared secret and lingering glance, had cracked open something primal within me—a wellspring of emotion that I could neither deny nor fully understand.

And so, I surrendered to sleep, a vessel adrift on the tumultuous sea of what ifs, my dreams a vivid tapestry of hope and fear inexorably woven together by the enigmatic artist of my affections.

As the first light of dawn crept through the curtains, I found myself wrapped in a cocoon of sheets, evidence of a night spent wrestling with a storm of thoughts rather than in peaceful slumber. There, in the quiet of the morning, my heart echoed with a longing that had grown too loud to ignore—a longing for Michael, for the sound of his voice, the warmth of his presence.

It had been days since our last encounter, days that had stretched into an eternity of waiting and wanting. The absence of his laughter, the absence of those insightful conversations that had become a balm to my soul, left a palpable void. Each moment away from him felt like a step away from the light he brought into my life.

"Enough," I murmured into the silence, a declaration more to myself than to the empty room. The liminality of longing had to end. Michael had become more than just a part of my days; he had become a necessity, his encouragement a catalyst that stirred the dormant parts of me to life. His belief in me filled the spaces within that had been shadowed by doubt, his words a gentle push towards becoming the person I aspired to be.

The woman who stared back at me from the mirror was one touched by the promise of something profound, a promise whispered in moments shared with Michael. The question wasn't if I was ready for him, but if I was ready to embrace the depth of my feelings, to dive into the unknown that love represented.

The realization dawned clear and bright: I wasn't just missing Michael; I was incomplete without him. The thought of another day passing without seeing him was unbearable. With a newfound resolve, I reached for my phone, the weight of decision pressing against my fingertips.

"Let's meet. I want to see you," I typed, each word a step closer to him, a step closer to us. The message sent, I allowed myself a moment of vulnerability, of hope. The anticipation of seeing him again, of sharing the same space and breathing the same air, ignited a spark of excitement—a beacon guiding me through the uncertainty of what lay ahead.

In sending that message, I acknowledged the importance of Michael's presence in my life, a presence that had become as vital as the air I breathed. The waiting would soon be over, and the thought filled me with a sense of purpose.

Today, I was not just Elena the dreamer; I was Elena, a woman ready to chase after what she desired, undeterred by the fear of falling. Today, I would see Michael again, and together, we would explore the depths of what we had begun to build. The words were out there, hanging in the digital ether, irreversible. A shiver raced up my spine, a cocktail of anticipation and angst. I threw on clothes without care, each article a shield against the chill of uncertainty.

"Whatever happens, you can handle it," I coached myself, repeating it like a mantra as I paced the length of my apartment.

"You've come through worse. You've battled addiction, fought tooth and nail for your sobriety. This is just a man. Just Michael."

Michael was more than a fleeting interest; he was the catalyst that rekindled a fire within me, a passion I thought was lost. Each moment with him, from the slightest touch to our shared laughter, stirred something deep inside me, a warmth that spread through every part of my being.

"Be brave, Elena," I whispered to myself, pausing in my anxious pacing. My heart echoed my words, beating with a fervor that spoke of hope, of desire. I was ready to embrace the chaos and beauty that awaited us.

The sudden vibration of my phone shattered the stillness of the room. With hands shaking from anticipation, I read his response. "Looking forward to it. See you soon." The words were simple, but they carried a promise, a confirmation of shared excitement.

A genuine smile lit up my face, a physical manifestation of the joy bubbling up inside me. I allowed it to fill me, pushing aside any lingering doubts. The future, with all its uncertainties, could wait. In this moment, I was consumed by the sheer potential of what lay ahead with Michael, the chance for something profound, something that resonated with the very core of who I was.

"See you soon, Michael," I whispered back to the empty room, the words a pledge to him and to myself. I was committed, heart and soul, prepared to navigate the upcoming journey with an open heart and a steadfast resolve. This marked the start of something new, our story, and I embraced it fully, eager for the chapters yet to be written.

Chapter Eleven

The first rays of morning light crept through the slats of my blinds, casting a warm, golden glow across the room. I stretched, feeling a delicious tingle of anticipation that had become as essential to my mornings as coffee. Today, Michael and I were meeting, and with each encounter, the substance of our exchanges seeped deeper into the fabric of my being.

I dressed with care, selecting a dress that matched my mood—bold yet understated, the color of ripe plums, hugging my curves in a silent promise of the woman I was becoming. The mirror reflected back an image of someone familiar but transformed, the quiet contours of my small-town life replaced by the chic sophistication of newfound confidence.

"Today," I whispered to myself, hazel eyes catching the light with a hint of mischief, "today could change everything."

I stepped out onto the bustling city streets, my heels clicking assertively against the pavement. The gallery Michael had chosen was nestled between high-end boutiques and gourmet eateries, its facade unassuming yet undeniably stylish. Inside, white walls stretched up to meet a ceiling lost to shadow, the perfect canvas for the vibrant artwork splashed across them.

Michael stood there, amidst the hushed murmurs of the early crowd, his dark hair and intense blue eyes drawing me in like gravity. He wore his charisma effortlessly, his smile lighting up as I approached, and it felt like coming home to a place I never knew I needed.

"Good morning," he greeted, his voice wrapping around me, warm and inviting.

"Morning," I replied, my own voice laced with a happiness that sounded strange to my ears—brighter, lighter, real.

We wandered through the gallery, pausing before each piece, losing ourselves in the colors, the forms, the raw emotions laid bare on canvas and sculpted in stone. Michael's insights touched something primal within me, as if he spoke directly to my soul, deciphering the language of my once-dormant dreams.

"Look at this one," he said, gesturing towards an abstract painting, swirls of crimson and sapphire dancing together in chaotic harmony. "The artist must have poured their entire heart into this creation. It's not just paint—it's their fears, their love, their very essence."

I nodded, my gaze transfixed by the intensity of the piece. "To create something so beautiful, they had to be willing to be vulnerable, to show the world what lies beneath the surface."

"Exactly." His approval sent a thrill through me. "It's the same with us, Elena. With every layer we peel back, we get closer to the truth of who we are."

Our conversation flowed seamlessly, touching on the dreams we held close and the walls we'd built to protect them. In the presence of such honest artistry, our own facades seemed trivial, unnecessary.

"Sometimes," I confessed, my voice barely above a whisper, "I'm scared that I'll wake up and find out all of this has been just another dream—that the person I am with you isn't really me."

"Then let's keep dreaming together," Michael said, his hand finding mine, a tangible lifeline in a sea of uncertainty. "Because I've never seen you more alive, more you, than you are right now."

His words anchored me, and I allowed myself to lean into the moment, into the possibility of an existence where vulnerability didn't equate to weakness, but to strength. Here, among the silent witnesses of paint and passion, I began to understand that intimacy wasn't just skin on skin; it was soul on soul, dreams entwined, a shared journey through the landscapes of our hearts.

The canvas before us was a riot of color, a chaotic dance of brushstrokes that pulled me into its turbulent world. Michael's voice, a gentle baritone, threaded through my thoughts as he mused on the artist's intention to capture the fervor of human emotion. Standing there, in the hushed reverence of the gallery,

I felt his words resonate within me, tapping into something raw and unexplored.

"Art," he said, his gaze never leaving the painting, "is intimacy made visible."

"Intimacy..." I echoed, the word feeling new and weighty on my tongue. "I used to think it was just about being close to someone. But now... with you, it's different. It's deeper."

"Depth is where the true beauty lies, Elena," he replied, shifting his gaze to meet mine, a corner of his mouth lifting in a knowing smile. "It's discovering the layers beneath the surface."

As we moved through the gallery, each piece spoke to me of potential and possibility—the same feelings Michael inspired in me. The more we shared, the more I realized how superficial my past encounters had been. They were like sketches, mere outlines of what I now craved: a masterpiece wrought from vulnerability and trust.

"Michael," I began, halting before an abstract that seemed to pulse with hidden life, "this... us... it's making me see things differently. For so long, I've been content with the shallow end, too afraid to dive deeper. But now, I want more. I want meaning, substance—"

"Passion," he supplied, his hand brushing against mine, sending ripples of awareness up my arm.

"Exactly," I affirmed, my voice stronger than I expected. "And not just here." I gestured to the space around us, the air vibrant with the silent energy of creation. "But out there, in the world. I want to create something lasting, something that will inspire others the way this"—I paused, sweeping my hand toward the artwork—"inspires me."

"Tell me," he urged, his presence grounding yet liberating.

I took a deep breath, the seed of a dream taking root. "An empire of galleries, not just spaces filled with art, but sanctuaries where creativity is nurtured. Where people can learn, grow, and express themselves freely. A place that fosters new talent and celebrates the courage it takes to share one's soul."

The excitement in his eyes mirrored my own. "You have the vision, Elena. And the passion to make it real. I've no doubt you'll create something extraordinary."

"Will you help me?" The question slipped out, naked in its hopefulness.

"Nothing would make me prouder," he assured me with a firm nod.

We stood side by side, our reflections mingling in the glass that protected a particularly evocative piece. I could see the future laid out before us, a tapestry woven from ambition and the tender threads of a bond only just beginning to reveal its depth.

"Thank you," I whispered, not just for his support, but for the awakening he'd stirred within me—a hunger for authenticity, for connections that transcended the physical and touched the very essence of who we were.

"Always," he whispered back, echoing his earlier promise, and in the quiet solidarity of that single word, I found the courage to chase my dreams.

The clink of ceramic mugs punctuated the hushed ambiance of the café as Clara and I settled into our secluded corner. My fingers wrapped around the warmth, a lifeline anchoring me in the now, before the torrent of my revelations.

"Clara," I began, my voice threading through the steam rising from my coffee, "I feel like every day with Michael unfolds a new layer of myself I didn't know existed."

She leaned forward, her eyes the embodiment of the safe harbor I'd come to rely on. "Tell me everything," she urged, her tone laced with genuine interest that coaxed my confessions from their hiding place.

"Being with him... it's not just about passion or even romance. It's like he sees right through to my core. Our conversations, they're not superficial; they're soulful, meaningful. He makes me want more—a deeper connection, an authentic life." The words poured out of me, a gentle river breaking its banks.

Clara nodded, her hand reaching out to squeeze mine. "It sounds like he's inspiring you in all the right ways," she said, her voice a soft caress against the vulnerability I laid bare.

I sighed, feeling the weight of past pretenses lifting. "And there's more. Today, in the gallery, surrounded by art that spoke of raw truths and hidden desires, I saw what I want for my future—an empire of galleries, not just as spaces to display art but as sanctuaries to nurture creativity and educate. Just like I envisioned before, but today, I am sure of it."

"Wow, Elena, that's incredible!" Her face lit up with the shared excitement of dreams unfurling. "You have this uncanny ability to make things happen. I can see it, your galleries changing lives, including your own."

"Really?" Doubt whispered its cold tendrils around my heart, seeking to choke the newfound ambition.

"Absolutely." She squeezed my hand tighter. "And I think I know someone who could be instrumental in making this dream a reality."

Before I could question her, the bell above the café door jingled, heralding the arrival of a woman whose presence seemed to command the very air around her. With sleek black hair and high fashion that draped her form with effortless grace, she approached us with a stride that was both determined and carefree.

"Meet Sophie Martinez," Clara introduced as the woman extended a hand towards me, her grip firm and full of promise.

"An absolute pleasure," Sophie said, her voice carrying the timbre of someone who wove creativity into every syllable. "Clara has told me so much about you, Elena. Your energy and vision, as Clara mentioned—it's exactly the kind of bold thinking we need more of in this city."

"Thank you," I murmured, taken aback by the immediate connection sparking between us. Her confidence was infectious, her gaze holding stories of her own trials and triumphs.

"Let's talk strategy," Sophie suggested, her enthusiasm undimmed. "There are grants, investors, spaces that cry out for the pulse of art to fill their empty chambers. And with your insight, we can make it resonate with voices yet unheard."

"Strategy," I echoed, the word solidifying into a tangible shape within my mind. Here was an ally, a fellow dreamer who saw the world not for what it was, but for what it could become.

"Exactly. You're not just building galleries; you're weaving a tapestry of culture and community. That's powerful," she affirmed, her eyes alight with a fire that matched my own.

"Sounds like we're embarking on quite the journey," I said, feeling the surge of adrenaline at the prospect of shared aspirations.

"More than you can imagine," Sophie promised, a grin spreading across her lips. "Buckle up, Elena. We're going to turn this city inside out with beauty, and nothing will ever be the same again."

"Nothing will be the same," I repeated, savoring the taste of transformation on my tongue. In that moment, surrounded by the clinking mugs and the murmur of patrons, I found solace in the thought that my former self—with her shallow encounters and stifling routines—was giving way to a woman whose dreams were as vast as the ocean and just as deep.

Stepping into the luminescent glow of the gallery, the air buzzed with an electrifying mix of anticipation and awe. The exclusive art opening, a masterpiece in itself, was Sophie's creation, and it swirled around us like a dream spun from the very essence of creative fervor. The walls were adorned with bold strokes and daring colors that dared you to look away, though you never could. I moved through the throngs of people, each piece beckoning me closer, whispering secrets of the artist's soul.

"Isn't this just electric?" Clara murmured, her voice barely rising above the symphony of conversation and clinking glasses. Her eyes sparkled, reflecting the vibrant tapestry of art that surrounded us.

"Absolutely," I replied, my heart swelling as I caught sight of an expansive canvas that seemed to capture the tumultuous dance of life and chaos. It was as if each piece called out to my own hidden desires, igniting them into something palpable, something real.

Sophie, ever the enchantress of the evening, flitted from group to group, her laughter as rich and compelling as the works she showcased. She approached, her energy magnetic, drawing us into her orbit. "Elena, what do you think? Does it speak to you?"

"It does," I confessed, my voice laced with newfound resolve. "It speaks of possibility, of worlds yet unexplored." My gaze lingered on an abstract that seemed to pulse with a hunger for more—more depth, more connection, a mirror to my own yearning.

"Then let's explore them together," Sophie said, her arm looping through mine, her conviction as infectious as her vision.

The evening unfolded like a series of revelations, each new introduction a potential thread in the tapestry I longed to weave. Influential figures from the art world, their faces etched with lines of passion and perseverance, offered not just pleasantries but doors to futures I was only beginning to envision.

Emboldened by the spirit of the night, I turned to Clara and Sophie, their presence both anchor and sail. "I want to create something like this," I began, my words tinged with the audacity of dreams. "An empire of art, where the new and the known converge, where we nurture talent and ignite minds."

Clara's eyes gleamed with pride, the bond of our shared history lending strength to my aspirations. "I've always known you were meant for extraordinary things, Elena."

"And I can already see it," Sophie added, gesturing expansively. "Galleries that don't just display art but celebrate it, workshops that don't just teach skills but awaken visions."

Their excitement cascaded over me, a torrent of affirmation and belief. We wove through the crowd, our dialogue a crescendo amid the backdrop of masterpieces, each word painting strokes of a future bright with promise.

"Imagine it," I said, my voice steady with determination. "A network of spaces alive with culture, with community. We'd be the heartbeat of the city, pulsing with creativity and growth."

"Your passion is your power, Elena," Clara said, her hand squeezing mine. "With it, you'll move mountains."

"Mountains, skyscrapers, whatever stands in your way," Sophie chimed in, her grin fierce and unwavering.

We stood there, a trio of dreamers set against a canvas of boundless potential, the night unfurling before us like a path paved with stars. And in that gallery, amidst the potent mix of art and ambition, I realized the depths of the journey I had embarked upon—a journey defined not by the addiction to superficial pleasures I once knew, but by the relentless pursuit of a life rich with meaning, crafted by my own hands.

"Let's make it happen," I declared, the words not just a statement but a vow, echoing through the charged space. "Let's make it all come alive."

The sharp clink of ice against glass punctuated the hum of conversation as I swirled my drink, a moody concoction that mirrored the twilight hues bleeding across the city skyline. Michael and I had claimed a corner at the rooftop bar, our latest urban sanctuary in a string of clandestine rendezvous that stitched together the fabric of our growing connection.

"Look at that," I murmured, gesturing toward the horizon where skyscrapers pierced the heavens, their lights winking like distant stars. The air was thick with the musk of ambition and whispered secrets, the energy of the city below pulsating in rhythm with my own quickening heartbeat.

Michael's gaze followed my outstretched hand, but it was clear his attention was more on me than the view. "Elena, every time I'm with you, this city feels... different. Like we're part of its story, not just passing through."

"Doesn't it?" I agreed, reveling in the reflection of the sunset on his intense blue eyes. "Each place we've been to holds a piece of us now."

"More than you know," he said, his voice dropping an octave, heavy with sincerity. He reached across the small table, brushing his fingers lightly against mine, sending a shiver up my arm. "I feel like I've shared more with you in these past weeks than I have with anyone in years."

His confession hung between us, raw and vulnerable, and I felt the walls around my heart crumble a bit more. "Me too, Michael. There's something about you that makes me want to open up, to share everything—even the parts of me I'm not proud of."

He leaned in closer, the intimacy of the moment wrapping around us like a cloak. "Like what?"

"Like my addiction," I said, the word tasting bitter on my tongue even as I forced it out into the open. "The rush of winning, the shopping sprees—they were a high, a way to fill something missing inside me."

His eyes softened, an ocean of understanding that threatened to pull me under. "We all have our escapes, Elena. Mine used to be work—drowning myself in it to avoid dealing with... well, life."

"Used to be?" I probed gently, recognizing the past tense, curious about the man behind the confident exterior.

"Before I met you," he admitted, a smile tugging at the corners of his mouth. "Now, I find myself wanting to face things head-on. With you."

The confession struck a chord within me, resonating with the sense of purpose I'd been nurturing. Our mutual vulnerabilities, instead of presenting chasms to leap over, became bridges connecting us on a deeper level.

"Thank you for trusting me with this, Michael," I whispered, squeezing his hand in appreciation, feeling the weight of his trust like a precious gemstone.

"Thank you for being someone worth trusting," he replied, his thumb tracing circles on the back of my hand.

The night deepened around us, the city's cacophony fading to a backdrop as we continued to share stories and dreams, intertwining our aspirations and fears until they were indistinguishable from one another. Each revelation, each shared secret, was another thread weaving the tapestry of our bond, richer and more complex with every layer.

Leaning back in my chair, I allowed the warmth of Michael's presence to engulf me, the sounds of the vibrant city rising and falling with our laughter. In those moments, amid the planning and dreaming, I felt the seeds of a new addiction taking root—the kind that didn't leave me hollow, but rather filled me with a sense of connection, of belonging.

"Let's promise each other something," Michael said suddenly, his voice earnest. "No matter how high we climb or how far we go, let's never lose this. This honesty, this rawness between us."

"Promise," I said without hesitation, the words sealing a pact that felt as significant as any business contract or vow. And as the city buzzed beneath us, I knew that whatever the future held, the foundation we were building would withstand any storm.

The silence of my apartment was a stark contrast to the lively chatter of last night, where Michael and I had peeled back layers of ourselves under the watchful gaze of twinkling stars. Alone now, I sat cross-legged on my velvet chaise, the soft fabric caressing my bare skin as the morning light painted my walls in hues of gold and amber.

My fingers hovered over the blank pages of my journal, the leather-bound confidant that held my whispered secrets and fragmented dreams. Today, it beckoned me to inscribe a new truth—one wrought from the realization of who I had become.

"Who am I?" I murmured, the question spilling into the quiet room. The echo of my own voice served as a reminder of the journey from obscurity, the path from longing to fulfillment. Each entry in my journal was a testament to the metamorphosis of Elena—the woman who once sought validation in empty pleasures, now finding solace in the depths of sincere connection.

I began to write, my pen dancing across the paper with a life of its own. "Gone is the girl who mistook attention for affection, who believed the lie that love was just a game of numbers," I scribbled fiercely. "In her place stands a woman awakened by the kind of intimacy that doesn't just touch skin, but ignites souls."

The words flowed like a river breaking free from a dam, carrying with them the sediment of my past selves—the versions of me that clung to the brittle highs of superficial encounters, mistaking them for joy. Now, though, I craved the richness of shared vulnerability, the intoxicating high of dreams entwined with another's.

"Michael has become the mirror through which I see my truest self," I wrote, reflecting on our conversations that delved into fears and aspirations with equal fervor. "His honesty strips me bare, leaving me exposed yet unafraid—because in his eyes, I see not judgment, but recognition."

With a final flourish, I closed my journal, the click of the latch sounding like the closing of one chapter and the beginning of another. I stood and walked to my desk, the scent of coffee and determination mingling in the air.

Before me lay the blueprint of what could be my legacy—a network of galleries that would serve as sanctuaries for the artistically hungry and the culturally curious. A place where talent could blossom from the nurturing soil of community and education.

As I sketched out plans for workshops and talent incubators, each stroke of my pencil felt like a promise to the future—an oath to provide what I once longed for: a space to belong, to grow, to connect beyond the superficial.

"Art is not just about observation—it's about participation," I whispered to myself, envisioning the lives that could change within the walls of my galleries. Like mine had, under the brushstrokes of authenticity and the canvas of genuine ties.

The hours slipped away as I lost myself in the logistics of leases and locations, marketing strategies and mentorship programs. This dream, once nebulous and distant, was taking shape under my hands, guided by a vision clear and bright.

"From obscurity to a life replete with meaning," I mused, leaning back in my chair. The prospect of it all was overwhelming, exhilarating—a potent cocktail of potential and purpose that left me intoxicated with ambition.

This was more than a business plan; it was a manifesto of transformation, etched in ink and infused with the essence of newfound connections—a testament to the woman I had become and the empire I was poised to build.

The clack of my heels on polished marble echoed like a metronome, keeping time with the racing pulse of my newfound determination. Boutique windows winked at me, their displays artful compositions of luxury and promise—each piece a potential thread in the tapestry of my emerging identity.

"Today is about celebration," I told my reflection as I paused before the gilded facade of an upscale store. The woman staring back held none of the hesitation that used to cloud her eyes. She was someone who knew her worth, who recognized the allure of depth over the fleeting charm of surface beauty.

I let my fingertips glide along the textures of silk and cashmere, selecting outfits not just for their cut or color, but for what they represented. Each garment was a choice, a declaration: I am here, I have arrived, and I will be seen.

"Exquisite taste, Ms. Elena," the attendant murmured as she folded my selections with reverent hands.

"Please, call me Elena," I insisted, offering a smile that felt as luxurious as the fabric pooling around me. Shopping had once been a salve, a way to fill the void with ephemeral things. Now, it was an affirmation.

Flushed with the thrill of self-indulgence, I emerged into the sunlight, bags swinging from my arms like trophies of a battle won—the battle to reclaim myself.

"Perfect timing, Elena," David's voice greeted me as I entered the café where we'd agreed to meet. His smile was a steady beacon, grounding amidst the heady swirl of my day.

"David," I sighed, settling into the chair across from him, my spoils of victory at my feet. "I feel like I'm finally stepping out of the shadows."

He nodded, his eyes reflecting pride and understanding. "You're ready for this. Now, let's talk strategy." His laptop opened between us, a bridge to the future I was impatient to cross.

"Location is key," I began, feeling the weight of every decision as if it were a stone set in the foundation of my dream.

"Somewhere vibrant, accessible, a place that throbs with the city's heartbeat."

"Agreed," David said, tapping away. "I've been scouting. There's potential near the arts district—foot traffic, a creative buzz. It fits your vision."

"Community engagement," I continued, leaning forward, driven by the fervor of my aspirations. "Art should be a dialogue, not a monologue. I want programs that invite participation, that challenge and nurture."

"Workshops, talks, scholarships?" he offered, each suggestion a building block.

"Exactly." My voice was firm, edged with the clarity of purpose. "This empire isn't just about displaying art—it's about creating a legacy of artists."

"We'll need to network, find patrons who share your passion," David reminded me, ever pragmatic amid my soaring dreams.

"Patrons..." I mused, rolling the word around my mouth like a rich wine. Once, I would have balked at such intimacy, at the thought of dependence on others. But now, I saw the strength in connections, the power in shared visions.

"Leave it with me," David assured, his confidence bolstering my own. "You focus on being the visionary. I'll handle the logistics."

"Thank you," I breathed out, gratitude mingling with anticipation. In the warm cocoon of the café, with my purchases a silent chorus of encouragement, I let myself believe in the possible.

"Anything else?" David asked, always thorough, always ready.

"Nothing for today," I replied, rising to leave, my mind alight with plans and possibilities. "Tomorrow, we build an empire."

"Then tomorrow it is," he smiled, and I carried that smile with me out into the evening, a talisman against the doubts that no longer held sway over the woman I had become—a woman capable of crafting a life as masterful and as meaningful as the art that inspired her.

The space around me, my home, felt transformed. It was as if the very walls, once silent witnesses to my solitude, was now filled with a new energy. This place, which had often echoed with the quiet of loneliness, now illuminated with the promise of something more.

It was my home, not because of the deed or the furnishings, but because it no longer felt empty. With the anticipation of change, each room bathed in a light of positivity that hadn't been there before. Love, or the promise of it, had seeped into the corners, filling up the spaces that doubt and uncertainty once occupied. It was as though Michael's presence, though not physical, had imbued my home with a warmth and a hope that made it feel complete for the first time.

The living room glowed with the soft hue of twilight, its elegance a soothing balm to my senses. I lowered myself onto the plush cream sofa, the gentle give of the cushions hugging me like an old friend. Before me lay the fruits of today's indulgence: glossy bags filled with textures and colors that spoke of a life luxuriously reimagined.

Each piece, a deliberate choice, was more than fabric or accessory; they were artifacts of transformation, imbued with the essence of who I was becoming. I ran my fingers over a silk scarf, its pattern a dance of vibrant hues, and felt a kinship with its bold defiance of the mundane.

"Confident, successful, cultured," I whispered to the quiet room, the words wrapping around me like the fine threads of my new wardrobe. The Elena reflected in the mirror now was one who commanded attention, not for vanity's sake but as a testament to her evolution.

Around me, the art adorning the walls—a curated mix of abstract expressionism and haunting portraits—echoed back my journey. They were the silent witnesses to the nights I wrestled with the demons of doubt and the seductive pull of old habits. Addiction, once a specter that clung to my heels, now found no purchase on the sleek marble floors of my new reality.

A soft sigh escaped my lips, a sound of contentment mingled with a flicker of ambition. It was not just about acquiring things; it was about crafting spaces where dreams could breathe, where talent could flourish under my care. An empire of art, built from the raw clay of my aspirations.

My mind danced back to Michael, his words a brushstroke across the canvas of our shared experiences. "To create is to be vulnerable," he had said, his gaze intense as we stood amidst the thrumming heart of the gallery. And wasn't that what I was doing? Exposing my deepest desires for a life rich in meaning, laying bare the blueprint of my soul?

"From obscurity to a life filled with art, love, and potential," I mused aloud, the mantra tethering me to this moment of clarity. I had stepped out of the shadows of an unremarkable existence, into a spotlight that didn't dazzle but rather illuminated the path ahead.

There was power here, in the solitude of my elegantly appointed sanctuary. Power in the silence that allowed me to hear the thrum of my own heartbeat, syncopated with the pulse of possibility. Tomorrow, I would step out again, shoulder to shoulder with allies like David, Clara, Sophie, and Michael, each believing in the vision I harbored within.

But tonight, I reveled in the private victory, in the tangible pieces of a new life that surrounded me. The bags whispered their encouragement, a choir of luxurious voices urging me onward. And in the stillness, I promised them—and myself—that this symphony of change was only the prelude to a masterpiece yet to unfold.

Chapter Twelve

The cursor on my laptop screen blinked mockingly, a silent challenge as I attempted to dive into the financial projections for my new business idea. Normally, numbers are my playthings, elements I command with ease to sketch the future I envision. But today, every figure, every calculation, seemed to thrum with an entirely different expectation, syncing more with the anticipation of the evening I had planned with Michael than with any fiscal forecast.

"Come on, Elena," I scolded myself, trying to rein in my wandering thoughts with a firmness that reverberated through the quiet of my minimalist home office. "Focus." My fingers danced across the keyboard in a determined burst of activity, yet underneath, my emotions swirled with a yearning intensity, pulling at me, urging me towards something beyond the numbers and plans.

I allowed myself a brief moment to think of him—Michael's laughter, the depth in his eyes when he shared his passions, the lively debates we fell into with ease. It wasn't just his appearance that captivated me; it was the way our minds met, challenged, and inspired each other.

With a sudden resolve, I shut my laptop, the final click echoing my decision to shift my focus. I got up and paced, the rhythm of my heels on the hardwood a sharp counterpoint to my racing heart. "I need something special for tonight," I murmured, the idea forming amidst the tumult of my thoughts.

That's when it struck me, clear and compelling. I moved towards my bookshelf, my hand automatically going to a rare art book, a piece we had once discussed passionately. It was perfect—a gift that was both personal and meaningful.

Holding the book, I felt a rush of anticipation, imagining Michael's delight, the possible closeness that might follow. This gift was a symbol, a declaration of our shared interests and budding connection.

With the book now wrapped and placed beside my purse, I glanced at my reflection, noticing the excitement that flushed my cheeks, anticipating not just the physical intimacy but the deeper exploration of the night ahead. "Tonight," I said, feeling a mix of determination and vulnerability, "we start to discover where this can go."

Taking a deep breath, I prepared myself. This evening was about more than just fleeting pleasure; it was a step towards something more meaningful, a blend of desire and depth I hadn't ventured into before.

As I turned off the office lights, stepping out into the evening, the book in my hand felt like a promise, a beacon for the night's possibilities. "Let's uncover some truths tonight, Michael," I thought, locking my door behind me, ready for whatever the night might reveal.

The anticipation bubbled up inside me as I prepared for the evening with Michael, my heart beating a little faster with every second. I decided on a stunning green dress from Gucci that David and I had found on a shopping spree last month. It was a piece that stood out in the store, and David insisted it was made for moments like this. Slipping into it, I felt as though I was wrapping myself in the excitement and promise of the night ahead.

To complement the dress, I chose velvet Manolo Blahnik heels, their texture as luxurious as the feelings swirling within me. The gold necklace I clasped around my neck was from David Yurman, a delicate piece that David had helped me pick, saying it mirrored my inner glow. Looking in the mirror, I saw not just myself but the sum of all the hopes and dreams I carried into tonight.

Every piece I wore was a memory, a step on the journey that had brought me here, filled with the laughter and confidence David and I shared on that day we shopped together. This wasn't just an outfit; it was a tapestry of moments, each thread woven with care and affection.

As I made my way to Michael's, the excitement was palpable, mixed with a sincere hope for what the night could unfold. The dress, the shoes, the necklace—all were symbols of a readiness to open my heart, to show Michael the depth of my sincerity, my willingness to explore what lay between us.

When the door swung open to reveal his welcoming smile, a wave of warmth washed over me. Here, in the dim light of the hallway, Michael's embrace spoke of acceptance, of beginnings. It was a silent promise that no matter where the night led, the sincerity of our connection, the feelings we were nurturing, were as real as the beating of my heart.

This moment, bought with laughter and chosen with care, was the beginning of something true, something deeply felt.I stepped across the threshold, carrying the art book carefully wrapped in silver paper, its ribbon glinting under the tasteful sconces that lined his walls. The space was a testament to Michael's eye for aesthetics—clean lines, bold artwork, yet every element curated to invite conversation and coziness. The thick pile rug underfoot cushioned the world away, and rich, velvety tones whispered from the corners of the room.

"Your place... it's beautiful," I breathed out, taking in the collection of sculptures and photographs that dotted the space with stories untold.

"Only the best for tonight." He watched me, his gaze like a brushstroke against canvas, painting layers of unspoken promise between us.

As the evening unfurled, we found ourselves nestled into the deep cushions of his couch, surrounded by the ambient hum of a city settling into night. Our dialogue meandered from the mundane to the profound, the kind of talk that stitches souls closer, thread by fragile thread.

"Tell me, Elena," he leaned in, his fingers tracing idle patterns on the armrest, "what dreams keep you awake at night?"

I hesitated, the weight of real vulnerability pressing against the facade I so often wore like armor. It was a question that demanded truth, not just surface confessions.

"I dream of creating something lasting," I admitted, the words spilling from a wellspring of ambition and fear. "Not just in business, but... in life. Connections that endure beyond the fleeting."

"Ah," he nodded, his eyes holding mine, "to leave a mark on the world and in the hearts of those we touch."

"Yes," I whispered, "exactly that."

Our conversation danced through the labyrinth of our aspirations, each disclosure peeling back another layer, revealing the rawness beneath. In the quiet spaces between words, I felt the air thicken with anticipation, a silent symphony of potential that played beneath our skin.

"Michael," I found myself saying, my voice barely above the murmur of distant traffic, "there's a part of me that's tired of chasing shadows. Of mistaking addiction for affinity."

He reached out, his hand capturing mine, a lifeline thrown across the chasm of my confession.

"Then let's chase the light together," he offered, his sincerity anchoring me to the moment, to him. "Let's find what's real and hold onto it with everything we've got."

The intimacy of the conversation wrapped around us like a cocoon, nurturing the delicate beginnings of something more profound than either of us had known. And in the sanctuary of Michael's living room, amidst the artifacts of his life and the echoes of shared secrets, I found myself on the cusp of transformation—a metamorphosis marked not by the fire of fleeting pleasures, but by the slow burn of genuine connection.

With a flourish, Michael pulled back a heavy velvet curtain, unveiling a wall adorned with art that seemed to pulse with life. My breath caught at the sight. Here, in the quiet grandeur of his apartment, was a collection that spoke of years spent seeking and savoring beauty.

"Is that—?" I began, stepping closer to a vibrant canvas.

"Delacroix," he confirmed, pride softening the edges of his voice. "La Liberté guidant le peuple. A reproduction, of course."

"Of course," I echoed, though I found the notion that Michael might house an original masterpiece within these walls not entirely implausible. He watched me as I took in the piece, my eyes tracing the determined figures charging forward, awash in the stormy hues of revolution.

"Your passion for art—it's infectious," I said, turning towards him. His fingers lightly grazed my arm as he guided me from one painting to the next, each accompanied by a story, a whispered secret from his past.

"Art speaks when words fail us," he mused, his gaze locked onto mine as we paused before a hauntingly intimate portrait by Klimt. "It's the rawest expression of our deepest selves."

"Like us," I ventured, "revealing pieces of ourselves without saying a word."

"Exactly," he replied, his touch lingering, inviting.

We settled onto the plush sofa, side by side, yet the space between us thrummed with an energy that felt tangible, almost electric. The air in the room coursed with unvoiced desires, thickening around us like a sensual fog.

"Michael," I murmured, drawn to the magnetic field of his presence, "there's something about you... it's different for me."

"Tell me," he whispered, his voice low and resonant.

"Every part of me is awake in your presence. You make me feel alive, seen... wanted." The confession tumbled from my lips, unguarded and true.

His hand reached for mine, and our fingers intertwined—a silent vow that pulsed through my veins. As he leaned in, the last distance closed, and his lips met mine in a kiss that ignited every starved corner of my being. It was a slow burn at first, then a raging inferno as our bodies melded into a chorus of heated caresses and fervent whispers.

Just like the first time we met, his hands traced the curve of my spine, pulling me closer. There was a reverence in his touch, a worship that seeped beneath the surface, reaching the parts of me long buried under layers of doubt and fear.

Our clothes became a memory, discarded on the path to a deeper truth. His body over mine felt like coming home—familiar, yet thrilling in its newness. With each movement, each shared breath, we explored the profound territory of desire and affection, mapping out a world where pleasure and emotion were inseparably entwined.

"Michael," I gasped, the sound swallowed by his fervent response, each stroke stoking the fire within. There was no holding back the tide, no dam strong enough to contain the flood of sensation that crashed over us. In the tempest of our joining, something shifted—the axis of my world tilting towards this man who made me feel known and cherished.

He moved with a purposeful intensity that left me breathless, every thrust a declaration, every moan an affirmation of the depth of our connection. The taste of his skin, the rhythm of his heartbeat, the strength of his arms wrapped around me—I imprinted them all, knowing this was a moment that would redefine me.

"Look at me," he urged, his blue eyes blazing with a passion mirrored in my own. Our gazes locked, and in that instant, the universe contracted to the space we occupied, to the sacred dance of two souls entwined.

The crescendo came, a powerful surge that swept us along, leaving us adrift in the aftermath, our bodies a testament to the profound act of communion we'd shared. Clinging to each other, spent and sated, we lay in silence, the reverberations of our union echoing through the stillness.

"Michael," I breathed, my heart full, "this is real."

"Real," he agreed, his voice a tender caress. "And just the beginning."

The moonlight spilled across the room, casting Michael's features in a soft silver glow as he spoke. His voice was a low hum, threading through the quiet of his apartment, touching on tales of youthful escapades and tenderly unfolding the layers of his past.

"Back in college, I thought I had it all figured out," he confessed, tracing the rim of his wine glass with a fingertip. The light danced in his eyes, reflecting a vulnerability that drew me closer.

I nestled into the curve of his arm, our bodies molding together on the plush sofa. "We all have those illusions," I whispered back, the laughter in my voice tinged with reminiscence.

"Tell me one of yours," he urged, his gaze never leaving mine.

"Alright," I acquiesced, feeling the weight of my own history press against my chest. "I used to dream of opening a little bookstore. Somewhere cozy, with worn leather chairs and that smell of old pages..."

"Sounds perfect," Michael murmured, his hand finding its way to mine, fingers intertwining in a tender clasp.

As the night deepened, our shared confidences wove a tapestry of intimacy, each story a thread binding us tighter. The space around us seemed charged, every breath we took laced with significance.

I leaned into him, my head resting against his shoulder, as the resonance of our shared secrets hummed between us. The physical closeness felt natural, yet there was an electric current of awareness running through my veins, a pulsing acknowledgment of the significance of this embrace.

"Michael," I said, my voice barely above a whisper, "there's something about you—about us—that feels... different."

"Good different?" he asked, his lips brushing the crown of my head.

"Profoundly so," I admitted, my heart thrumming a staccato rhythm against my ribs.

In his hold, I felt a yearning blossom—a longing not just for the heat of his touch, but for the warmth of his soul. It was a desire that eclipsed any fleeting pleasure I had known before, a craving for communion that delved beyond flesh, seeking solace in the very essence of another being.

"Michael, I want..." My words trailed off, but he understood, his blue eyes piercing through to the core of my hesitance.

"Everything," he filled in, his voice a rich timbre that vibrated within me. "You want everything, Elena, and I want to give it to you."

Our lips met in a kiss that was a promise and a discovery rolled into one—the taste of him intoxicating, emboldening me to explore further, deeper.

"Michael," I gasped, my fingers digging into his shoulders as the world narrowed down to the searing point of contact between us. "You make me feel alive—truly, deeply alive."

"And you, Elena," he groaned, his movements deliberate, achingly slow, "you make me feel like I've finally come home."

Our union was a dance of shadows and moonlight, of whispered pledges and fervent cries that echoed off the walls, marking us, changing us. This was more than passion; it was an unveiling of souls laid bare, a testament to a longing fulfilled and a future that beckoned with open arms.

Waking up next to Michael was like opening my eyes to a new world. The morning light crept in, casting a soft glow on his sleeping face, and in that peaceful moment, everything felt different. He looked so serene, a stark contrast to the vibrant, passionate man I had come to know. Watching him there, I felt a warmth spreading through me, a sense of contentment I hadn't known before.

The night we had shared was amazing, beyond what words could capture. It wasn't just about the physical connection, though that was undeniable. It was the laughter, the conversations that flowed effortlessly, the way he looked at me as if I was the only one in the room. I had never felt so understood, so cherished.

Lying there, I realized how full I felt, as if Michael had filled up spaces in me I didn't even know were empty. The satisfaction wasn't just physical; it was emotional, a deep-seated feeling of being exactly where I was meant to be. For the first time in a long while, I didn't feel the urge to question or doubt. I just allowed myself to be, to feel.

I traced my fingers lightly over his cheek, careful not to wake him. He shifted slightly, a soft sigh escaping his lips, but remained asleep. I couldn't help but smile, taking in the sight of him, memorizing the feel of his skin under my fingertips.

After a moment, I gently kissed his forehead, a silent thank you for the night, for the feelings he had awakened in me. I felt a pull to stay, to wake him with whispers of promises and plans. But something within me chose this quiet departure, a way to savor the sweetness of the night a little longer, to leave us both wanting more.

So, without another word, without waking him, I quietly got out of bed, dressed, and left his apartment. The early morning air was crisp against my skin, a reminder of the world outside our bubble. As I walked away, I carried with me the warmth of his embrace, the memory of his smile, and a heart full of possibilities.

This was an acknowledgment of something beginning, something neither of us could yet define but both eagerly anticipated. And as I stepped into the day, I knew that what Michael and I shared was a rare find, something to cherish, to explore. I left his side, but took a piece of that warmth with me, stepping into the daylight full and satisfied, ready for whatever came next..

With each step away from his apartment, I became acutely aware that I was no longer the woman who measured worth by social standing or sought solace in the ephemeral. In Michael's arms, I had glimpsed a future where genuine affection and mutual respect were the cornerstones of connection.

The streets were empty as I walked, wrapped in reflections of the night before. Every memory, every whispered confession, and every caress seemed to confirm that my life was irrevocably altered. I had tasted the essence of something pure, a love not marred by the addictive pursuit of fleeting pleasures but grounded in the profound discovery of another's soul.

My heart raced with the realization that this was only the beginning. Michael and I, we had found something rare—something worth cherishing and nurturing. And as the first rays of sunlight kissed the horizon, I stepped forward, ready to embrace whatever came next.

Closing the door behind me, the familiar scent of my apartment greeted me like an old friend. It was strangely comforting after the intensity of Michael's place, a sanctuary where my scattered thoughts could settle into coherence. I kicked off my shoes and padded across the cool hardwood floor, feeling the ghost of his touch still lingering on my skin.

I sank into the embrace of my plush armchair, letting the softness catch me as I closed my eyes and replayed the evening in my mind. The taste of red wine danced on my tongue, a reminder of our laughter as we shared stories between sips. With each recollection, I peeled back the layers of my attraction to Michael, dissecting the emotional anatomy of what drew me to him.

It wasn't just desire that pulsed through my veins when I thought of him; it was a connection that dove deep beneath the surface, reaching into the hidden caves of my heart that I had sealed off long ago. This wasn't a fleeting thrill or a means to fill the void left by my past indulgences; this was a river that flowed with shared dreams and vulnerabilities, carving out a path through the rocky terrain of my soul.

"Michael," I whispered into the quiet room, tasting the name, feeling its weight and promise. His image, so vivid in my mind's eye, brought a warmth that radiated from within. We had traversed the landscape of each other's bodies with a reverence that spoke volumes, our silent conversation punctuated by gasps and moans that echoed off the walls of his bedroom, narrating a tale of longing finally fulfilled.

My past affairs, now distant shadows, paled in comparison to the depth of what Michael offered. There was no empty high, no craving for the next hit of pleasure. With him, I found sustenance, something wholesome and nourishing that sustained me far beyond the ephemeral rush. Each caress, each kiss, was imprinted with significance, etching a story of genuine affection into the canvas of my being.

Lying back, I let the fatigue of the night wash over me. My body was tired but satiated, every muscle humming with the memory of our union. As sleep beckoned, I surrendered to its call, a smile playing on my lips. In the tapestry of tangled sheets and whispered confidences, I had discovered a new texture of intimacy, one where respect and understanding were woven together with threads of passion.

And there, on the precipice of dreams, I understood that with Michael, I was embarking on a journey not just of the flesh but of the spirit. We were two souls converging on a path that promised mutual growth and discovery, our hearts beating in sync with newfound purpose.

I tried to surrender to a nap, cradled by the serenity that comes with the recognition of something real. There was no looking back, only forward, toward a horizon rich with the colors of a love that promised to be as enduring as it was profound.

Sunlight peeked through the blinds, casting a golden haze across my eyelids. Consciousness stirred within me, gently coaxing my senses awake. I stretched languidly, muscles singing a sweet song of exertion from the night before. With each movement, memories of Michael's touch flickered behind my closed eyes—tender yet fervent, a testament to our newfound intimacy.

I rolled over, the empty space beside me a stark reminder that I was alone in my bed. Yet, I felt anything but solitude. There was a presence, an essence of Michael lingering like a subtle fragrance in the air. The warmth of his skin seemed to still radiate from the sheets, and I wrapped myself in them, savoring the comfort they offered.

My thoughts wandered to the intricate dance of our conversations, how words had flowed between us with ease, weaving a tapestry of shared dreams and vulnerabilities. His voice, a soft baritone, had filled the spaces of his apartment, now etched into my mind as clearly as if he were whispering in my ear at this very moment.

"Good morning," I murmured to the quiet room, a private acknowledgment of the shift within me. It wasn't just the aftermath of passion that warmed my cheeks; it was the recognition of something deeper. The pleasure I found in Michael's arms was different—it wasn't a salve for loneliness or a quick fix for desire. It was the kind of connection that fueled not just the body but also the soul—a rare find that I had longed for without truly understanding its absence.

Sitting up, I wrapped my arms around my knees. The business plans that had consumed my thoughts yesterday seemed less daunting now. They were no longer just tasks to be accomplished, but pieces of a larger puzzle of my life that suddenly had more dimension, more color. Michael had become a part of that picture, contributing strokes of inspiration and support that enriched the canvas.

"Focus," I whispered to myself, recognizing the need to channel this clarity into action. The energy coursing through me was electric, a current that demanded to be harnessed. I wanted to build, to create—not just in terms of my career but in the fabric of my relationship with Michael. It was a delicate balance, one that required the same careful attention and dedication I gave to my business endeavors.

I swung my legs over the edge of the bed, feet touching the cool hardwood floor. The chill of the morning snapped me into full alertness, a physical echo of the emotional awakening taking place within. As I stood, I caught sight of my reflection in the mirror—eyes bright, a flush on my cheeks, a woman transformed by the promise of genuine affection.

"Today is a new chapter," I affirmed, letting the words fill the space around me. The longing that tugged at my heart was no longer a void to be filled with fleeting pleasures but a path to be explored, hand in hand with someone who saw me for who I truly was, beyond the accolades and achievements.

I moved towards my closet, selecting attire that mirrored my mood—sophisticated yet approachable, a blend of business savvy and personal warmth. Today, I would step back into the world not as Elena the entrepreneur alone but as Elena the woman who had discovered a profound connection, one that promised to shape her journey in ways she was only beginning to understand.

And so, I continued my day, ready to embrace both the challenges of my work and the unfolding story of Michael and me. The balance would be intricate, but I was eager to navigate it, armed with a newfound sense of purpose that was as exhilarating as it was grounding. This was the start of something real, something transformative—and I was wholly, unreservedly open to its potential.

Chapter Thirteen

The clinking of fine crystal and the low hum of cultured voices wrapped around me like a velvet cloak as I stepped into the grand ballroom. My heels clicked against the marble floor, each step resonating with the pulsing excitement and gnawing nerves that warred within my chest. The chandeliers cast a golden glow over the venue, turning everyone beneath them into gilded figures of high society.

"Deep breaths, Elena," I whispered to myself, plucking at the hem of my sleek black dress. "You belong here."

My fingers grazed the delicate fabric, the sensation grounding me as I let my gaze drift across the room. Men in tailored suits and women in haute couture dresses mingled effortlessly, their laughter tinkling through the air like a foreign language I was only beginning to decipher.

I allowed the current of bodies to carry me forward, slipping into the stream of conversation with a smile painted on my lips. One deep inhale steadied my fluttering heart, the scent of expensive perfume and aged whiskey acting as an invisible brace against the swell of intimidation that threatened to capsize me.

"Stunning event, isn't it?" a silver-haired gentleman commented, his eyes appreciative as they swept over me.

"Absolutely," I agreed, matching his ease with practiced poise. "Elena Callahan," I introduced myself, extending a hand that he took with a firm, confident grip.

"Ah, the name precedes you. I've heard whispers of your ventures. Ambitious," he remarked, a knowing tilt to his voice.

"Thank you," I said, allowing a hint of pride to seep into my words. "I'm always looking to learn from those who have paved the way."

We discussed market trends and investment opportunities, his insights sharp and shrewd. Each word he spoke was like a piece of a puzzle I was determined to complete, and I found myself fitting them into the framework of my aspirations.

"Excuse me for a moment," I said, after we'd exhausted the topic. With a polite nod, I glided away, weaving through clusters of elites with a newfound determination. The aim was clear; seek out the influencers, the decision-makers, the quiet puppeteers of commerce and industry.

"Ms. Callahan, isn't it?" A woman with a voice like honey and eyes that missed nothing addressed me, her perfectly manicured hand resting lightly on my arm. "I've seen you navigate this room. You have an aura of someone who knows exactly what she wants."

"Perhaps I do," I responded, letting the edges of my mouth curl into a sly grin. "And maybe it's about finding the right people who want the same things."

"Then we might be of use to each other," she suggested, her statement laced with the promise of mutual benefit.

"Indeed," I affirmed, the exchange of hidden agendas as intoxicating as the wine that flowed freely from cut-glass decanters.

The evening stretched on, a dance of ambition and strategy. I savored each interaction, each connection formed in the web I spun with meticulous care. This was more than networking; it was a ballet of intellect and will, where every step, every turn, carried the weight of future success.

As I moved through the crowd, my confidence swelled. I was no longer just Elena Callahan; I was a contender, a force to be acknowledged. And tonight, I laid the foundation of an empire that would rise from the very conversations I cultivated under these opulent chandeliers.

With my glass of champagne in hand, I mingled through the crowd, savoring the excitement of our little game. The room was alive with the chatter of the city's elite, but my attention was on the thrilling play of pretending we were strangers, Michael and I.

Then, his voice, deep and resonant, cut through the noise, a familiar thrill that sent shivers down my spine. "I've heard your business plan is quite the disruptor," he said, playing his part perfectly.

I turned, feigning surprise at finding Michael there, his distinguished salt-and-pepper hair and commanding presence a stark contrast to the masquerade of our game. "Disruptive, yes," I responded, my heart racing with the joy of our secret. "Change is overdue, wouldn't you say?"

He leaned in, his interest not just an act. "Change is indeed progress's lifeblood," he agreed, his blue eyes sparkling with a mix of amusement and genuine curiosity. "Tell me more," he urged, as if we were meeting for the first time.

So, I shared, letting my enthusiasm and dreams flow freely in a way that only he could inspire. He listened intently, his nods and probing questions a dance we both knew well, yet it felt new and exciting under the guise of our game.

"Your perspective," he mused, playing along but also speaking his truth, "is refreshingly unjaded. You're not just in the game; you're looking to change it entirely."

I couldn't help but smile, buoyed by his acknowledgment. "Isn't that the essence of innovation?" I replied, our eyes meeting in a silent acknowledgment of the game and something deeper.

"Indeed," he raised his glass to me, a gesture filled with layers of meaning, a salute to our shared ambitions and the electric connection between us.

Sipping my champagne, I reveled in the richness of the moment, our game adding a layer of intrigue and connection to an already deep bond. This wasn't just a conversation; it was an affirmation of the unique, playful, and profound relationship Michael and I shared.

In the crowd, in the heart of our game, we found a new way to celebrate and explore the depth of our connection, a secret dance only we knew the steps to. The night unfurled like a ribbon in the wind, and I found myself amidst a huddle of entrepreneurs.

Their stories were tapestries of triumph and loss, woven with threads of gritty determination. A woman with sleek black hair recounted her ascent, her failures as illuminating as her successes. A man, his suit sharp as his wit, shared the sacrifices made at the altar of ambition. Each narrative was a lesson, a map of pitfalls and peaks.

"Adaptation," the woman said, her gaze piercing, "is survival. But knowing when to pivot and when to persevere— that's the art."

"True," the sharply-dressed man added, "but without passion, even the soundest strategy is hollow. You have to believe, or no one else will."

Their words were a mirror to my own journey. Adaptation had been my shadow since the day fortune smiled upon me with a slip of paper bearing numbers of change. Passion, however, had always been the pilot light within me, flickering, sometimes threatened by gusts of reality, but never extinguished.

"Your story," they pressed, turning to me, hungry for the fresh ink of an unfolding tale.

I shared, my voice steady, my narrative raw. The addiction of comfort in known misery, the vertigo of sudden change, the seductive dance with ambition—it all spilled out, my confession to these kindred spirits.

"Brave," the woman murmured, her approval a soothing salve.

"Resilient," the man agreed, his nod solidifying my place among them.

In their reflections, I saw myself—a mosaic of the woman I was and the entrepreneur I was becoming. With each insight absorbed, I felt my foundation solidify, my aspirations taking on new dimensions, informed by their wisdom, yet uniquely my own.

The event was a crucible, and I emerged tempered, the heat of their experiences forging my resolve. As I walked around mingling, the sparkling air kissed my cheeks, whispering promises of the chapters yet to be written. And I walked forward, my steps sure, my heart ablaze with the fire of validation and motivation.

The laughter swelled, a symphony of ambition and desire wrapped in layers of silk and the clink of crystal. In the midst of it all, I took a step back, my eyes drifting beyond the masquerade of smiles and handshakes. The grandeur that filled the room was blinding, yet within its golden glow, shadows played—a silent ballet of influence and manipulation.

"Can you believe the gall?" A voice dripped with venom, slicing through my reverie.

I turned, finding myself facing Marianne DeLour, her sleek black hair a stark contrast to the ivory gown hugging her slender frame. Socialite. Gatekeeper. Her gaze bore into me, as if challenging the very space I occupied.

"Excuse me?" My heart quickened, but my voice carried a calm I hardly felt.

"Darling," she tipped her head, the word laced with derision, "this event is not for the... how shall I put it? Faint-hearted entrepreneurs."

My throat tightened, the specter of old insecurities beckoning. Yet, somewhere within, a switch flipped—the latent electricity of newfound self-assuredness surging forth. I smiled, not out of submission, but as an armor forged from every rejection, every sleepless night entwined with dreams and fears.

"Perhaps, Marianne," I began, each word deliberate, "true courage lies in embracing vulnerability, in daring to bring new visions to life amidst the doubt. It's easy to remain ensconced in comfort; it takes bravery to chase a dream."

Her eyes narrowed, a hint of surprise flickering behind her icy facade. Around us, the chatter dimmed, the air thick with anticipation—high society's appetite for drama insatiable.

"Your words carry weight, Elena," she conceded, her tone softer, but still edged like a blade. "But do they bear fruit?"

"Let them speak for themselves," I replied, my confidence blooming like a nocturnal flower, unafraid of darkness. "In time, you'll see the orchards I've sown."

A murmur rippled through the crowd, whispers painting the air with intrigue. Marianne regarded me anew, respect threading the fine line between her brows. I had not just weathered her storm; I had navigated it with the poise of one who knows the tempest within.

"Very well," she said, a begrudging smile tugging at her lips. "It seems there's more to you than meets the eye. I look forward to your harvest, Elena."

And with a nod, she retreated into the throng, leaving in her wake a trail of murmurs and a sense of victory hard-won. I stood taller, the chains of doubt melting away, replaced by the warmth of recognition.

Tonight, surrounded by the glittering echelons of power, I had not only observed but participated in their intricate dance. I had been seen, heard, and acknowledged—not as an outsider looking in, but as a player on this chessboard of high stakes and higher aspirations. The event continued to swirl around me, but now it did so with a different rhythm—one that matched the steady beat of my own burgeoning legacy.

I slid my phone from the silk folds of my clutch, a discreet confidant in the palm of my hand. Beneath the chandeliers casting prisms on the walls, I tapped into my notes, a digital scribe capturing the whispered alchemy of success. Every conversation was a thread in the intricate tapestry of industry, and I wove them into my vision with meticulous care.

"Never underestimate the power of an unexpected partnership," an entrepreneur with eyes like polished coal advised, his words laced with the smoke of experience.

"Indeed," I murmured, my fingers dancing over the screen, enshrining his insight. The weight of my future business pulsed at my fingertips, each note a stepping stone paving my path to prominence.

"Risk is the price of entry for any significant reward," another chimed in, her laughter tinged with the heady intoxication of risk. She wore her successes as effortlessly as the diamonds at her throat.

"Absolutely." My voice was steady, but inside, adrenaline coursed through me, a silent symphony to their chorus of ambition. This was more than networking; it was an intimate tango with fate, and I was determined not to miss a step.

As the evening waned, I found a quiet corner to reflect, the hum of the gathering softening to a reverent hush. My phone lay heavy with the night's harvest, each line a promise etched in pixels. I scrolled through the notes, feeling the pulse of potential in every word. I had come here tonight seeking validation, but what I found was far greater—an inner conviction that roared louder than any approval.

The grandeur of the event became a backdrop to my rumination. These encounters, these connections—I had not just made them; I had crafted them with the finesse of a master jeweler setting precious stones. Each individual was a jewel in the crown of my burgeoning empire, their wisdom facets that caught the light of possibility.

I rose, my departure unnoticed by the clusters of guests still ensnared in their own ambitions. The air was cool against my skin as I slipped outside, the stars overhead bearing witness to the silent vow that caressed my soul. This was not the end of an evening but the beginning of an era.

"Tonight, you were more than enough," I whispered to myself, the high society's applause a fading echo behind the closed doors. My heels clicked on the pavement like a metronome keeping time with my quickening heartbeat. I had arrived uncertain, threading my way through a labyrinth of doubt. But now, as I walked away from the shimmering lights of the venue, I did so with the poise of one who had not only traversed the maze but claimed it as her own.

Elena, the respected figure. Elena, the visionary. Elena, the woman who would turn the whispers of tonight into the legacy of tomorrow.

Chapter Fourteen

The keys of my laptop danced beneath my fingertips, each stroke a tiny heartbeat echoing through the quiet of my apartment. I was alone but not lonely, surrounded by the silent company of ideas and aspirations that cascaded from my mind in a relentless stream. The gentle glow of the screen illuminated my face, casting shadows that played upon the walls like specters of the future I was determined to manifest.

"Let's make you real," I murmured to the business plan laid bare before me, an intricate tapestry of dreams woven with pragmatic threads. Hours slipped away as I delved deeper, refining concepts, carving out strategies, and polishing every sentence until it gleamed with purpose. My eyes were heavy with determination, my soul alight with a fire kindled at tonight's event.

I was sculpting something meaningful, a testament to my journey from the shackles of addiction to the liberation of empowerment. Each idea was a step further from the woman who once found solace in the numbing embrace of ephemeral pleasures. Now, I sought fulfillment in creation, in the tangible progress of building something greater than myself.

The dawn chorus had yet to begin its symphony when I finally leaned back in my chair, stretching muscles tense with the labor of intellectual childbirth. The document before me was more than a business plan; it was a map of my evolution, charting a course from who I was to who I dared to be.

"Time for some fresh eyes," I whispered, my voice raspy with fatigue. I gathered the mentors and advisors in my mind, their faces a pantheon of guidance. Michael, with his piercing blue eyes that saw through pretense, would be my cornerstone of critique. His insights would cut sharply, yet always with the intent to sculpt rather than scar.

I composed an email, attaching the digital embodiment of my aspirations. "Your thoughts would mean the world," I typed, my heart thrumming with a cocktail of anticipation and vulnerability. This was more than asking for feedback; it was an invitation to witness my bare ambitions, unadorned by the armor of bravado.

As I hit 'send,' a shiver coursed through me—a mix of adrenaline and the raw exposure of sharing my innermost plans. It was an act of trust, a surrender to the collaborative process that had become my crucible of growth. Michael's response would either be balm or acid on the open wound of my endeavors.

"Be brutal," I added in a postscript, sealing my fate with those two words. The masochistic part of me craved the sting of honest critique, knowing that pain was often the precursor to progress. I yearned for the growth that came from such exchanges, hungry for the wisdom to navigate the labyrinthine path ahead.

With the deed done, I closed my laptop and stepped onto my balcony, welcoming the cool caress of predawn air. The city lay below, a mosaic of light and shadow, mirroring the duality within me—the struggle between ambition and fear, confidence and addiction's whispering ghosts.

"Today, you are more," I vowed to the reflection in the glass door, my own hazel eyes meeting the challenge. The woman staring back was no longer a passive participant in her life but the architect of her destiny. And though the road ahead promised trials and tribulations, I knew I was ready to meet them head-on.

"Bring on the daylight," I said, a smile curving my lips, my spirit undeterred by the enormity of what lay ahead. For in the pursuit of passion and purpose, I had already triumphed over the greatest adversary I would ever face—myself.

The cursor blinked on the spreadsheet, a silent metronome to my racing thoughts. Columns of numbers and deadlines stretched before me like soldiers in formation, each representing a different battle in the war I was waging for success. I leaned back in my chair, rubbing the tension from my temples, feeling the weight of self-doubt teetering on the edge of my resolve.

"Fuck it," I muttered under my breath, not one to be cowed by fear. "I can do this." My voice, though quiet, cut through the silence of the room—sharp, definitive. I began typing, segmenting my grand plan into smaller objectives, immediate and tangible. 'Market Research - Complete by March,' ' Development - May,' 'Investor Pitch - July.' The tasks took shape, each with its own deadline, transforming the nebulous into the achievable.

A chime from my phone broke the stillness—a reminder that I had set for myself. Yoga class. A promise of serenity amidst the storm of ambition that raged within me. I hesitated, my fingers hovering over the keyboard, torn between the urge to continue working and the need to honor my commitment to self-care.

"Balance, Elena," I recited the mantra that had become my lifeline. "You're no good burned out." With a deep breath, I saved my work and closed the laptop, standing up to stretch my cramped muscles. The familiar pull of guilt tried to ensnare me, the old addiction of workaholism whispering seductively that I could do just a little more before taking a break.

I changed into leggings and a loose tank top, tying my hair back as I prepared to step away from my empire-in-the-making. Each movement was an act of defiance against the part of me that equated rest with weakness, pleasure with frivolity.

In the yoga studio, surrounded by the hum of tranquil music and the scent of sandalwood, I found my center. Each pose was a testament to the strength of my body, a stark contrast to the cerebral battles I fought daily. As I moved, I focused on my breath, inhaling purpose and exhaling doubt. Here, there was no networking, no power plays, no snobbery— just the purity of existence, the connection to something greater than the sum of my aspirations.

"Let the day's challenges flow off you like water," the instructor's voice washed over me, a calming balm to the intensity that so often consumed me.

Later in the day back at my desk, the glow of the computer screen greeted me like an old friend—or perhaps a sparring partner. I reviewed the notes I had discreetly taken on my phone during the event, integrating the insights gleaned from conversations with industry titans into my business strategy. With each addition, my plan grew more robust, infused with the collective wisdom of those who had tread the path before me.

"Who knew schmoozing could be so...enlightening?" I chuckled to myself, acknowledging the irony. In the pursuit of connections, I had found more than just potential backers—I had stumbled upon mentors, kindred spirits, and the realization that my self-worth wasn't tethered to social ladders or financial statements.

"Tomorrow is another day," I whispered, powering down for the night. As I slipped between the sheets, the soft fabric caressed my skin, a sensual reminder that pleasure too had its place in the tapestry of life. And somewhere between wakefulness and dreams, I surrendered to the night's embrace, recharging for the battles yet to come.

The first blush of dawn painted the horizon with a promise as I stood by the window, the cool glass a stark contrast to the warmth spreading through my chest. My hands clasped around a steaming mug of coffee, its rich aroma mingling with the scent of determination that seemed to linger in the air.

"Another day, another battle," I murmured, sipping the bitter liquid that jolted my senses awake, mirroring the adrenaline that now coursed through my veins. The challenges that had once loomed like insurmountable mountains now appeared as mere stepping stones on my path to triumph.

My reflection stared back at me, a woman transformed by her own resolve. The vulnerability that had clung to my skin, an uninvited shadow, was shedding, leaving behind the sheen of newfound confidence. I had grappled with the demons of self-doubt, each victory etching deeper lines of fortitude across my soul.

"No fear," I declared to my mirrored counterpart, a smile curving my lips. It was a raw acknowledgment of the internal strife I'd battled, the nights spent wrestling with the seductive whispers of insecurity that sought to lure me into a lull of complacency.

The room around me was silent, save for the rhythmic tapping of my fingers against the porcelain mug. Yet, within that silence thrummed a symphony of ideas—a cacophony of inspired strategies and refined plans that demanded expression. My business was more than a dream; it was a testament to my evolution, a narrative woven from the threads of every encounter, every setback, every revelation.

"Let's do this," I breathed out, setting the mug down with a decisive click against the wooden surface of the dining table. The fabric of my blouse clung to my skin, a sensual reminder of the physicality of my journey—the late nights, the tireless work, the unrelenting drive that fueled my ambition.

I strode towards my workspace, the familiar hum of my laptop greeting me, a harbinger of the tasks that awaited. The glow of the screen illuminated the darkness, casting a halo of light that seemed to consecrate the moment. Each keystroke was a declaration, a commitment to the future I was sculpting with my own hands.

"Every 'no', every door slammed in my face, they're just the prelude to a 'yes' that will change everything," I wrote to my journal. The taste of past rejections lingered, a bitter tang that no longer soured my essence but instead served as a potent reminder of my resilience.

With each passing hour, the sun climbed higher, its rays chasing away the shadows that had once clung so stubbornly to my world. My phone buzzed intermittently, messages from mentors and would-be collaborators punctuating the morning. But this was my time—my sanctuary of solitude where I could nurture the seeds of potential into a garden of success.

"Stay focused, Elena. You've got this," I coached myself, reviewing the milestones laid out before me. The weight of expectation was a familiar burden, one I now carried with pride rather than apprehension. I had indulged in the intoxication of validation, savored the sweet high of recognition, but I knew the true test lay in the sustainability of my vision.

As this chapter of my life drew to a close, I felt the stirrings of a new beginning. I was ready to step into the light, to embrace the contours of a destiny that I had shaped with my own two hands. A renewed sense of purpose ignited within me, a flame that would not be extinguished.

"Bring it on, world," I said, a fierce whisper cutting through the clarity of the morning. "I'm ready for you."

Chapter Fifteen

The horizon blushed with the soft touch of dawn as I stepped out onto the balcony, greeted by a crisp breeze like an old friend. Below, the city stretched out, a tapestry of waking life woven from steel and ambition. There, in my sky-kissing penthouse, I perched between two worlds—the woman I was and the one I had become. My fingers traced the rim of the porcelain mug, the heat of my coffee seeping into my skin, grounding me.

"Another day, Elena," I whispered to myself, a ritual of acknowledgment for the empire I had built from the ashes of anonymity. The art world, once an impenetrable fortress, now swung its gates open at the mention of my name.

I inhaled deeply, savoring the rich aroma of the Arabica blend, each sip an indulgence in the life I had crafted. A life that seemed to pulse with the rhythm of the city below—unpredictable, vibrant, alive. Yet, the liquid warmth couldn't quite reach the cold tendrils of loneliness that coiled around my heart. No amount of caffeine could jolt away the yearning for something more profound than accolades and balance sheets.

"International Art Fair," I murmured, the words an incantation for the future looming on the horizon. There was power in being chosen, in being seen—not as the uncertain girl from a nowhere town but as a visionary, a voice, a force. It was a milestone that marked how far I had come, yet it also cast a shadow over the fragility of my own reflection.

I leaned against the railing, the metal cool against my silk robe. My gaze drifted across the skyline, skimming over rooftops and searching for answers in the creeping sunlight. What did it mean to transform? To shed your skin and emerge anew, only to find that success was as intoxicating as the finest wine—and just as likely to leave you empty?

"Damn it, Elena," I chided myself, "this isn't the time for doubt." But the nagging persisted, the fear that beneath the polished exterior, the unresolved cravings of my past lurked, ready to surge at the slightest crack in my resolve.

I set the mug down with a clink that shattered the morning stillness. Enough introspection; there were galleries to oversee, artists to champion, a legacy to sculpt with my own two hands. Yet even as I steeled myself for the day ahead, I couldn't shake the sense that every step forward was haunted by the specter of addiction—that seductive whisper promising escape, offering oblivion wrapped in a velvet bow.

"Is it enough?" The question slipped out, a vulnerable admission to the city that bore witness to my triumphs and my fears. Was my empire enough to fill the void, to silence the cravings, to keep the darkness at bay?

The sun crested the horizon, bathing my face in golden light—a silent benediction for the battles fought and the ones still to come. And in that moment, I made a silent vow: to face the challenges head-on, to embrace the beauty and the scars, and to remember that true strength lay in vulnerability.

"Today, you soar," I declared, my voice steady, my resolve unbreakable. With one last glance at the awakening city—my city—I turned back inside, ready to conquer the art world, one masterpiece at a time.

The phone's vibration broke through the fortress of my solitude, shaking me out of my reverie. I glanced at the screen: Michael. His name alone sent a pulse of anticipation through my veins, a warmth that soothed the jagged edges left by my last battle with temptation.

"Can't wait for our weekend," his message read, punctuated by a heart emoji, the digital shorthand for affection in our hectic lives. It was a lifeline, a reminder of what I had built beyond the canvases and gallery walls—a love that was both sanctuary and celebration.

I typed back swiftly, "Me neither. Needing this escape with you." The words were true, every letter a stitch in the fabric that wove our lives together. Our relationship, once a cautious dance of new beginnings, had become a partnership as intricate and resilient as the masterpieces lining my gallery's walls.

In the quiet hum of my penthouse, I allowed myself a moment to linger on the thought of our getaway. A cabin in the mountains, the world pared down to the essentials: us, nature, a crackling fire. No spreadsheets, no strategy meetings—just Michael's blue eyes reflecting the flames, seeing into the parts of me I had yet to put on display.

My mind already projecting to the weekend, I slipped into something more professional—a tailored black dress that hugged my frame without constriction, an armor of sophistication—and made my way to the gallery.

The familiar scent of oil paint and varnish greeted me as I stepped inside, the air charged with the silent energy of potential. My team awaited, gathered around the polished mahogany conference table that I once thought was too grandiose for someone like me. Now, it felt like a command center from where I led my empire.

"Morning, everyone," I greeted them, my voice carrying the weight of authority softened by genuine camaraderie. They returned the greeting, a chorus of voices harmonizing in the shared pursuit of art and ambition.

"Let's talk expansion," I said, confidence swelling in my chest as I outlined the vision that had been keeping me up at night. "Our brand has power, influence. It's time we extend our reach—new cities, new communities."

Heads nodded, pens scribbled across notepads as I detailed the idea of opening galleries in other metropolises, each space a nexus between culture and connection. These weren't just rooms with walls to hang art; they were havens for creativity, platforms for voices yearning to be heard.

"Imagine the impact," I continued, painting the future with my words, "we'll be curating experiences, fostering dialogues. Art is the language, and we... we will be its amplifiers."

Questions and suggestions filled the room, a symphony of logistics and dreams. We dissected locations, demographics, potential artists—a mosaic of decisions that promised growth and new challenges.

"Remember," I concluded, meeting each gaze with the intensity of my own, "we're not just expanding a business. We're cultivating a movement. Every new gallery is another chapter in our story, another chance to touch lives."

As the meeting dispersed, I was left with the echo of our plans, the resonance of what we were building. And in that space between the spoken word and silent contemplation, I understood that this empire—my empire—was more than just a testament to success. It was a testament to survival, to overcoming the siren call of darkness with a brighter, enduring light.

"Today, you soar," I whispered to myself, the mantra becoming my talisman against the heady lure of old habits. With each victory, each step forward, I proved to myself that the past did not define the horizon. That my journey—our journey—was one of perpetual ascent.

The hum of my gallery was a living thing—a pulsing heart of ambition and artistry. I stood at the core, my own heart beating in tandem with the thrumming energy of creation that surrounded me. My team's voices wove through the air, carrying ideas like dandelion seeds on the wind, each one pregnant with potential.

"Expansion is more than geography," I mused aloud, folding my hands atop the polished conference table. "It's cultural infiltration, a silent revolution."

"Exactly," Jenna, my lead curator, agreed, her eyes alight with shared fervor. "We're not just opening galleries; we're planting seeds for social change."

As the fervent nods rippled around the room, the vibration of my phone against the tabletop felt like an intrusion. Apologetically excusing myself, I stepped away, thumb swiping across the screen to reveal an unexpected name—Lila, from a lifetime ago.

"Hello?" My voice was cautious, a tendril reaching into the past.

"Elena! It's been ages!" Lila's voice burst forth, a geyser of warmth tinged with something else—hope? Desperation?

"Too long," I replied, though the tendrils of my old life often wrapped around my thoughts, uninvited. "What's up?"

"It's about the community center here. We're struggling, Elena. And everyone keeps talking about how you made it big in the city—the art, the culture you've created." Her words were hurried, tripping over themselves in their urgency.

"I remember the center," I confessed, my thoughts drifting to the concrete walls that had cradled my first dreams. "Tell me what you need."

"Support, guidance... maybe even a collaboration?" There was a tremble in her plea, and I felt the weight of our shared history, the roots of my origin story growing entwined with hers.

"Let me see what I can do," I promised, already envisioning vibrant murals replacing peeling paint, art breathing new life into the stagnation of forgotten places.

"Thank you, Elena. Really, thank you."

Ending the call, I leaned against the cool glass pane of the nearest window, the cityscape sprawling before me like a canvas awaiting my touch. Yet, as I pondered Lila's request, the lure of my beginnings beckoned, a siren song blending with the symphony of my current life.

"Troubling news?" Jenna's voice interrupted my reverie, her approach soft but insistent.

"An opportunity," I said, turning back to face her, "to bridge the divide between my past and present."

Before she could respond, another alert shattered the momentary stillness—a text message from an artist whose reputation preceded him. A man whose work ignited debate and inflamed passions, both in admiration and outrage.

"Shit," I muttered under my breath, reading the words that stated his desire to exhibit in my gallery.

"Who is it?" Jenna asked, leaning in to catch a glimpse of the message.

"Adrian Serrano," I said, the name tasting like forbidden fruit on my tongue.

"Wow, he's huge! But controversial..." She trailed off, her expression mirroring the conflict within me.

"His work is provocative; it challenges, disturbs. Hosting him could be a coup or a catastrophe." My mind raced, calculating risks and rewards, the potential for discourse and dissent tangling together.

"Can we handle the backlash?" Jenna pressed, her question cutting to the heart of my hesitation.

"Can we afford not to try?" I countered, the prospect sparking a fire in my belly. "Our empire was built on pushing boundaries, wasn't it?"

"True," Jenna conceded, "but this is playing with fire."

"Sometimes," I said, my gaze returning to the city that bore witness to my evolution, "you need to burn the old to illuminate the new."

"Then let's light it up," Jenna said, resolute, and I couldn't help but smile at her audacity.

"Light it up," I echoed, my decision made.

Adrian Serrano's a big deal in the art world, known for art that really makes you think and talk. When he called me, it was a pretty huge moment. He's not just anyone; his art's about challenging norms, kind of like what I'm trying to do with my gallery.

"Your gallery's exactly where my next show should be," Adrian told me over the phone. His voice was friendlier than I expected, making the whole conversation feel more personal.

I was thrilled, of course. But there was a catch. I had plans with Michael for a quiet weekend away—our little escape from everything. Adrian's request meant canceling that, and it wasn't easy to decide. "I need to meet this weekend," Adrian said, "to make sure we're on the same page for the exhibition."

"Let me figure a few things out," I told him, already knowing what I had to do but dreading the conversation with Michael.

Telling Michael wasn't easy. "I've got to cancel our weekend," I said, hating that I had to bring work into our time. "It's for the gallery. Adrian Serrano wants to work with us."

Michael was quiet for a bit, then said he got it, that my work was important. But I could tell he was disappointed. It's tough, trying to balance my career and our relationship.

I threw myself into getting ready for the meeting with Adrian, knowing this could really put my gallery on the map. But I kept thinking about Michael and how understanding he was. It made me realize just how much I'm juggling and how much I rely on his support.

Meeting with Adrian could change everything for my gallery. It's exciting but also a bit scary, knowing I'm sacrificing personal time for it. But I hope it'll be worth it, both for my career and for everything Michael and I are building together.

As the weekend approached, I found myself entangled in a whirlwind of emotions—nervousness intertwined with anticipation, shadowed by a pang of guilt for postponing plans with Michael. Despite this, his unwavering support shone through, easing the sting of disappointment. Yet, the focus had to shift; Adrian Serrano's visit loomed on the horizon, promising to pivot "Art Unleashed" towards an unprecedented chapter.

When Adrian arrived, his demeanor was serene, betraying none of the revolutionary fervor his art was known for. He lavished praise on "Art Unleashed" for its daring ethos, explaining his decision to exhibit with us was driven by our shared vision of challenging the conventional. It was affirming, hearing such words from an artist of his caliber—like a beacon of validation in the often murky waters of the art world.

As we delved into the heart of our meeting, our conversation flowed effortlessly from one topic to the next—outlining his exhibition, discussing the layout, lighting, and promotional strategies. It was a dance of ideas, each of us contributing, refining, and aligning our visions until they were in perfect harmony. There was a synergy between us, a mutual understanding and respect that transcended the usual artist-gallery relationship.

With the exhibition blueprint set, the next phase was to bring our plans to fruition. Guided by David's experienced hand, we began orchestrating a grand opening event that would do justice to Adrian's work and mark a significant milestone for

"Art Unleashed". Every detail, from the installation progress to coordinating with vendors, was meticulously overseen by me. It had to be perfect, a night to remember, a celebration of art's power to provoke and inspire.

Choosing my outfit for the opening became a reflection of my personal journey and the stakes involved in this exhibit. After much deliberation, I settled on an Alexander McQueen gown that struck the perfect balance between elegance and boldness. The dress, accompanied by carefully selected accessories, wasn't just attire; it was a statement, an extension of the gallery's and my own ethos.

Michael's support during this hectic period was my rock. His presence, whether offering a listening ear or a reassuring smile, was a constant reminder of the strength found in partnership. He stood by my side, a testament to the enduring power of mutual respect and love.

Now, with everything in place, all that remained was the anticipation of the grand opening. The gallery was set to unveil not just Adrian Serrano's provocative works, but also "Art Unleashed"'s commitment to pushing boundaries and challenging perceptions. As I reflected on the journey that led to this moment, I felt a deep sense of accomplishment and readiness for whatever the night would bring.

Chapter Sixteen

After a week that felt like a whirlwind of non-stop work and mounting excitement for the upcoming launch, I finally found a moment of respite. It was time to spend some much-needed quality time with Michael. This pause in our bustling lives felt like a breath of fresh air, a chance to reconnect and share in the anticipation and joy of what we had been working towards. The world around us seemed to slow down, allowing us to savor the simple, profound moments that we too often took for granted.

The clink of ice against glass punctuated the silence in our penthouse as I poured Michael a scotch, his favorite way to unwind. He should have been home by now. A glance at the clock heightened the unease already spinning in my stomach. The date today—our anniversary—had slipped through the cracks of a calendar choked with meetings and deadlines.

"Shit," I muttered to myself, the word a serrated edge cutting through the quiet. How could I have forgotten? Was it the thrill of the chase, the relentless pursuit of more success that numbed me to these crucial personal milestones?

The door clicked open and there he was, Michael, looking every bit as weary as I felt, the lines of stress etched into his handsome face. His tie hung loose around his neck, a silent testament to the battles fought in boardrooms.

"Happy anniversary, babe." His voice was low, tinged with something that sounded like disappointment—or was it hurt?

"Michael, I—" My throat tightened around the words, a confession strangled before birth. "I'm sorry, I forgot."

A flash of something crossed his eyes. Not anger, but something deeper, a chasm opening between us. We were two planets drifting in separate orbits, our own successes casting shadows over the shared light of our relationship.

"Looks like we both did," he said, shrugging off his jacket and collapsing onto the sofa. "Guess that's what happens when work is your mistress."

His words were a gut punch, leaving me winded. I joined him on the couch, seeking his warmth, but found only the chill of distance.

"Are we losing ourselves to this?" I asked, the fear of losing him making my voice tremble.

"Maybe," he confessed, swirling the amber liquid in his glass, a slow storm gathering in the confines of crystal. "Or maybe we're just evolving, Elena. But we can't keep going like this."

The truth of it settled heavy on my chest. Our love, once an all-consuming blaze, had dwindled to embers under the cold draft of ambition.

"Let's fix this, Michael. We need to find a way back to each other." My plea hung between us, my hand reaching for his.

He met my grasp, his fingers a lifeline. "We'll figure it out. We always do."

But doubt lingered, a specter at the feast of our love.

Though Michael pretended it didn't bother him, I could sense his embarrassment over forgetting our anniversary. In light of that, I decided to meet with Clara and Sophie. It felt necessary to step away, to seek the comfort and understanding of friends who had become my confidants through the highs and lows of my journey.

"Girl, you're walking a tightrope with no safety net," Clara's voice cut through the fog of my thoughts as I recounted the evening to her and Sophie.

"I can't believe I forgot our anniversary," The admission hung in the air between us, a blend of disbelief and regret flavoring my words.

We sat in a cozy corner of my favorite wine bar, the soft glow of candlelight playing across their concerned faces. They were my touchstones, reminders of a life less complicated by the trappings of success.

"Love isn't a ledger, Elena. You can't balance it like your accounts," Sophie chimed in, sipping her pinot noir. She knew about balancing acts; her marriage had survived a stormy sea of addiction and come out stronger on the other side.

Clara raised her eyebrows, a gentle nudge of surprise in her gesture. "That doesn't sound like you, Elena. You're usually on top of everything."

"I know," I admitted, the weight of my neglect pressing down on me. "I've been so focused on chasing the next big thing... I didn't see what I was sacrificing. With the gallery opening and everything with Adrian, my mind's been elsewhere."

Sophie reached across the table, her hand offering silent support. "Michael understands, doesn't he? He knows how much this means to you."

"He does, but that's not the point. I hate that I let something so important slip through the cracks," I admitted, feeling the weight of my oversight.

Sophie smiled, her warmth enveloping me like a comforting blanket. "Then make it up to him, Elena. You two have been through so much together. This is just a small bump in the road."

"Communication, babe. It's cliché because it's true," Clara said, her own experiences with infidelity lending wisdom to her words. "Talk to him. Really talk. And listen, too. Find out what he needs, what you need."

"Compromise doesn't mean weakness," Sophie added softly. "It's choosing the path together, even if it means stepping off the one you're on."

Their advice was a balm, soothing the raw edges of my guilt. Michael and I had built an empire, each in our own right, but it was time to build bridges back to one another.

"Thanks, you guys," I said, feeling the stirrings of resolve within me. "I think I know what to do."

"Good," Clara raised her glass, a smile tugging at her lips. "Now, let's toast to fixing fuck-ups and finding the way back to love."

We clinked glasses, the sound a bright note in the melody of friendship and understanding. Tomorrow, I would face Michael, armed with fresh perspective and determination. Tonight, I would lean on the strength of these women who had weathered their own storms.

"Here's to love and the messy, beautiful fight to keep it alive," Sophie declared, and we drank deep.

The scent of oil paint and turpentine lingered in the air, a heady mix that always seemed to stir something deep within me. Michael stood at the center of my penthouse studio, his hands covered with streaks of cobalt blue and cadmium yellow, his eyes reflecting the chaos and beauty of the canvas before him.

"Michael," I began, my voice steady even as my heart raced with the vulnerability of what I was about to propose. "We've been ships passing in the night for too long."

He paused, brush mid-stroke, and turned to face me. His gaze held mine, searching, as if he could see straight through to the tangle of emotions I'd been wrestling with.

"Let's create something together," I said, the idea blossoming like the peonies in the crystal vase by the balcony door. "Not just art, not just business, but moments. Let's set aside time for creative dates. Evenings where we explore new mediums, blend our passions. It's time our love had its own renaissance."

The corners of his lips curled upward, a silent acknowledgment of the metaphor that so aptly captured our relationship. He set his palette down and wiped his hands, crossing the room to where I stood, vulnerable yet resolute.

"Art brought us together, Elena," he murmured, his arms wrapping around me in a warm embrace. "It's only fitting it keeps us connected. You're my muse, my confidante, my partner in every sense. Yes, let's do this—creative dates, you and I, reclaiming 'us' amidst the canvases and the clay."

I exhaled a breath I didn't realize I'd been holding, relief flooding through my veins like the first rays of dawn after a turbulent night. We were more than just two individuals excelling in our respective fields; we were collaborators in life's grand design.

As we stood there, entwined in the soft light of the studio, inspiration struck like a lightning bolt. The struggles we'd faced, the tension between our ambitions and our affections, they weren't unique to us alone. There were others out there, couples grappling with the same delicate dance of love and career, intimacy and independence.

"Michael," I said, pulling back slightly to look up into his eyes, "what if we opened the gallery for more than just exhibitions? What if we hosted couple's art therapy sessions? A space for connection, exploration, healing. We can guide them, use our journey as a blueprint..."

"Help them paint their stories," he finished for me, understanding instantly. His excitement was palpable, his belief in me, in us, a force that propelled my ambition into new realms.

"Yes, exactly." My mind raced with the possibilities, the logistics already forming amidst the fervor of newfound purpose. "Art has been my sanctuary, our sanctuary. We can share that, offer it to those who are searching for a way back to each other."

"Then let's make it happen," Michael said, the promise in his voice sealing our pact.

Together, we would turn the gallery into an oasis for lost souls seeking reconnection, using brushes and colors as tools to mend frayed bonds. As we sketched out plans for our first session, our conversation ebbed and flowed with the ease of two artists lost in collaborative creation. We were designing not just a series of events, but a tapestry of experiences that would weave our personal narratives with those of others, crafting a legacy interlaced with passion, growth, and the enduring power of love.

The golden light of dawn streamed through the floor-to-ceiling windows of my gallery, casting long shadows that danced with the promise of a new beginning. I stood amidst the buzz of early risers, local artists whose hands were already stained with hues of hope and ambition.

Standing amidst the flurry of activity, I took a moment to address the team, my voice carrying a blend of gratitude and excitement. "This day marks the beginning of something extraordinary—a collective journey that transcends individual aspirations," I said, gesturing to the gathering of talented souls who had come together under the banner of Art Unleashed..

The initiative I unveiled was simple yet groundbreaking: Art Unleashed. A project sponsoring local talent, providing materials, space, and exposure. We would transform city walls into murals, empty lots into sculptures, and neglected neighborhoods into open galleries. It was more than art; it was a heartbeat, a revival.

"Art is not a solitary act," I continued, my passion reverberating off the walls adorned with eclectic masterpieces. "It's a conversation, a collective breath. With Art Unleashed, we breathe life back into places forgotten."

Applause erupted, a symphony of support that fueled my purpose. The following days were a whirlwind of positive press. Articles praised the initiative, social media buzzed with anticipation, and the city itself seemed to hum with newfound vibrancy.

But with the spotlight came shadows I hadn't anticipated.

One evening, after a long day of planning and promotion, I returned to my penthouse to find an envelope slid under my door—a stark anomaly against the polished hardwood. Inside, a single sheet of paper bore words that sent a chill down my spine: "Not all art is welcome here. Stop now, or else."

My hands trembled as I read the thinly veiled threat. Was it because of the controversial artist I'd recently decided to exhibit? Or someone who despised the inclusive embrace of Art Unleashed?

"Michael," I murmured into the phone, my fingers tight around the handset as I recounted the message. His response was swift and protective, his voice a solid anchor in the tumultuous sea of my fears.

"We'll handle this, Elena. Together," he assured me, his tone leaving no room for argument. "I'll be there first thing in the morning. We're increasing security at the gallery. No one threatens what you've built."

I wanted to lean on his strength, to let his resolve wash over me, but a part of me resisted. This empire, these initiatives— they were extensions of my soul, and the thought of them being targeted awakened an unfamiliar defiance within me.

"Thank you," I whispered back, a fusion of gratitude and determination settling in my chest. "We won't let fear overshadow our creation."

That night, sleep eluded me. I wandered through the darkened rooms of my home, each piece of art a testament to struggle and triumph. I had fought too hard, come too far to cower before faceless intimidation. My past, riddled with addiction and uncertainty, had taught me resilience. Now, it would be my shield.

As dawn broke once again, casting its first tentative light upon the city I loved, I knew the battle ahead would be fraught with complexities I had never imagined. But as I looked out onto the horizon, I also knew I was ready. Ready to fight for every stroke of paint, every chiseled detail, every artist's dream.

This was my legacy, a tapestry woven from the threads of creativity, community, and courage. And nothing, no threat or challenge, would unravel what we had begun to weave.

The evening air was a symphony of city sounds as I stood alone in the quiet sanctuary of my office. The world outside buzzed with life, but within these walls, I could breathe. My gaze lingered on the canvas before me—a turbulent sea of color and emotion that mirrored the storm inside me.

"Chaos often breeds life, when order breeds habit," the artist had once said. His words clung to me, a mantra for the unpredictability that had become my constant companion.

I leaned back against the cool leather of my chair, letting the silence envelop me. How strange it was to be at the helm of an empire that had risen from the ashes of my former life. With every success, the stakes grew higher, the falls more perilous. Yet here I was, stronger than the doubts that had once shackled me.

"Prepared" wasn't a strong enough word. No, I was fortified by the love of Michael—his intense blue eyes that saw through my armor, his embrace that promised solace. And my friends, whose loyalty was the bedrock upon which I built my dreams.

"Are you ready, Elena?" Michael's voice cut through the stillness, warm and grounding.

"Always," I replied, not just to him, but to myself.

Together, we walked into the opening night of my gallery. in where the private viewing of Adrian's new exhibit was about to commence. The hum of conversation crescendoed as we entered, a tide of anticipation and admiration washing over us.

For the grand opening, no detail was overlooked. The gallery was a vision of luxury and sophistication, with opulent decorations that mirrored the vibrancy of the art on display. Exquisite floral arrangements added a touch of natural beauty, while strategic lighting accentuated the striking features of each piece.

Dressed in a stunning gown from Alexander McQueen, complemented by delicate Cartier earrings, I felt like a manifestation of the gallery's spirit—bold, transformative, and undeniably elegant. My attire was a statement, not just of personal style, but of the significance of the occasion.

Clara, Sophie, and David were integral to the evening's success, each playing their role with grace and efficiency. David's expertise in setting the perfect ambiance, Sophie's infectious energy, and Clara's meticulous attention to detail ensured the event unfolded without a hitch.

Michael's presence was a source of strength and encouragement. His support, evident in his proud gaze and reassuring smiles, underscored the importance of our shared journey. The event was not only a celebration of art but a testament to the bonds that had fortified along the way.

As guests arrived, the gallery came alive with the buzz of conversation and admiration. Reporters and photographers mingled with artists and art lovers, each eager to capture the essence of Art Unleashed. The air was thick with anticipation, as everyone awaited the unveiling of a project that promised to redefine the city's relationship with art.

"Your vision is breathtaking," a colleague whispered, her eyes wide as she took in the vibrant array of artworks.

"Thank you," I murmured, my heart swelling with gratitude. Each piece told a story, each brushstroke a testament to the community we'd crafted. This wasn't just art; this was life— messy, beautiful, and unapologetically raw.

Laughter rippled through the room, punctuated by the clink of glasses and the soft shuffle of footsteps. My friends, family, and colleagues moved around me, their faces illuminated by the soft glow of the gallery lights. They were the colors in my palette, the inspiration that drove me forward.

"Cheers to Elena," Michael announced, raising his glass. "To her tireless spirit and the path she's forged."

"Cheers!" echoed through the space, a chorus of support that wrapped around me like a blanket.

The speeches were heartfelt and inspiring, with every word echoing the gallery's mission to democratize art and inspire communal transformation. As I took the podium, the weight of the moment settled over me—a blend of pride, responsibility, and boundless hope for the future.

"Our vision for Art Unleashed is simple yet profound," I declared, my voice steady and clear. "We believe in the power of art to unite, to heal, and to embolden. Today, we invite you to join us in this journey, to witness the awakening of a city reborn through the strokes of creativity."

The applause that followed was a resounding affirmation of our shared dream. As the evening progressed, the gallery thrummed with energy and excitement, each guest captivated by the promise of Art Unleashed.

I watched them all, these people who had become part of my journey. Their engagement with the art was intimate, each one finding a piece of themselves reflected in the canvases. It was then I understood—the triumphs, the challenges, they were all threads in a larger tapestry.

This was more than an opening; it was the dawn of a new era—an era where art was not confined to galleries but woven into the fabric of everyday life. And as the night drew to a close, I stood amidst the remnants of celebration, deeply moved by the realization that Art Unleashed was not just a gallery but a beacon of change, illuminating the path toward a more vibrant, united, and artistically enriched world.

As the night drew to a close, I stood amidst the remnants of celebration, the lingering conversations, and the emptying wine glasses. The threats that loomed outside felt distant, inconsequential even. We were creating something imperishable, something that would outlive fear and ignorance.

"Let them come," I thought fiercely, a fire igniting within me. "We'll face them together."

And in that moment, surrounded by the enduring power of creativity and connection, I was unbreakable.

Chapter Seventeen

This was our moment, a celebration of our hard work and commitment. Between my relentless dedication and Michael's unwavering support, we had earned this escape. For someone who had never experienced the luxury of flying, let alone on a private jet, this was monumental. But I wanted to do this for him, to share this new chapter of adventure and luxury, all thanks to the life-changing windfall. Gratitude filled me as we stepped onto the plane, "Thank you, lottery," I thought, "for transforming my world."

The runway lights blurred into streaks of luminescence as the private jet's engines roared with an unspoken promise of adventure. I watched Michael's face, his eyes wide with disbelief, the corners of his mouth twitching into a smile that he tried to suppress—a futile effort against the overwhelming joy bubbling inside him.

"Are we really doing this?" His voice was a mix of childlike wonder and the deep timbre that always sent a shiver down my spine.

"Oui, mon amour," I replied, my own excitement making my heart race. "Paris is waiting for us."

He laughed, the sound mingling with the hum of the aircraft as it ascended into the star-speckled abyss above. The cabin's intimate ambiance cloaked us in seclusion from the world we left behind, a bubble of our own creation where secrets whispered and true selves revealed without hesitation.

"Tell me again why you're spoiling me like this," Michael said, leaning closer across the rich leather seats that enveloped our bodies in luxury.

"Because life is too short for what-ifs and too vast for never-haves." My words were sincere, tinged with the knowledge of how quickly fortunes could turn—how addiction to routine could stifle the dreams that now danced freely between us.

"God, Elena, when you say things like that..." He trailed off, his gaze intense, blue eyes reflecting a soul that had known the weight of guarded walls now crumbling at the touch of genuine connection.

I reached out, tracing the line of his jaw—a familiar path that still thrilled me. "We're here to make memories, to chase the dreams we've been whispering about between the sheets, in those vulnerable hours before dawn cracks open the sky."

"Speaking of dreams," he began, our fingers intertwining, "I can't wait to see the Louvre with you, walk along the Seine, just... breathe in the same air as centuries of artists and lovers."

"Me neither. And to think, this is just the beginning." The hint of more to come laced my words, a promise not just of this weekend but of all the days and nights beyond, where the mundane would no longer be our master.

"Let's toast to beginnings then." Michael signaled the attendant, who promptly appeared with two flutes of champagne, the bubbles catching the light like tiny stars being born in our glasses.

"To us," he declared, his voice steady yet imbued with an emotion that spoke of battles fought and won.

"To us," I echoed, the cool crystal against my lips, the liquid gold a harbinger of the opulence and decadence that awaited.

As the jet cut through the night, cleaving the darkness with its silver wings, we shared our dreams. There was a rawness to our conversation, a stripping away of pretenses that could only happen in these suspended moments between earth and sky. We talked of future businesses, philanthropy, and art; of healing old wounds and painting our lives with broad, vibrant strokes.

"Michael, I want to build something lasting, meaningful— not just wealth but a legacy." My voice carried the fervor of newfound purpose, a stark contrast to the small-town girl who once believed the world ended at the county line.

"I know you will, Lena. You've got this fire in you that's going to change the world." His affirmation was a balm, soothing the lingering sting of insecurity, the addiction to doubt that sometimes clawed its way back up my throat.

"Only if you're by my side," I admitted, allowing vulnerability to tint my words, showing him the parts of me still tethered to fear.

"Always," he vowed, and the certainty in his tone wrapped around me like a blanket woven from threads of trust and understanding.

And as we journeyed across the Atlantic, cocooned in the quiet luxury of the jet, the dawn began to sketch the first lines of Paris on the horizon—a canvas awaiting the bold strokes of two souls embarking on an adventure that would redefine their very essence.

The tarmac was a blur beneath us as we touched down, the private jet's tires kissing French soil with a whisper that seemed to say, "Bienvenue." I slid my hand into Michael's, feeling his fingers intertwine with mine, a silent echo of our affections. The cool Parisian air enveloped us as we stepped off the plane, carrying scents of baked bread and the distant murmur of the city's heartbeats.

"Welcome to Paris," I breathed out, unable to keep the grin from my lips as I watched Michael draw in the sights, his blue eyes wide with the childlike wonder I so cherished.

"Christ, Elena, you've really outdone yourself." His words were a husky chuckle, laden with admiration and disbelief. He pulled me close, his arms encircling me. "I can't believe we're here."

"Believe it," I whispered back, pressing into his embrace.

The drive through the winding streets was a symphony of colors and sounds, the very essence of Paris unfolding before us. We arrived at our hotel, a beacon of opulence with its gilded doors and marbled foyer.

Our suite was a testament to love's grandeur, with a view of the Eiffel Tower that stretched heavenward, mirroring the peak of what Michael and I shared.

"Look at this..." I guided him to the window, letting the cityscape steal his breath away. The tower punctured the skyline, its iron lattice a symbol of structural and emotional strength—a steel counterpart to the resilience of our relationship.

"Every time I think I know you, you surprise me even more," he murmured, his voice catching slightly as he kissed my temple softly.

"Only the best for us," I said, meaning every word. This was about more than luxury; it was about marking the heights we had reached together, about celebrating the climb from my own depths of addiction and doubt, and reveling in the freedom of our ascent.

Our first day in Paris was a tapestry woven with the golden threads of exploration and intimacy. Hand in hand, we meandered through Montmartre, our steps echoing on the cobbled stones that had borne the weight of countless dreamers before us. Each art studio we entered was a portal to another's soul, and we lingered over canvases splashed with color and life, reflecting the vibrancy of our own feelings.

"Imagine the stories behind these," Michael mused, gesturing towards an abstract piece that captured the chaos and beauty of existence in every stroke.

"Like us—our story is here too, isn't it? In the layers and the contrasts," I replied, tracing the lines of paint with my gaze, seeing parallels in the tumultuous journey that had led us here.

"Exactly like us," he affirmed, his voice a tender rumble as he pulled me into his chest. "Complex, beautiful, and utterly real."

We stole kisses in secluded alleyways, our lips meeting with the fervor of discovery and the reassurance of familiarity. Each caress was a reminder of where we'd been and where we longed to go, the taste of him igniting the ever-present hunger within me—a hunger that now craved connection as fervently as it once craved escape.

"God, I love you," I confessed against his mouth, the words spilling forth unbidden but certain.

"Je t'aime," he echoed back, his French imperfect but achingly sincere.

Our laughter mingled with the pulse of Paris as we continued our way through the city's veins, each moment an imprint on the fabric of our souls. And as the sun began to dip below the horizon, casting shadows that danced alongside our own, I knew that this city, this man, and this love were the masterpieces of my once-unpainted life.

The Seine lapped gently at the sides of the boat, a soothing rhythm that underscored the hum of Parisian nightlife. Michael's hand was warm in mine as I led him onto the polished wooden deck of the private vessel. His surprise—a mix of childlike wonder and adult appreciation—etched itself into my heart.

"Mon amour, you didn't have to do this," he marveled, his eyes reflecting the shimmering lights that danced across the water.

"Ah, but I did," I whispered, wrapping my arms around his waist from behind, resting my chin on his shoulder. "Paris is not just a city; it's an experience, and I want us to live it together."

The boat began its slow drift down the river, and the Eiffel Tower blossomed into view, a lattice of light stretching into the night sky. We stood there, wrapped in each other's embrace, the monument's grandeur making our own world feel both minuscule and infinitely significant.

"I've never felt so alive," he admitted, turning to face me, his hands finding the small of my back. "With you, Elena, every moment is magnified, intensified."

"Isn't that what life should be? A series of vivid moments, like brushstrokes on a canvas?" I mused, feeling the pulse of my own desires grow bolder with his touch.

"Indeed," he agreed, pressing his lips to mine in a kiss that tasted of promise and the sweet tang of champagne.

We talked of everything and nothing as the city paraded by, our voices mingling with the soft burble of the river. Each landmark we passed was a testament to endurance, to history—a mirror to our own journey through the murky waters of addiction and into the clarity of shared purpose.

"Look, the Louvre..." Michael pointed out the grand palace, its glass pyramid aglow, an anchor amidst the waves of time.

"Tomorrow," I promised, "we'll lose ourselves in its corridors, explore the depths of human creativity."

"And Notre-Dame?" he asked, a playful twinkle in his eye.

"An exploration of faith—of what we choose to believe in," I said, thinking of the strength we'd drawn from one another during the darkest of times.

"Like us," he affirmed, understanding my unspoken thoughts. "Believing in us when all else seemed lost."

As the night deepened, we found solace in the quiet corners of the city, sharing a croissant in the solitude of a park bench, its flaky layers crumbling between our fingers—a metaphor for the way we'd picked apart our pasts, layer by layer, to forge something new.

"Simple pleasures," I sighed contentedly, watching a lone leaf flutter to the ground, its descent a silent ballet.

"Are often the most profound," Michael completed my thought, always in sync, even in silence.

The weekend stretched before us, a tapestry of cultural marvels and intimate discoveries, each moment a thread woven into the fabric of our being. We would return home with more than souvenirs; we carried a renewed sense of self, a love deepened not just by pleasure but by the recognition of our worth beyond the ephemeral.

"Paris will always be a part of us now," I said as the boat docked, the city's heartbeat echoing our own. "A chapter in our story, written in light and shadow."

"Let's keep writing it," Michael replied, his voice low and earnest, his lips finding mine once more under the benevolent gaze of a thousand Parisian stars.

The silk sheets whispered against our skin, a cool contrast to the heat we generated between us. Our nights in Paris had become the canvas for our passion, each touch painting strokes of desire and longing that deepened our connection. Michael's intense blue eyes held mine in the dim light, reflecting a vulnerability we'd only just begun to explore.

"Tell me your dreams," he murmured, his fingers tracing the contours of my face as if committing every detail to memory.

In the sanctuary of our suite, with the Eiffel Tower piercing the night sky outside our window, I allowed myself to unravel before him. My voice was barely above a whisper, "I dream of a life where this"—I gestured around the opulent room and then back to us intertwined—"isn't just an escape but a reality."

He nodded, understanding the weight of my admission. The addiction of these highs was real, and the fear of returning to the monotony of everyday life loomed large. Yet, there was hope here, nestled in the warmth of his embrace.

"Let's make it our reality," he said, conviction lacing his words. There was no judgment in his gaze, only the shared acknowledgment of our mutual longing to blend our lives into something resilient and beautiful.

"Could we?" I asked, the possibility tasting like the vintage wine we'd shared at dinner.

"Anything is possible with you, Elena," he replied, sealing his promise with a kiss that spoke of futures yet written.

We dressed leisurely for dinner that evening, the sensual energy of the night still clinging to our skin. Michael chose a restaurant renowned not just for its cuisine but for the intimacy of its setting—a place where conversations could unfold undisturbed.

"Here's to new beginnings," I toasted, raising my glass as we settled into the hushed ambiance.

"To us," he echoed, his glass chiming softly against mine.

Over plates of coq au vin and boeuf bourguignon, we ventured into territories of conversation we'd only skated around before. We talked of blending our lives, of finding a home together where the walls knew no echoes of loneliness or the coldness of solitude. With each course, our dialogue wove a future rich with shared purpose.

"Imagine waking up to the smell of coffee and knowing it's just the start of all we can share," I said, caught up in the tapestry of a life interwoven with his.

"Or coming home to you after a long day, finding solace in our little world," Michael added, his hand finding mine across the table.

"Will it always feel like this?" I asked, the question tinged with the raw edge of my past addictions—the relentless chase of a high never meant to last.

"Better," he assured me, squeezing my hand. "Because it'll be real. Built on more than fleeting moments. On trust, on dedication... on love."

As dessert arrived, a decadent chocolate fondant that melted under our spoons like our resolve under Parisian influence, I felt the last of my reservations dissolve. Here, with Michael, I discovered the courage to believe in a dream that extended beyond the city's romantic allure, beyond the addictive rush of new experiences.

"Let's do it. Let's blend our lives into a masterpiece," I declared, the words a vow spoken from the depths of newfound intimacy.

His smile was a mirror to my heart—full of promise, full of tomorrow. "Together," he affirmed, and Paris, with all its lights and shadows, became the witness to our pledge.

"Where are we going?" Michael's voice was playful, but I sensed the underlying current of curiosity.

"Trust me," I said, a smile tugging at my lips.

Finally, standing at the center of the bridge, the Eiffel Tower punctuating the horizon like an exclamation of all we had shared, I pulled the lock from my pocket and handed it to him. Our initials—E & M—were etched into the shimmering surface, a testament to what we were choosing to create.

"Shall we?" I asked, my heart pounding with a cocktail of excitement and fear, no longer from the addictive thrills I once craved, but from the weight of commitment that felt as heavy and as sweet as the golden locket in his hand.

His fingers brushed mine as he took the lock, and something electric passed between us. With a nod, he secured it onto the bridge's railing, clicking it shut with a finality that resonated deep within my bones. We tossed the key into the Seine, watching as it surrendered to the river's embrace, and I felt a release, a letting go of the past that had clung to me like the scent of cigarettes on a barfly's clothes.

"Forever is a long time," he said, turning to face me, the depth of his blue eyes more profound than the waters that ran beneath us.

"Forever is made up of nows," I replied, my voice steady even as my insides quivered. "And every 'now' with you is a brushstroke on the canvas of us."

"Then let's paint a masterpiece," he whispered before his lips captured mine, sealing our promise with a kiss that held the fervor of every artwork we'd admired, every whisper shared, every shadowed corner of addiction I'd fought to step out of.

Beneath the Parisian sky, we wrote the beginning of our next chapter—not with words, but with presence, with connection, with love that dared to claim eternity as its playground. And in that moment, I knew that every high and low that had brought me here was essential; they were the dark hues that made the bright ones sing on the vast, unfolding mural of my life with Michael.

The tangle of sheets whispered beneath our fingers as we packed, the woven memories of nights spent in the embrace of Paris and each other. Our luxurious suite, with its grand view of the Eiffel Tower, now bore the sweet chaos of two lives intertwining amidst open suitcases and scattered clothing.

"Can you believe we have to leave all this?" Michael murmured, folding a shirt with a precision that matched his sharp, dark attire.

I zipped my bag shut, my hands lingering on the fabric—a soft, delicate cashmere I would never have touched before the windfall that had uprooted my life. "Paris is just the beginning," I said, my voice tinged with a mix of melancholy and anticipation.

He crossed the room, his presence filling the space between us, and wrapped his arms around me. "Every moment here with you... it's been more real than anything I've ever known."

"More real than those boardroom battles you love?" I teased, leaning back to meet his gaze.

"Infinitely," he replied, his lips curving into a smile that crinkled the corners of his intense blue eyes. "You've shown me that there's more to life than conquests and accolades."

"Good," I whispered, "because I need you—us—to be about more than just escapades or exotic locales." My voice wavered as I spoke of needs, my history with Alex—a man who embodied the antithesis of depth—casting shadows in my mind.

"Hey," Michael said, tipping my chin up with a gentle finger. "I'm here for the quiet mornings and the stormy nights too. For every addiction you fight, every dream you chase."

"Promise?" The word felt heavy, laden with the weight of my past and the fears for what lay ahead.

"Promise." His affirmation was a balm, soothing the raw edges of my vulnerability.

The journey to the airport was a blur, the city passing by like a series of impressionist paintings—vivid, yet somehow distant. We slipped into the leather seats of the private jet, the hum of the engines a backdrop to our shared silence.

As the plane ascended, leaving Paris to become a sparkling jewel in the night sky, Michael pulled out a notepad, his salt-and-pepper hair catching the cabin light. "So, where to next?" he asked, his pen poised.

"Somewhere quiet... maybe a cabin in the woods? Or a beach house where the only soundtrack is the ocean," I suggested, yearning for the simplicity that my new life often eclipsed.

"Let's do both. We'll wake up to the sunrise over the water and get lost among the trees when we crave solitude." He scribbled down our ideas, his hand steady, his resolve clear.

"Sounds perfect." I leaned against him, feeling the thrum of the jet match the rhythm of my heart. "But let's not forget about home. Movie nights, cooking together... those moments matter just as much."

"They're what make everything else worthwhile," he agreed, his hand finding mine, linking our futures with a simple touch.

"Michael?"

"Mmm?"

"Thank you. For understanding me. Thank you for everything." I breathed in the scent of him, a mixture of cologne and something innately his, something that spoke of safety and challenge all at once.

"Thank you for letting me into your world. For trusting me with your heart, your fears... your love."

Our conversation drifted then, from grand adventures to mundane pleasures, each plan a testament to our commitment, each quiet aspiration a reflection of the love that had grown, fierce and tender, within the city of lights.

And as the sky shifted from velvety black to the soft blush of dawn, I realized that Paris had been but a prelude to the symphony of our lives—a melody composed of highs and lows, played with the fervor of shared passion and the quietude of intimate understanding.

The wheels of the private jet kissed the tarmac with a whisper, a stark contrast to the thunderous pulse that still raced through my veins. We were home. The air felt different—

denser, laden with reality—but as I glanced at Michael, his blue eyes weary yet alight with the same fervor that fueled our Parisian nights, I knew we carried back with us an invincible thread woven from the city's romantic tapestry.

"God, I'm beat," he murmured, stretching his arms, the motion causing his shirt to cling to the contours of his well-defined chest. His voice was gravel and silk, sending a shiver down my spine despite my own exhaustion.

"Me too," I admitted, my body aching in places I never knew could feel so deliciously sore. The afterglow of our lovemaking lingered on my skin like the memory of sunlight.

We shuffled off the plane, hand in hand, a silent pledge between us. The terminal was nearly empty, echoing with the soft clatter of our footsteps. Our shadows danced ahead of us, entwined and inseparable.

"Remember that tiny café?" I asked, the corners of my mouth lifting with the recollection. "The one with the croissants that melted on your tongue?"

"Impossible to forget." He squeezed my hand tighter. "It's the simple things, isn't it? Those shared bites, your laughter spilling into the morning air—that's what I'll treasure most."

"Those moments are the threads that keep the fabric of us strong," I said, feeling the weight of truth in my words.

Outside, the night had settled like a cloak over the landscape, familiar and comforting. The drive home was quiet, a reflective space where thoughts meandered and tangled with the hum of the engine.

Once inside my apartment, the silence enveloped us like a cocoon. We moved together in a slow dance of routine—discarding shoes, keys tossed onto the table, each act stripping away the veneer of adventure to reveal the raw, tender vulnerability beneath.

"Let's not unpack tonight," Michael suggested, his hands finding my waist. "Let's just be. Here. Now."

I nodded, suddenly overwhelmed by the intensity of everything we'd experienced, the depth of emotions that threatened to spill over. Paris had been a dream, but this—our life, our struggles, our future together—was vividly real.

He pulled me close, and I buried my face in the crook of his neck, inhaling the scent that was uniquely him, a mixture of cologne and the faintest hint of paint from his latest canvas. It grounded me, reminded me of who we were beyond the intoxicating haze of the City of Light.

"Michael," I whispered, my voice breaking with the confession I'd carried across the ocean, "I need you more than the thrill of escape. More than Paris. You anchor me when the cravings claw at my soul."

His lips pressed against my forehead, a balm to the confession that laid bare my fears. "Elena, I am here, through every high and every low. We will face your demons together, love stronger than any addiction."

Chapter Eighteen

I was about to lean in for a kiss, intoxicated by the proximity, when a sliver of white at the foot of my door caught my eye. A note? My heart stuttered with a curious beat, the laughter dying in my throat as I stooped to retrieve it.

"Hey, what's that?" Micheal straightened, his playful curiosity shifting to concern at the sudden change in my demeanor.

I unfolded the paper, my fingers tremoring slightly. The world around me seemed to dim, the words scrawled across the page screaming louder than the silence that engulfed us. It was Alex's handwriting—uneven, aggressive—a visual echo of his volatile nature that I knew all too well.

"Who's it from, Elena?" Micheal's voice broke through the shock that held me captive, his tone laced with a hint of alarm now.

I couldn't speak; the words would not come. The note—its threat inked in a familiar hand—was a ghostly punch, knocking the wind out of me. I was momentarily paralyzed, the joy of moments ago now a distant memory replaced by a cold dread pooling in my stomach. "I'll get you back, you're mine, or else.." was written.

Micheal looked up at me, his eyes searching for an explanation I wasn't yet ready to give.

"Alex," I finally whispered, the name tasting like ash in my mouth.

The note slipped from my trembling hands, floating down to land softly on the concrete. My past, which I thought I had buried deep enough, had clawed its way back to the surface with a vengeance. And standing there, under the harsh glare of the porch light, I felt the first thread of the life I'd built start to unravel.

I lifted my gaze to meet his, seeing the protective fire in his eyes, the need to shield me from whatever darkness lurked behind that slip of paper. But this was a shadow not even Michael could chase away. "It's... it's a threat," I confessed, feeling the weight of each word, heavy and foreboding.

"From your ex?" His hands clenched at his sides as if grappling with an invisible enemy. I'd never seen him like this—anger pulsing just beneath his skin, a fierce protector ready to battle demons he didn't understand.

"Michael, I..." The rest of the sentence died on my lips. How could I explain the complexities of a past relationship that had left scars invisible to the naked eye?

"Jesus, Elena! Does he have any reason to do this?" The raw edge in his voice startled me, so different from the gentle warmth I was accustomed to.

"None that I can think of," I replied, my mind racing with possibilities. But they were just smoke—formless and obscure.

"Does he want to get back with you? Is that what this is about?" Michael's jaw was set, his anger a palpable force that seemed to push against me.

"No!" The word erupted from me, fierce and certain. "It was over long before you. He's not part of my life, Michael. He hasn't been for a long time."

"Then why—"

"I don't know!" The admission shattered the last of my composure. Frustration, fear, and a profound sense of helplessness collided within me, leaving me breathless.

"God damn it, Elena." Michael ran a hand through his hair, a gesture of vexation that sent chills down my spine. "This changes things. It's not just about us anymore."

"Please, Michael." I reached out, needing to bridge the distance his anger had created. "Don't let this—"

But he stepped back, out of reach, his expression one I couldn't read. I knew then that the fragile fabric of trust between us had been torn, perhaps irreparably, by the ghost of a relationship I thought had died long ago.

"Michael, please," I begged, my voice raw with the strain of defending myself against an unseen accuser. "Alex was a part of my past—a chapter that's been closed for a long time."

"Was it?" Michael's eyes were two storm clouds, dark and swirling with suspicion. "Or is this note proof that the story isn't over? That he still has some hold on you?"

My heart pounded against my ribcage, each beat echoing the hurt in his words. "You know that's not true. I've been open with you about everything—about him, about us. Why would I hide now?"

"Because people keep secrets, Elena!" His shout bounced off the walls, amplifying the distance between us. "Secrets that can destroy what they claim to love!"

"Dammit, Michael." The taste of tears mingled with bitterness on my tongue. "I fought too hard to get away from Alex and his manipulations, not being loved or cared, his indifference. I've worked too damn hard to build something real with you to let it crumble because of him."

"Worked hard?" He scoffed, the sound like acid etching glass. "Is that what you call it? What about the nights I caught you staring into nothing, your mind obviously miles away? Was that just work, or were you thinking of him?"

"Never!It was never about him! He never even crossed my mind! How could you say that?" I felt so helpless, not knowing how to make him believe, scared of losing what we have.

"Fuck!" Michael raked his fingers through his hair, his features contorting with frustration. "I can't compete with a ghost, Elena. I won't be the one standing here, waiting for the other shoe to drop."

"Then don't wait!" The words erupted from me, a volcanic release of pent-up fear and anger. "If you can't trust me, if you can't see that I'm fighting every day to stay free from that life, to build something precious something meaningful with you—then maybe you should leave!"

For a moment, we stood there, our breaths mingling in the charged silence. The air was thick with the weight of unspoken truths and the sharp tang of impending loss.

"Maybe I should," he said quietly, the tempest in his eyes giving way to a cold resignation.

"Michael—" But he held up a hand, stopping me mid-plea.

"Save it, Elena. Just... save it." His voice was devoid of the warmth I had come to cherish, replaced by a chilling finality.

The door slammed shut behind him, leaving me in a void of my own making. Alone in the shell of a home we'd built together, I could feel the foundation crumbling beneath me. The remnants of his presence mocked me from every corner—his jacket draped over a chair, the lingering scent of his cologne, the faint indent on the pillow where he used to lay his head.

"Damn you, Alex," I whispered into the emptiness. "Damn you for haunting me still."

And as the night crept in, swallowing the last vestiges of daylight, I crumpled to the floor, a solitary figure amidst the ruins of a love that may have just breathed its last.

Tears streamed down my cheeks, hot and unrestrained, as I buried my face into the worn fabric of the couch cushion—Michael's favorite spot. His absence was a gaping hole in the room, echoing back my sobs with cruel indifference. I held myself tightly, rocked by the tremors of heartbreak that threatened to tear me apart from the inside.

"Was any of it real?" The question hung heavy in the air, mingling with the ghost of our shared laughter, now tainted by the acrid burn of doubt. How could something so steady, so full of promise, crumble so swiftly under the weight of a past I thought I had buried deep enough?

Alex. His name seared through my mind like a brand, igniting memories I fought so hard to suffocate. I remembered his touch—a dangerous cocktail of pain and pleasure—a reminder of a time when I was lost to the addiction of him. His love had been my drug, potent and destructive, leaving scars too deep to ever really fade.

I unfolded the note once more, smoothing out its creases as if by doing so I could iron out the chaos it had brought into my life. The letters danced menacingly before my eyes, each word a lash from Alex's invisible whip, dragging me back to the darkness I'd escaped. What did he want? Was this retribution for leaving him, or a twisted attempt to draw me back into his world—a world I barely survived?

The room felt colder, emptier, as if even the walls mourned the love they had witnessed. Michael's angry words echoed in my ears, the hurt behind them almost palpable. He didn't understand, couldn't understand, the chains that once bound me to another. And how could I blame him? To him, the Elena caught in Alex's toxic orbit was a stranger, someone he couldn't reconcile with the woman he thought he knew.

"Where did I go wrong?" I mused aloud, the whisper seeming sacrilegious in the stillness. My reflection stared back at me from the darkened windowpane—a specter of the person I had become, haunted by the shadows of who I used to be.

I sank deeper into the couch, letting the silence envelope me. The future we had envisioned, Michael and I—full of hope and free from the sins of yesterday—seemed like a naive dream now. The foundation of trust we built had fissures wide enough for doubt to pour through, filling the cracks with uncertainty and fear.

"Can we survive this?" But there was no answer, only the relentless echo of my own voice. The night stretched on, a canvas painted with regrets and what-ifs, each stroke a vivid reminder of the fragility of love and the enduring grip of addiction. The threat from Alex wasn't just a warning; it was a test—one that had already begun to unravel the delicate tapestry of my recovery, and perhaps, the very fabric of my relationship with Michael.

The glow of the early morning sun did little to warm the chill that had settled deep within my bones. I wrapped my arms around myself, the once comforting silence of my home now a deafening cacophony of unanswered questions and what-ifs.

Michael's words still ricocheted through my mind—sharp, stinging with betrayal and disappointment.

"Can we even get past this, Elena?" The image of his intense blue eyes, usually so full of warmth but then burning with accusation, flickered before me. Our last conversation hung in the air like a ghost, haunting the space between us that seemed to stretch wider with each passing second.

I paced the room, the rhythmic creak of the floorboards underfoot punctuating the turmoil swirling inside me. Each step was aimless, a futile attempt to outrun the loneliness nipping at my heels. Michael had been my rock, my shelter against the storm that raged within me—a storm Alex had reignited with a few cruel strokes of a pen.

"Was it all a lie?" The question slipped from my lips, raw and vulnerable. My reflection in the mirror winced back at me; the dark circles under my hazel eyes were a stark testament to the sleepless nights spent agonizing over the consequences for my future.

"Fuck!" I slammed my fist against the wall, the pain a welcome distraction from the ache in my heart. The thought of losing Michael, of facing the world without his steady presence, was unbearable. But it wasn't just about him. It was about me—about who I'd become and who I still had to be.

"Get your shit together, Elena." But the words were empty, a mantra void of conviction. How could I piece myself back together when I felt so irreparably broken?

Days blurred into one another, each as gray and indistinct as the next. The outside world beckoned, life continuing its relentless march forward, but I remained cocooned within these walls, shackled by despair. Food lost its taste, the shower became an adversary, and my bed a siren calling me to the depths of isolation.

"Alex... why did you want to destroy me? Is this your victory?" Alex's passive nature, once endearing, now revealed itself as a sinister undercurrent, capable of dragging me back into the abyss I fought so hard to escape.

"Michael..." His name was a prayer, a plea for redemption I wasn't sure I deserved. He was out there somewhere, probably nursing his own wounds, questioning if the woman he loved was nothing more than a façade.

"Am I even worth fighting for?" The bitter inquiry lingered, unanswered. Yet, the silence spoke volumes.

"Maybe this is it," I muttered to the emptiness, "the beginning of the end." The thought should have terrified me, but instead, a numbness had taken hold, a detachment from the very essence of life.

"Is this how it feels to lose everything?" The question was rhetorical, the answer etched in the hollow feeling that consumed me. Time ticked away, mocking me with its indifference, as I lay there, a shell of the person I once was, drowning in a sea of depression and disbelief, with persistent a nausea that hasn't gone away for days

Chapter Nineteen

The moment my eyes fluttered open to the intrusion of morning light, a leaden exhaustion clung to my bones. I rolled onto my side, cradling my head in hands that trembled with a weakness that was becoming all too familiar. The queasiness that roiled in my stomach had morphed from an occasional nuisance to a relentless specter that haunted my mornings.

"Push through it, Elena," I muttered to myself, swallowing back the bile that threatened to rise. I'd become adept at ignoring the signals my body screamed at me, burying them under the mountain of work that never seemed to diminish.

"Come on, you've survived worse," I chided myself as I pushed through the morning routine like a soldier marching to battle—undaunted, unwavering. But privately, I wondered what kind of war I was waging against myself.

For what felt like forever, I barely left my house, feeling lost and empty. David, Sophie, and Clara didn't give up on me, though. They kept calling and coming over, trying to help me through this rough patch. But without Michael, everything seemed pointless. He was my rock, and now he was gone.

Clara came over one day, and we talked for hours. Her words were kind but firm, reminding me of the strong person I used to be—the one who started her own business, who wasn't afraid to chase her dreams. That's when something clicked in me. I realized I couldn't let this breakup ruin me. I had faced tougher times and come out stronger.

Taking a deep breath, I decided it was time to get back up. Time to step back into the world and take on whatever came my way, even if I had to do it by myself. Michael was a big part of my life, but he wasn't everything. I had my friends, my business, and my own strength. Getting out of bed, I knew it wouldn't be easy, but I was ready to face it. After all, I'm Elena, and I don't give up easily. So, I opened the door, ready to start fighting for my life and dreams again.

"Are you sure you're up for this?" Sophia's voice, laced with concern, broke through the veil of my concentration as we traipsed through the boutique-lined streets. A day out with Sophia and Clara should have been a balm to my frayed nerves, a rare indulgence in normalcy.

"Of course," I lied smoothly, plastering on a smile that felt more like a grimace. My reflection in the shop windows hardly recognized me—a pale imitation of the vibrant woman I once took pride in being. My mind, obsessed with the thought of Micheal and what we had, couldn't think of anything else.

"Let's try these on!" Clara exclaimed, her enthusiasm undimmed by the world's weight. She thrust a collection of garments into my arms, fabrics that whispered promises of transformation. But as I slipped into the dressing room, each piece betrayed me, hugging curves that were not there before, pinching at the waist where there had always been space.

"Nothing fits," I murmured, the words hollow as they bounced off the mirror. "I don't understand."

"Hey, are you okay in there?" Sophia's voice pierced the curtain, tinged with worry.

"Uh, yeah, just... nothing seems to fit right." The admission felt like defeat, and I braced myself against the cool wall, a chill seeping into my skin. "I've just been feeling so off lately."

"Off how?" Clara's voice pierced the thin dressing room curtain, her words sharp with worry.

"I've been nauseous, so nauseous. And not just in the mornings. Plus, I've been exhausted. It doesn't matter how much I sleep," I continued, the symptoms I'd been ignoring now aligning like stars in a constellation I hadn't wanted to recognize.

There was a pause, filled with the rustling of clothes and the muted sound of the mall outside, before Sophia's voice cut through with a suggestion that felt like a cold wave, "Elena, do you think you might be pregnant?"

The word 'pregnant' hung in the air, heavy and fraught with implications. A chill ran down my spine as I processed her words, my heart racing with the sudden influx of possibilities.

"Take a test, Elena. It's the only way to be sure," Clara's suggestion came through the curtain, softer now, tinged with an understanding that seemed to reach out and wrap around me in a gentle embrace.

A test. The idea was both terrifying and necessary. A definitive answer to the question that had started to form, unbidden, in the back of my mind. "Yeah, maybe I should," I finally agreed, my voice barely a whisper.

The curtain whisked aside as I stepped out, met by the supportive gazes of Clara and Sophia. Their faces were a mixture of concern and encouragement, a silent promise that no matter what the test revealed, I wouldn't have to face it alone.

"Let's go," Sophia said, her determination clear. She led the way, her steps resolute, as Clara fell in step beside me, her presence a comforting reminder that friendship was a lifeline, especially in moments like these.

As we made our way to the pharmacy, the reality of my situation began to sink in. The possibility of pregnancy was no longer an abstract concept but a potential pivot in the path of my life. The myriad of emotions swirling within me—fear, anticipation, hope—were a tumultuous sea, and I was adrift, clinging to the lifeline my friends offered.

The fluorescent lights of the pharmacy seemed too bright, casting everything in stark relief as we navigated the aisles. Finding the pregnancy tests felt surreal, each box a harbinger of a future I hadn't planned for. My fingers trembled as I selected one, the weight of the decision pressing down on me.

"We're here for you, Elena, no matter what," Clara said, her voice steady. Her hand found mine, squeezing gently, a beacon of support in the sea of uncertainty that threatened to engulf me.

"Yeah, we've got you," Sophia echoed, her arm looping through mine, solidifying the circle of our friendship. Their unwavering presence, the strength they lent me, was a tangible thing, warming the cold tendrils of fear that wrapped around my heart.

"Can I help you find something?" The clerk's voice jolted me from my thoughts.

"Uh, no. I've got it, thanks," I mumbled, ducking down an aisle before she could glimpse the unease in my eyes. My hands hovered over the array of pregnancy tests, each promising accuracy, ease, results. I scoffed at their certainty, feeling anything but sure as I scooped up different boxes, each one a possible key to a new chapter—or the end of the life I knew.

At the checkout, I avoided the cashier's eyes, the test a declaration of my current chaos hidden in a small, unassuming box. The walk back was a blur, my thoughts a whirlwind of 'what ifs' and 'then whats.'

"Have a nice day," she chirped mechanically as I all but snatched the bag from her hands and hastened out into the brisk air that did little to cool my burning skin.

I needed to do this part alone, I had to. So I told Sophie and Clara I'd give them a call once I did the test and parted ways. My pace quickened on the way home, the streets a blur. I felt every curious glance like a prying into my private turmoil. By the time I reached my apartment, my breaths came fast and uneven, mirroring the tumult inside.

The key turned in the lock with an echo too loud for the silence awaiting me. Dropping my purse by the door, I made my way to the bathroom, the sanctuary where so many truths had been faced in the reflection of its mirror.

Carefully, I laid out the boxes on the cold marble countertop, each one a silent judge. My hands were steady now, driven by a compulsion for answers. I followed the instructions meticulously, the clinical language a stark contrast to the whirlwind of scenarios spinning through my mind.

"Five minutes," I whispered to myself, setting the timer on my phone. Those digits transformed into a chasm of time, a void where my usual distractions held no power. There was nothing to do but wait, and waiting was a cruel game for a mind shackled by what-ifs.

The white tiles beneath my feet were a blank canvas where I projected my fears—a mosaic of addiction's grip, the chaos of unmet dreams, and the fragility of newfound love. Could I be a mother? Would Michael understand, or would he see this as a brushstroke too erratic for our carefully composed picture?

"Shit," I cursed under my breath, the walls of the room closing in. The scent of antiseptic cleaner mingled with the sweet fragrance of my anxiety. I perched on the edge of the bathtub, elbows on knees, head in hands. This sterile space was a far cry from the vibrant world outside, where I'd spun my life from grey monotony to technicolor dreams.

The alarm's shrill call startled me back to the present, my breath hitching as I reached for the stick that held my future. My gaze transfixed on the single window of my fate, knowing that once seen, it could never be unseen.

The silence was deafening, the kind that echoed through the hollows of my chest. My fingers trembled as they clutched the plastic herald of change; two pink lines stark against the pallor of my hand, unwavering and resolute. Pregnant. The word ricocheted through my mind, an unfamiliar guest that refused to leave.

"Fuck," the curse slipped from my lips, a helpless acknowledgment of the turmoil within. I sat on the cold bathroom floor, back against the tub, knees drawn up to my chest. A strange amalgam of emotions churned in my gut—fear knotted with threads of wonder, uncertainty shackled to a burgeoning sense of awe.

My life had been a canvas of muted tones until Michael strode in with his palette of vibrant hues. He painted strokes of confidence over my insecurities, sketched dreams where there were voids, and now, perhaps, added a new life to our shared masterpiece. But how could I tell him? After what we've been through? After all this time? After how stupid Alex destroyed us with a simple note?

I closed my eyes, letting the waves of emotion crash over me. His face came unbidden to my mind's eye, those intense blue eyes that seemed to see right through to my soul. We'd danced through galleries, sipped wine in dimly lit corners of the world, and reveled in the raw beauty of creation. Art, travel, love—all swirling together in a dizzying waltz of passion and possibility. But now, not speaking for what, a month? Or even more?

"Can we really do this?" I whispered to the reflection of a woman in the mirror, her hazel eyes wide with the weight of her revelation. She—no, I—was at the precipice of something monumental. Each brushstroke of our love had led to this point, and now a baby, a tiny, unformed being, might be the next delicate line in the sketch of our lives.

"Michael," the name fell like a prayer or perhaps a plea. His presence, always so grounding, suddenly felt vital, necessary to anchor me in this storm of realization.

A baby. Our baby. It was a concept as daunting as it was intoxicating. The potential of a little one interwoven into the tapestry of our existence filled me with a fierce protectiveness I'd never known.

"Will you still want me, want this, when you know?" The question hung in the air, unanswered, a specter of doubt amidst the certainty of the test in my hand. Michael's love was a given, but what shape it would take in the face of this news was a mystery yet to unravel.

"God, I need you," I murmured, clutching the porcelain edge of the bathtub for support. The thought of telling him made my heart race, a mix of desire and dread. The reality of our situation, its implications stretching far beyond the confines of this small room, loomed large.

I stood, shaky legs barely supporting the weight of my newfound knowledge. A future unfurled before me, ripe with promise and peril. "Together," I promised the reflection, "we'll face whatever comes." With a deep breath, I prepared to step out of the solitude of the bathroom and into the unfolding story of us.

I paced the length of my living room, each step a silent question echoing off the walls. The city lights outside cast a soft glow through the sheer curtains, wrapping me in their hazy embrace as if to soften the blow of my racing thoughts.

"Am I even ready for this?" I whispered into the void, envisioning a future that was both foreign and unsettlingly near. Motherhood was a mantle I never imagined draping over my shoulders, yet now it seemed to hover, waiting for me to slip beneath its weight.

"Can you do this, Elena?" I asked my reflection in the windowpane, seeking affirmation from the woman who stared back with uncertain eyes. She was me, but this new role felt like a stranger's outline I was being asked to fill. "How will you tell him? Will he come back, accept this?"

A sigh escaped me, fogging up the glass—a momentary cloud over the clarity I so desperately sought. Michael's face came to mind, his intense blue eyes always filled with unwavering support. But would they hold the same warmth when I shared my news? His love was a sanctuary, but could it expand to encompass the life growing inside me?

"Your career, Elena," I chided myself, fingers tracing the patterns on an embroidered cushion. My work was more than a job; it was my passion, my identity. Could I reconcile the demands of motherhood with the unyielding pull of ambition?

"Clara," I exhaled her name like a lifeline, picking up my phone with hands that trembled slightly. Clara had been there through every twist and turn, her wisdom a beacon when my path seemed darkest.

"Hey, it's me," I said, my voice steady despite the storm within. "Can we talk?"

"Of course, Elena. What's going on? You sound... different." Her voice was a soothing balm, her intuition sharp as ever.

"Clara, I'm—I think I'm pregnant," I admitted, the words tumbling out in a rush, raw and exposed.

"Wow, Lena, that's... Are you okay? How are you feeling about it?" There was no judgment in her tone, only concern.

"Scared, confused, and a million other things. I don't know if I can do this, Clara. And Michael... what if he doesn't want this? What if I can't be the person they need me to be?"

"Listen to me," she said firmly, her voice cutting through my fears. "You are stronger than you realize. This is big, yes, but you're not alone. And Michael, he loves you. He's not going to run away from this."

"But my career, Clara. I've worked so hard, and now—"

"Your career will adapt, just like you will. You're not the first woman to face this, and you won't be the last. You've got this, Elena. But whatever you decide to do, I'm here for you. We'll figure this out together."

"Thank you, Clara. I needed to hear that. I feel like I'm on the edge of something huge, and I'm terrified of falling."

"Then we'll build a net, Elena. You're not falling. You're flying. Remember that."

"Okay," I murmured, the knot in my chest loosening ever so slightly. "Okay."

"Talk to Michael. Be honest with him. And then, let's meet tomorrow. We'll sort through everything, one step at a time."

"Tomorrow," I echoed, a plan taking shape amidst the chaos. "Thank you, Clara. For everything."

"Anytime, Lena. Anytime."

I ended the call, my heart still a wild rhythm against my ribs. But Clara's words were a mantra, ringing with truth and possibility. I wasn't alone. With a newfound resolve, I knew what I had to do. Tomorrow would come with its own challenges, but tonight, I would face Michael, and together, we'd step into our future—one fraught with uncertainty, but also shimmering with promise.

Chapter Twenty

The flicker of the candle flames cast a soft, undulating light across the walls of my living room. Each wick I lit was a small prayer, an invocation for courage. The scent of jasmine began to infuse the air—an aroma chosen for its calming properties, though my hands still shook with each match struck.

I placed the last candle on the mantelpiece and stepped back, watching the shadows dance in a slow, hypnotic rhythm. My heart matched their tempo—a staccato beat that spoke of fear and longing.

With each breath I drew, I felt the weight of my secret pressing against my chest, a physical manifestation of the emotional burden I could no longer carry alone.

"Tonight," I whispered into the quiet of the room, a promise to myself as much as to Michael, "everything changes."

I glanced around the space that had witnessed the ebb and flow of our love—laughter echoing off the walls, bodies entwined in passion's embrace, and now, the silent testament of separation. The couch, once our sanctuary, seemed like an island in a sea of uncertainty. I fluffed the cushions mechanically, trying to dispel the vivid memories that clung to them, reminders of nights spent chasing pleasure with abandon.

Pleasure. The word echoed in my mind, tainted with irony. What started as an exploration of joy had morphed into a craving, an addiction to moments of escape from the emptiness that gnawed at me. But the fleeting highs left behind an aching void, one that begged to be filled with something deeper, more substantial.

"God," I muttered, running a hand through my hair, "let this be right."

As the doorbell echoed through the house, a shiver traveled down my spine. This was it—the precipice of change. And I stood on its edge, peering into the depths of the unknown, about to leap.

"Michael," I breathed out, steeling myself as I moved toward the door. The air felt thick with anticipation, charged with the electricity of a storm about to break. Every step felt like a journey, every second stretched long with the gravity of what I was about to reveal.

"Be brave," I told my reflection in the hallway mirror, her eyes wide with a vulnerability I couldn't mask. Tonight, I'd bare my soul to him, peel back the layers of pretense and touch upon a truth that could either bind us together or sever what ties remained.

"Be brave," I repeated, and with a deep breath, I reached for the door handle, ready to step into our future, wherever it might lead.

The click of the lock disengaged, and the door swung open to reveal Michael. He stood there, a silhouette against the twilight sky, his intense blue eyes immediately seeking mine. They were the ocean in a storm—beautiful yet terrifying in their depth. My heart pounded as if it knew to brace itself for the impact of his gaze.

"Hey," he said, stepping inside, a tentative smile playing on his lips.

"Hi," I replied, my voice a whisper lost in the space between us. The word felt inadequate, a poor vessel for the surging emotions that threatened to spill over.

We moved through the hallway, a dance of uncertainty, into the living room where flickering candles cast shadows that played upon the walls. This room had once been our sanctuary, filled with laughter and whispers of dreams shared on the couch that now seemed like a relic from another lifetime.

"Nice ambiance," Michael commented, his sharp features softening in the warm light. But the compliment hung awkwardly in the air, tethered to the tension that neither of us could deny.

"Thank you," I managed, my fingers nervously tucking a rogue curl behind my ear. I watched him take a seat, every movement deliberate, a testament to the control I both admired and feared might crack under the weight of my confession.

There was a silence, profound and heavy, that draped around us like a thick blanket, smothering the small talk that might have eased us into this moment. My pulse echoed in my ears, a relentless reminder of what I needed to say. I perched on the edge of the armchair across from him, the fabric unfamiliar beneath my fingertips, though I'd chosen it myself not two years ago.

"Michael," I started, the name a key turning the lock on my resolve. "There's something I need to tell you." My voice trembled, betraying the emotion that swelled within me, a tide that rose with each word.

He leaned forward, his brows knitting together in concern. "Everything okay?" he asked, his tone steady, a lighthouse in the brewing storm of my psyche.

I hesitated, the words a lump in my throat. How does one say the unsayable? How do you share a truth that alters everything?

"Michael... I'm pregnant."

The words hung in the air, raw and exposed, echoing off the walls and filling the room with a new gravity. That single sentence shifted the very foundation of the space we occupied, charged with the power of creation and the fragility of the unknown.

His face was a canvas of unspoken thoughts, a silent tableau that held the brushstrokes of our past and the outline of an unforeseen future. The candlelight flickered across his features, casting him half in light, half in shadow—a perfect metaphor for the duality of this revelation.

"Say something, please," I whispered, my heart a drumbeat against my ribs, begging for reassurance. I searched his face for any clue, any hint of what lay behind those stormy eyes, desperate for an anchor in the chaos of my emotions.

Michael's stillness became its own entity, filling the room like a dense fog. His gaze locked onto some distant point beyond the walls of my carefully curated living space, and I felt every second of his silence etching itself into the marrow of my bones. The candles I had lit with such precision now seemed absurdly inadequate, their flickering flames dwarfed by the enormity of my confession.

"Michael?" My voice was barely a thread in the heavy tapestry of our shared silence. The ambient sounds of the city beyond my window—a siren wailing in the distance, the muffled laughter of passersby—felt alien, a world away from the intimacy of this moment.

He blinked, slowly, as if surfacing from the depths of an ocean. His intense blue eyes met mine, and I saw the tempest brewing within them—a storm of emotions he couldn't quite name, much less articulate. Shock, certainly, but beneath that, layers of feeling that defied easy categorization. He swallowed hard, Adam's apple bobbing, and when he spoke, it was with a voice that resonated with the effort of processing the unexpected.

"Wow, Elena...this is...a lot." His words were tentative, each one measured and released with care, as though they were fragile things that might shatter upon impact.

I bit my lip, tasting the metallic tang of anxiety. The room seemed to contract around us, the air growing thick with the weight of his reaction—or lack thereof. I needed him to say more, to break through the ambiguity with something concrete, something I could hold onto.

"Talk to me, Michael. Please. I can't stand this silence." Desperation edged my plea, a rawness that scraped against the polished façade I'd worked so hard to maintain since my life had been upended by fortune and change.

He leaned back, running a hand through his dark hair, the gesture achingly familiar. Then, as if reaching a decision, he leaned forward, closing the gap between us. His hand found mine, warmth seeping from his skin into my cold fingers.

"I'm here, Elena. We're in this together," he said, and the sincerity in his tone was a balm to my frayed nerves. "It's unexpected, sure. But if there's one thing I know about us, it's that we're at our best when we face challenges head-on."

His acceptance was a shore I hadn't realized I'd been seeking amidst the tumultuous sea of my fears. In the span of those few sentences, he offered not just words, but a promise— a commitment that stretched beyond the barriers of my uncertainties.

"Really?" The word was a whisper, a prayer for confirmation.

"Really." His affirmation was as steady as the pulse thrumming in my veins. With the simple clasp of our hands, he bridged the chasm of our separation, anchoring me once again in the possibility of 'us.'

"Thank you," I breathed, allowing myself a momentary respite in the strength of his grip, the solidity of his presence. There were a thousand questions yet to be asked, a myriad of fears to be faced, but in the shelter of his acceptance, I found a flicker of hope that perhaps, together, we could navigate the uncertain path ahead.

My fingers still entwined with Michael's, I led him to the plush depths of the sofa, our shared sanctuary in times past. The flickering candlelight cast dancing shadows upon his face, revealing a vulnerability I had seen only on rare occasions.

"Michael," I began, my voice barely above a whisper, "these last months without you... they've been like wandering through a fog. A relentless gray that dulled everything."

He squeezed my hand gently, urging me to continue. His eyes, those deep pools of blue, held mine with an intensity that both comforted and unnerved me.

"I know what you mean," he said, his voice rough around the edges. "There was this hollow feeling, a void where you used to be. Work, friends, it all seemed like a play I was watching from the back row. Detached. Meaningless."

The raw honesty of his words cut through the remnants of my defenses. How could it be that even in absence, we mirrored each other's emotions?

"Every day felt like a battle against the silence that you left behind. It was deafening, Michael," I confessed, turning my gaze to the flicker of a solitary candle. "Some nights, I'd come home and just sit here, half-expecting you to walk through the door, ready to fill the space with your laughter, your warmth."

"God, Elena, I missed you." His voice broke on my name, and he reached out to cradle my cheek, his touch igniting a familiar fire within me. "I missed us. The way you challenge me, the way you laugh, the way you look at me like I'm the only one in the world who can understand you."

"Did you ever..." My question trailed off, the fear of his answer lodging itself in my throat.

"Did I ever what?" He prompted, thumb stroking my cheekbone.

"Did you ever find someone to fill the emptiness? To make you forget, even for a moment?"

"Never," he said firmly, leaning forward so his forehead rested against mine.This word enveloped me in a strength I desperately needed.

"I missed you, Michael," I pleaded, my voice laced with a yearning that transcended the physical. "I missed you and I love you."

"I love you too. Always," he vowed, his lips claiming mine with a fervor that spoke of lost time and reclaimed moments.

Our clothing became a memory, and the world outside ceased to exist as we rediscovered each other's bodies, each touch a testament to the depth of our connection.

As the night unfolded, every kiss, every caress, wrote a new chapter in the story of us—one where the future brought new hopes in our relationship.

In the aftermath of our rekindled passion, the flickering candles cast a warm glow across the room, illuminating the vulnerability that now lay bare between us. We were nestled in an embrace on the couch, Michael's arms wrapped around me as if to shield me from the world outside. My head rested against his chest, and I could feel the steady beat of his heart, grounding me in the reality of what was to come.

"Michael," I began, my voice barely above a whisper, "I'm scared." The confession hung in the air, raw and palpable.

"Talk to me, Elena." His fingers traced patterns on my back, soothing yet insistent.

"This baby... it changes everything. I don't know if I'm ready. What if—" My fears spilled out, a torrent of uncertainties about motherhood, our relationship, and the future that loomed ahead. "What if I lose myself in this? What if I can't be the woman you need?"

He cupped my face in his hands, his blue eyes searching mine with an intensity that stirred a mixture of fear and comfort within me. "Elena, listen to me. This child is a part of us—of our love. And no matter what doubts you have, I want you to know that I am here. Fully committed. To you, to our baby, to whatever life throws our way."

"Michael, I—" My throat tightened with emotion, the weight of his words anchoring me even as they set me adrift in a sea of new feelings.

"Shh," he murmured, pressing his lips to my forehead. "We're in this together. You won't lose yourself because I will be right here, reminding you of who you are every step of the way. You're strong, Elena, stronger than you even realize."

His reassurance was a balm to my anxious soul, and in his embrace, I found the courage to face the unknown. His presence was my harbor in the storm, and as we sat there, entwined in each other's arms, I felt a glimmer of hope piercing the veil of my fears.

"Thank you," I breathed out, my body relaxing against his. "For believing in us, even when I struggle to."

"Always," he replied, his voice a vow that echoed in the depths of my heart. "We'll navigate this together, love. Each challenge, each joy—we'll meet them as one."

The night deepened around us, but in Michael's arms, I found a sanctuary where the demons of addiction and the specters of past mistakes could not reach me. Together, we would forge a path through the uncertainty, bound by love and the shared promise of a future filled with meaning beyond the superficial allure of wealth and status.

As the candles burned lower, casting elongated shadows across the walls, I allowed myself to lean into the comfort of his words, feeling for the first time that maybe, just maybe, I could be the person he saw in me—the woman capable of weathering the storms of life, of motherhood, of love—with him by my side.

The silence had settled, a soft blanket around us, when Michael's voice cut through, practical as always. "We need to think about where we'll live," he said, his gaze steady. "This place..." His eyes roamed the small space, appreciative yet concerned.

"Is nice but we need to have something bigger maybe, something to call our's." I finished for him, the reality of it sinking in. The walls seemed to close in at the thought, and I felt a twinge of loss for the first time. This had been my sanctuary, but it could not be the nest for our growing family.

"Exactly." He leaned forward, elbows on knees, intensity lining his features.

Topic after topic we talked —insurance plans, maternity clothes, baby furniture—the future began to take shape, not just as an abstract fear, but as a tangible, exciting reality. Our conversation wove a tapestry of hope, each thread a commitment to our shared life.

Then, without warning, he stood, pulling me to my feet. "Enough planning for tonight," he declared, his voice low and laced with a different kind of intent.

"Michael?" I questioned, breathless as his hands found my waist, drawing me close.

"Let's not forget to live in the present, Elena." His lips trailed a path along my neck, igniting a fire within me that had nothing to do with fear or the future.

"Here," he murmured against my skin, "now."

My response was a whisper of fabric falling to the floor, a gasp as his mouth claimed mine with a passion that spoke of deep, enduring connection. We moved together, lost in a dance as old as time, each touch reaffirming the bond that tied us to one another.

"God, I've missed you," he groaned, his movements deliberate, worshipful.

"Me too," I managed, my fingers tangling in his salt-and-pepper hair, anchoring myself to the moment, to him.

Our bodies united in a rhythm of love and longing, every sensation heightened by the knowledge of the life we would soon bring forth. In this act of union, there was no addiction, no haunting past—only the raw purity of two souls entwined.

"Michael," I only managed to say, the world narrowing down to the electric connection between us, a current that surged and pulsed, driving us to the brink and beyond.

"I love you," he said, his own release a testament to the power we held over each other, a power that was tender as much as it was fierce.

Afterward, we lay entangled, the candles reduced to flickering stubs, casting a warm glow over our sated bodies. Our hearts beat a shared rhythm, a silent vow that whatever came next, we would face it together—with love as our compass and unwavering trust as our guide.

I reached for Michael's hands across the coffee-stained table, feeling the calluses on his fingers that told stories of hard work and dedication. His eyes met mine, a stormy blue sea that I found myself adrift in, seeking direction.

"Michael," I began, my voice steadier than I felt, "I think we need to... learn. To prepare for this baby. Together."

His nod was immediate, decisive. "Parenting classes," he said, echoing my thoughts. "And talking to friends who've been through this. We won't just wing it, Elena."

It was the action plan I craved, something concrete amid the swirling uncertainty. "I could ask Laura about her experiences," I suggested. "She always has such practical advice."

"Good idea," he agreed. "And I'll talk to John. He's got three under his belt; if anyone knows how to juggle life and kids, it's him."

The tension that had been coiled tight within me began to unravel. Here we were, sketching out a future in penciled lines, ready to erase and redraw as life demanded. It was terrifying and exhilarating, knowing that every step forward was one we would take together.

"Michael," I said, my heart swelling with gratitude, "I can't do this without you."

"Hey." He squeezed my hands gently, pulling me back from the edge of an emotional precipice. "You will never have to. We are a team, remember? For better or for worse."

Tears pricked at the edges of my vision, not of sorrow but of overwhelming love. In his presence, I felt fortified, capable of facing down the demons of doubt and the specter of addiction that always lurked in the shadows of my mind.

"Promise me," I whispered, "that no matter what happens, we'll stay united. That our love will be the compass guiding us through every challenge."

"Promise," he said solemnly, sealing the vow with his thumb brushing against the back of my hand.

"Even when it's hard," I continued, needing to lay bare every fear, "even when I feel like I'm losing myself to this... to motherhood or slipping back into old habits. Promise me you'll remind me who I am, Michael. Who I'm meant to be."

"Every damn day," he swore fiercely. "I'll be here to remind you of your strength, your passion, and the incredible journey you've embarked on. And Elena..." His gaze held a flame that burned away all lies, "if you ever fall, I will pick you up. Every time, no matter how many times it takes."

"Thank you," I breathed, allowing the gravity of our pledge to sink in, to root itself deep within me. The road ahead would be fraught with sleepless nights and testing moments, but it would also be paved with laughter, first steps, and shared dreams coming to fruition.

"Let's make a pact," Michael said, his voice firm with resolve. "To embrace the uncertainties, the mess, the beauty of it all, with love and unwavering support for each other. Let's promise to grow—not apart, but closer with every challenge."

"Let's," I echoed, the word a talisman against the fear, a beacon of hope in the enveloping night.

We sealed our promise with a kiss that spoke of commitment, a tangible affirmation of our mutual support. As his lips moved with mine, I felt the foundations of our future solidify—an edifice built not merely of brick and mortar but of trust, understanding, and an unbreakable bond that the trials of life would only strengthen.

"Tomorrow," I whispered, my voice steady despite the storm of emotions brewing within me, "we should start telling them. Our families, our friends... about the baby."

Michael nodded, the corners of his mouth lifting in a cautious smile, one that carried the weight of reality and the brightness of hope. "Yeah. It's time they knew. We're starting a new chapter, Elena. Together."

"Optimism," I said, the word feeling like a promise in itself. "We'll need it by the boatload."

"Then we'll buy a whole fleet," he replied, his tone light but his eyes serious. He understood, as did I, that optimism wasn't just a luxury—it was our lifeline.

"Can we do this?" The question slipped out, tinted with vulnerability, hanging in the air between us like the delicate aroma of the extinguished candles.

"We already are." His assertion was firm, a rock amidst the swirl of uncertainty. "We're doing it now."

With the night winding down, Michael rose from where we sat entwined on the couch. Standing before me, his hand extended, he helped me to my feet, his touch grounding me. Our fingers lingered together, reluctant to part even as he turned towards the door.

"Michael," I called out softly, halting his departure.

He paused, then turned back, his silhouette framed by the doorway. His intense blue eyes searched mine, reading the unvoiced plea that trembled on my lips.

"Stay," I said, not a request but an invocation, summoning him back to me.

In two strides, he closed the distance, his arms encircling me with a strength that promised safety, a haven from past regrets and future fears. Our bodies molded together, a perfect fit born from trials weathered and battles fought side by side.

"Tomorrow," he murmured against my hair, "we face the world. But tonight, let's just be us."

His scent enveloped me, a blend of cologne and the undeniable essence of him—masculine, comforting. My arms tightened around his waist, clinging to the solidity of him, to the reality of us in a world where nothing else seemed certain.

"Us," I echoed, savoring the sound of the word, the concept, the truth of it.

We swayed slightly, lost in the embrace, each heartbeat a silent vow. As he finally pulled away, his hands rested on my shoulders, thumbs brushing the bare skin at the base of my neck, leaving trails of warmth.

"Goodnight, Elena," he said, his voice low and laced with the depth of our connection.

"Goodnight, Michael." My reply was a whisper, a tender endnote to the symphony of our evening.

Watching him disappear into the night, I leaned against the doorframe, the chill of the air no match for the heat lingering in his wake. A single tear escaped, tracing a path down my cheek— not of sorrow, but of overwhelming gratitude. For his acceptance, for the love that tethered us, for the life that grew within me.

As the silence of the house wrapped around me, I closed my eyes, envisioning the faces of those we would soon confide in, the shared joy and inevitable worry. My hand drifted to my belly, a protective gesture, and I allowed myself to dream of the days ahead, of the laughter and first steps, of the unwritten stories waiting to unfold.

And above all, I held onto the certainty of Michael's embrace, the promise that whatever tomorrow brought, we would face it heart to heart, soul to soul, together.

I sank into the couch, its cushions holding me like the remnants of Michael's embrace. My fingers traced the fabric, still warm from where he sat, discussing futures and fears with a courage that seemed to pulse from his very being. The candles flickered their last dance, casting shadows that played upon the walls like the quiet doubts flickering at the edges of my mind.

The room was silent now, save for the soft crackle of waning flames, yet it echoed with the residue of our confessions, our laughter, our tentative plans whispered with an audacity that only love could justify. I let out a breath I hadn't realized I'd been holding, the air leaving my lungs in a slow, deliberate release as if to make room for the swell of emotions within me.

Memories of the evening cascaded through me—a tender torrent of words and silences, touches that spoke louder than any declaration. Michael's eyes, those deep pools of blue, had held my gaze with such intensity, reflecting back at me not just the woman I was but the mother I would become. His acceptance, unspoken yet unequivocal, fortified my spirit against the specter of past demons that clawed at the fringes of my newfound joy.

Wine glasses perched on the coffee table, one half-empty, the other barely touched—mine. I reached for it, my hand hovering, then pulled away. Not tonight. Tonight was for clarity, for the raw and unadulterated truth of this life growing inside me, this life we created. The taste of victory over vice was sweeter, more intoxicating than any vintage I'd known.

"Be strong, Elena," I murmured to myself, a mantra to chase away the shadows. "For you, for him, for the little heart beating its own fierce rhythm beneath yours."

My thoughts turned to the future, a tapestry yet unwoven, threads of fear entwined with those of anticipation. Would I recognize myself in this new role, or would the essence of who I am unravel, thread by delicate thread? The question hung in the air, unanswered, a challenge to my evolving identity.

Yet, amid the uncertainty, there was a steadfast pillar—Michael. His love, a constant through the chaos, reassured me that no trial was insurmountable. Together, we were a force unto ourselves, a union that would weather the storms of doubt and bathe in the light of each small triumph.

With a deep, steadying breath, I rose from the couch, snuffing out the candles' final glow. Darkness settled around me, a blank canvas upon which we would paint our tomorrow. And as I made my way to the sanctuary of my bedroom, I carried with me the spark of an unshakable conviction.

We were embarking on a journey neither of us could have envisioned, a path fraught with challenges and blessed with miracles. But whatever lay ahead, I knew one immutable truth: with Michael beside me, hand in hand, we were invincible.

Chapter Twenty-One

The scent of pine and sea salt mingled in the air, weaving through my senses as I watched the coastline unfurl from the balcony of the secluded beach house. Michael had whisked me away under the pretense of a weekend retreat, a chance to escape the relentless pace of our lives. But his eyes, the color of a stormy ocean, hinted at deeper intentions.

"Beautiful, isn't it?" His voice was a low thrum beside me, sending ripples across the calm surface of my apprehension.

"Stunning," I agreed, my gaze not on the horizon but on the man who seemed to see through the facade I'd so carefully constructed. The empire I'd built stood tall, yet here, it felt as though its foundation lay bare for him to scrutinize.

"Come here." He wrapped an arm around my waist, and we stood in silence, watching the waves crash against the rocky shore. The rhythm was soothing, almost hypnotic, lulling my racing thoughts into a semblance of tranquility.

"Michael..." I began, the words catching like driftwood in a tide. "I can't stop thinking about what this means—for us, for me."

He turned me gently, his hands framing my face with a tenderness that belied the strength in his fingers. "Elena, I know you're scared. You've been thrown into the deep end more times than anyone should be. But every time, you've swum, not sunk."

"Sometimes, amidst all this chaos, I feel like I'm barely keeping afloat," I confessed, my voice a mere whisper against the symphony of the crashing waves.

He stepped closer, his gaze locking with mine, a storm of sincerity within his eyes. "Let me be your anchor, Elena," he said, his voice deep and unwavering. His thumb gently traced the contour of my jaw, a simple gesture that somehow managed to anchor me to the present, to him.

Before I could muster a response, he took a step back, and with a grace that seemed almost rehearsed, he descended to one knee. My heart raced, pounding against my chest with the ferocity of a caged bird seeking freedom.

"Michael?" I managed to utter, a cocktail of astonishment and trepidation swirling within me.

"Shh," he whispered, his eyes gleaming with unshed tears as he retrieved a small, velvet box from his pocket. Slowly, he opened it, and inside lay a ring of breathtaking beauty—a piece I had once admired at Harry Winston, its 10-carat diamond sparkling with a life of its own, , an exquisite testament to elegance priced at a small fortune.

"Elena, I love you. Not merely for who you are today or the mother you will be, but for the incredible journey we've undertaken together. I wish to stand by you, through every trial, every victory, and every simple moment that makes up our life. Will you marry me?" His proposal was a poem, each word a brushstroke painting our future together in hues of endless love.

Tears streamed down my face, each droplet a reflection of the joy and love overflowing within my heart. This moment was more than a proposal; it was a sacred vow, a testament to his unwavering faith in us, in our shared dreams and intertwined destinies.

"Michael," I breathed out, my voice trembling with emotion. "Yes. A thousand times, yes, I will marry you."

Gently, he slid the ring onto my finger, a symbol of our eternal bond, fitting perfectly as if it were made just for me. Rising, he enfolded me in his arms, and in that embrace, I found a haven, a promise of forever. Our kiss was a seal on the vow we'd just made, a sweet surrender to the love that bound us.

Enveloped by the twilight, with the stars witnessing our union, I understood that whatever the future held, Michael's love would be my guiding light, as constant and enduring as the ceaseless sea whispering secrets to the night.

The ring on my finger caught the firelight, casting prismatic dances across the walls of our secluded cabin. I lay nestled in Michael's arms, the warmth of his chest a reassuring fortress against the chill of the night air. The world outside faded to a distant murmur, and in this cocoon of love, I found the courage to let go.

"Michael," I murmured, my voice a soft echo in the quiet room, "this feels like a dream."

He brushed a curl from my forehead, his touch gentle. "It's our reality now, Elena. Every bit of it."

I turned to face him, the intensity of his gaze grounding me. The vulnerability we shared was raw, unfiltered by the facades we presented to the outside world. We were just two souls, stripped bare and bound by a promise.

"Talk to me," he urged, his thumb tracing the line of my jaw. "Tell me what you're feeling."

"Everything," I confessed, the word slipping out with a shaky laugh. "Fear, excitement, love... It's overwhelming, like I'm standing at the edge of a cliff, ready to jump into the unknown."

"Let's jump together." His words were a vow, spoken with the certainty that only true partnership could offer. "Tell me about the future you see, Elena. Our future."

So we talked, our voices weaving through the night, crafting a tapestry of hopes and dreams. I spoke of my empire, the business that had become an extension of my identity, and my fears of it consuming me. He listened, his fingers lacing with mine, a silent pledge of support.

"Your success is incredible, but it doesn't define you, Elena. Not to me," he said. "You're more than your achievements.

You're the woman I love, the mother of my child. We'll find balance."

"Family," I whispered, the word carrying the weight of both yearning and trepidation. "I want our child to grow up knowing they are loved, surrounded by passion for life, not just the pursuit of success."

"Passion," he echoed, a smile playing on his lips. "Like the passion that brought us here, to this moment?"

"Exactly," I replied, my heart swelling as his hand found its way to my still-flat belly, an intimate connection to the life we created.

We explored each other, bodies and minds entwined, surrendering to the ebb and flow of desires and confessions. As moonlight spilled through the window, bathing us in its ethereal glow, I felt the addictive pull of his touch, a craving that went beyond physical need. It was the hunger for a shared life, for moments stolen from the relentless march of time.

"Promise me," I said between breaths, "that no matter how hectic life gets, we'll always find our way back to this—to us."

"Always," he assured me, sealing the vow with a kiss that stole the very air from my lungs.

Our conversation meandered through the corridors of the night, touching on travel, art, the books we would read to our child, and the laughter we would share. We painted a picture of our future in strokes of aspiration and affection, a masterpiece of mutual dreams.

"Michael," I admitted as dawn tiptoed across the sky, "I've never been so scared of anything as much as I am of this—of being a mother. But with you, I feel like I can do anything."

"Then let's do everything," he replied, his voice a whisper against my skin. "Together."

As the first light of morning crept over the horizon, we lay entangled, sated by love and the promises made in the dark. The ring on my finger glinted anew, a symbol of our commitment, a beacon for our shared journey. And in the quiet afterglow, I finally allowed myself to embrace the full spectrum of joy that flooded my soul, knowing our next chapter was waiting to be written.

The warmth of the sun had nothing on the incandescent joy blooming in my chest. My hand, adorned with the glinting symbol of Michael's love and promise, trembled slightly as I found David's contact and pressed call. The phone barely had time to trill before his voice came through, a lifeline of excitement meeting mine.

"David, we're engaged!" The words burst from me like birds freed from a cage, soaring high on currents of elation.

"Congratulations! This calls for a celebration!" His response was a mirror of my own fervor, and I could almost see his smile through the phone, knowing it matched the stretch of my own lips.

"Absolutely," I agreed, my mind spinning with the dizzying array of possibilities. "We want an engagement party that tells our story—the journey me and Michael have been on."

"Let's make it unforgettable," he said, his tone rich with the promise of unbridled creativity. I knew then that this celebration would be drenched in significance, every detail a testament to the love that had reshaped my once predictable life.

I ended the call with David, my heart hammering a rhythm of anticipation, and dialed Sophie next, the screen blurring a little as my emotions swelled.

"Sophie, it's official—we're getting married!" I could feel the smile stretching across my face, muscle memory from years of sharing secrets and dreams with her.

"I'm so happy for you both," she replied, her voice a warm blanket enveloping me. Her words were more than mere congratulations; they were an affirmation of the future I'd dared to envision.

"Clara, you won't believe it—he asked, and I said yes!" I told our other confidant, the words spilling out like fine champagne, effervescent and heady.

"You two are meant for each other," Clara declared, her sincerity wrapping around me like a protective shawl. It was as if she saw into the very soul of our relationship, acknowledging the profound connection that Michael and I shared—a bond strong enough to weather my inner storms.

Their voices, laced with genuine affection and jubilation, were anchors grounding me amid the swirling tide of my new reality. As I sat there, curled on the couch with the afternoon light spilling across the room, I reflected on the journey ahead. The engagement party would be a mosaic of our experiences, a tapestry woven from threads of shared tastes and memories.

This wasn't just a party; it was a declaration—a bold statement that despite the addiction shadows lurking at the edges of my newfound happiness, I stood defiant, ready to embrace a lifetime of love and challenge with Michael by my side.

"Let's start with the guest list," David said , his tone practical yet tinged with excitement. His suggestion anchored us, and together we began to weave the fabric of the occasion. Each name we listed was a thread in the tapestry of our shared history, a reminder of the community we had built together.

"Michael loves that truffle risotto from the little place on Main, remember?" Sophie suggested, her memory igniting a spark in our culinary discussions. We delved into the menu, each dish a nod to the flavors and moments that had defined our relationship—a silent acknowledgment of our refined palates and the simple pleasures we found in food.

"Clara, can you handle the decorations? You've always had an eye for beauty," I asked, already envisioning the ambiance she would create. A soft chuckle resonated on the line, affirming her agreement. Her artistic flair promised an atmosphere as intoxicating as our love.

"Of course, darling. Think fairy lights, soft fabrics... a Midsummer night's dream," she mused, her voice painting pictures in the air.

"Let's set a date," I said, heart pounding with the weight of decision. "Something soon, to capture this freshness, this... giddiness."

"Next Saturday?" David proposed, the question hanging amidst our collective breaths.

"Perfect," Sophie and Clara echoed, their assent wrapping around me like a warm embrace.

"Next Saturday," I repeated, the words etching themselves into reality. Three weeks to celebrate, to declare to the world that despite the darkness I'd fought, love had emerged victorious. My heart raced, not just with the thrill of planning, but with the knowledge that this engagement party was more than a festivity—it was a testament to survival, to finding joy beyond the seductive pull of ephemeral highs. With Michael, with my steadfast friends, I was scripting a new chapter—one where the demons of addiction became mere footnotes in a larger narrative of triumph and unconditional love.

"Thank you," I whispered, though I wasn't sure they understood the depth of my gratitude. "For everything."

"Anything for you, Elena," they replied, their voices a chorus of unwavering support. And in that moment, surrounded by the love of those who had seen me at my lowest and still believed in my heights, I knew there was nothing we couldn't face together.

The twilight seeped in through the slats of the shutters, casting a soft glow over the room as we nestled into the crook of the sofa. Michael's arm was a secure band around my waist, his fingers tracing idle patterns on the fabric of my sweater. I leaned back against him, feeling the rise and fall of his chest with each breath, the steady beat of his heart beneath my ear.

"Can you believe it?" I whispered, the words spilling out like the first drops of a long-awaited rain. "An engagement party... us."

His chuckle vibrated through me, a warm rumble that soothed the edge of anxiety that never quite dulled inside me. "I can," he said. "It's just the start, Elena. A prelude to every celebration we'll have from here on out."

The vision of our future parties unfurled in my mind—anniversaries, birthdays, all the milestones marked with laughter and shared glances. Yet, beneath the shimmering surface of these dreams lurked the shadow of my past indulgences, the temptations that once threatened to erode all I held dear.

"Michael," I began, my voice a hesitant thread, "you know my struggles, the addictions that..."

"Shh," he interrupted gently, pressing his lips to my temple. "I know where you've been, love. But I also see where you're going. You're stronger than any of those demons."

His affirmation was a balm, but old fears clung to me, barnacles of doubt that no amount of reassurance could fully pry loose. I turned within his embrace, meeting the steady blue of his eyes. They were deep pools of understanding, reflecting back an image of myself that I still struggled to recognize—the woman who triumphed over her fragility, who dared to love fiercely despite the scars.

"Every day with you is a celebration, Elena. Remember that." His words were a vow, a promise etched into the very air we breathed.

I nodded, allowing the truth of his statement to sink in, to fill the spaces between my ribs. Our kisses then were tender, a physical manifestation of our commitment, mingling breaths and the taste of mutual resolve.

"Let's make every detail of this party a testament to that—to us," I said, my resolve hardening like steel tempered in fire.

"Absolutely," he agreed, his hand finding mine, lacing our fingers together. "And when the time comes, we'll stand before everyone we love and declare it: that we're more than the sum of our pasts, that together, we are infinite."

The night grew heavy around us, a blanket of stars watching silently from the sky. We stayed there, entwined, until the moon climbed high and our conversation faded into whispers, into breaths, into the silent language of bodies that had learned to speak volumes in the quietest of moments. In his arms, I found not just refuge, but a rallying cry—a call to face the coming days with bravery, with the certainty that whatever life brought our way, we would face it as one.

The gentle caress of dusk illuminated the room as I adjusted the flowing skirt of my Vera Wang gown, its ivory silk fabric whispering against my skin with every movement. A blend of anticipation and elation pulsed through me, my heart aflutter at the thought of the evening ahead. Michael, positioned by the window, cut a striking figure in his bespoke Tom Ford suit, the dark fabric enhancing the broadness of his shoulders and the lean line of his frame. His gaze, lost in the shifting hues of twilight, held a depth of emotion that mirrored the complex tapestry of colors painting the evening sky.

"Ready?" His voice was steady, a grounding force in the storm of my emotions.

"Almost." I took a deep breath, feeling the weight of the evening ahead. The news we were about to share was more than an announcement; it was the unveiling of a new chapter, a leap into a life we had only dared to dream of.

The doorbell rang, its chime slicing through the quiet anticipation. Michael offered his hand, and I slipped mine into it, drawing strength from his touch. Together, we moved toward the living room, where the faces of our friends and family awaited—each one a thread in the tapestry of our lives.

"Thank you all for coming," I began, my voice slightly trembling despite my best efforts. Michael squeezed my hand reassuringly, his presence a reminder of the partnership that anchored me. "We've gathered you here because we wanted to celebrate our engagement with you. And also, we have some wonderful news."

A collective inhale filled the room, a symphony of expectation. I caught sight of Alex, standing off to the side, his expression unreadable. Once, his laid-back demeanor would have calmed me, but now, it was Michael's unwavering gaze that steadied my heart.

"Michael and I are going to have a baby," I announced, the words hanging in the air like a delicate promise.

The room erupted into cheers and applause, the warm embrace of shared joy enveloping us. Our loved ones swarmed around us, their hugs and congratulations a balm to the lingering shadows of doubt that had haunted me.

"Little Elena running around, eh?" someone joked, and laughter bubbled up around us, a soothing melody that chased away the lingering fears of addiction's grip on my past.

"Or a little Michael," another chimed in, and my fiancé beamed with pride, his eyes alight with visions of our future child.

As the evening wore on, the undercurrent of anxiety that had once dictated my every move seemed to ebb away, replaced with a sense of belonging, of being rooted in something greater than myself. Michael's hand remained a constant on my back, his touch a silent vow of support through every step of this journey.

"Here's to family," I said later, lifting a glass filled with sparkling water, honoring the choice to stay clear-headed amidst the celebrations.

"To family," they echoed, and the clinking of glasses was like a chorus of affirmation, a testament to the new life within me and the love that surrounded us.

I leaned into Michael, allowing myself to be fully present in the warmth of his embrace, the beat of his heart syncing with mine. In his arms, I found more than safety; I found the courage to face the tides of change, fortified by the love that promised to buoy us through the storms to come.

"And to beginnings," Michael added softly, his lips brushing against my ear, sending shivers down my spine. "Every day with you is a new beginning."

"Every day," I whispered back, and together, we turned to face our friends and family, our smiles mirroring the happiness that shone back at us, a reflection of the life we were building, moment by precious moment.

Chapter Twenty-Two

The scent of fresh peonies mingled with the subtle aroma of new fabric as we stepped into the Chanel boutique, a palace of haute couture that made my heart quicken with anticipation. David was at my side, offering his arm and a reassuring smile that told me he was in this adventure as much as I was.

"Ready to find 'the one'?" he quipped, his eyes gleaming with shared excitement.

I laughed, the sound bubbling up from a place of newfound joy. "I thought I already did that when Michael proposed," I said, but my gaze was already caressing the rows of gowns, each whispering promises of bridal perfection.

"Ah, but a dress...that's the true love story today," David teased, guiding me deeper into the boutique's embrace.

Our reflections danced in the mirrors as we moved, my long curls bouncing with each step. Today, they fell freely, framing my hazel eyes that now scrutinized every detail of the gowns before us. The high ceilings and soft lighting cast an ethereal glow on the fabrics, turning the room into a canvas where futures could be painted in silken threads.

"Charming, but not quite you," David said, dismissing a gown adorned with too many frills for my taste.

He knew me well. Our laughter filled the space as we recounted tales of my small-town past—how I'd once believed that such luxury was beyond my reach, how I'd drowned those dreams in bottles of cheap wine, believing them to be foolish.

"Look at you now, Elena," David said, his voice lowering, touched by the weight of our shared history. "Look how far you've come…" His hand swept over the array of designer labels, and I followed it with a sense of surreal wonder.

"Michael would love you in this," he pointed out, drawing my attention to a Givenchy creation that seemed to glow with its own inner light. Its elegance was understated, the kind of beauty that didn't scream for attention but rather waited to be discovered—an echo of the woman I was learning to see myself as.

"Would he?" I murmured, my hand trembling slightly as I reached out, the silk cool and smooth beneath my fingertips. The sensation sparked a memory of Michael's touch, grounding and gentle, guiding me through the maze of my insecurities.

"Let's try it on for size, shall we?" David's encouragement was a lifeline, pulling me back to the present.

In the changing room, the confines of my old life shed away with my clothes. Slipping into the gown felt like stepping into a dream, one where addiction's chains lay broken at my feet, and self-doubt was nothing more than a distant shadow.

I emerged, the skirt flowing around me like water. David's sharp intake of breath was all the validation I needed.

"Damn, girl. You're every bit the goddess I always said you were," he said, his words laced with pride. This was more than just finding a dress; it was about stitching together the fragments of who I had been, who I was, and who I would become.

"David," I started, my voice catching with emotion, "do you remember when I told you I couldn't afford to dream? When hope was as worn and frayed as the couch I crashed on?"

"I do," he whispered, his eyes misty. "But look at you now, rising from it all like a phoenix. Michael is a lucky man."

"Thank you, for being here, for everything." The words were inadequate, but they carried the weight of my gratitude.

"Always," he promised, and we stood there, amid the glamour and the echoes of my past struggles, bound by something far stronger than blood.

"Let's find the dress that says 'Elena,'" he declared, his voice steady once more, and I nodded, eager to continue the hunt, knowing that each step was a step toward the future—a future where love was the fabric that held all pieces together.

The light poured through the high windows of the Dior boutique, bathing the ivory gowns in a celestial glow. My fingertips grazed the fabrics, each whisper-soft touch a caress that sent shivers up my spine. I was searching for more than just silk and lace—I was seeking a reflection of the woman I had become.

"Try this one, Elena," David urged, his voice a tender nudge back to reality. He held out a dress that seemed to capture the very essence of sunlight, its intricate beading sparkling like dewdrops at dawn.

As I slipped into the gown, it clung to my curves with an intimate familiarity, as if it had been crafted with me in mind. The mirror before me held not just my image but the journey etched deep within my eyes. Here was the culmination of years spent clawing my way out of addiction's dark embrace, of learning that love could be a salve rather than another vice.

"Oh my God," I breathed out, the word a prayer and a profanity all at once. "It's perfect."

David stood beside me, our reflections side by side. His nod was solemn, reverent. "It's you, Elena. It's everything you've fought for, every goddamn step you took to get here."

"Michael won't know what hit him," I said, half-joking, half-awed by the truth of it. Michael, who had seen past the chaos to the heart of me, who had offered his hand not to pull me from the depths but to accompany me on the ascent.

"Let's not forget the wedding planner." David's reminder was gentle, laced with the laughter we had shared throughout the day. "Someone has to orchestrate this fairytale."

"Right." I nodded, reluctance threading through my excitement. Letting go, even to a professional, meant trusting someone else with the narrative of our love.

We stepped out of the boutique, the dress bag in my hands a talisman against the surge of nerves. Choosing a planner felt like handing over a piece of my soul, but wasn't that what this was all about? Trust, vulnerability, the merging of two lives into a singular, beautiful tapestry.

"Whoever it is will have their work cut out for them," I mused aloud, the corners of my mouth lifting in anticipation. "I want magic, David. Not the sleight of hand I used to fall for, but something real. Something as raw and authentic as the life I'm living now."

"Then we'll find someone who gets that, who gets you," David promised, his arm around my shoulders in a protective embrace. "And if they don't deliver, they'll answer to me."

"Let's hope it doesn't come to that," I laughed, the sound bubbling up from a place of newfound joy. Together, we would craft a celebration not just of a union, but of survival, of the hard-won triumph of love over every demon that had once danced in my blood.

"Here's to new beginnings," I whispered, the Dior gown a tangible promise of the vows I would soon make under a canopy of stars.

The scent of freshly cut grass mingled with the calm, soothing ripple of the lakeside – a symphony to nature's own heartbeat. I stood there beside Michael, our hands entwined, as we gazed upon the canvas where our wedding would take place. The planner, Vivienne, sketched visions in the air with her hands, painting images of elegance poised between dreams and reality.

"Imagine," Vivienne's voice was a whisper, "lanterns floating like stars above you, the soft glow reflecting in the lake's embrace. A canopy of lights, an aisle adorned with your favorite lilies and roses, leading to the moment where two souls become one."

I squeezed Michael's hand, feeling the pulse of his excitement mirroring my own. This was it – the blend of grandeur and intimacy that spoke not only of our love but of the journey that had brought us here. The reflections in the water seemed to dance with possibilities, each shimmering wave a nod to the future.

"Every detail matters," I said, my voice laced with conviction. "From the centerpieces to the vows we exchange, it has to be...us. Not just a spectacle for guests but a testament to what we've overcome."

Michael nodded, pulling me close for a moment that was ours alone amidst the planning chaos. "It will be, Elena. Because it's not about the lights or the flowers. It's about the strength of our love, strong enough to pull us from the depths of our pasts into something beautiful."

"Can we really do this?" I asked, not just about the wedding, but about the life awaiting us beyond it. "Can we build a life that's free of the shadows?"

"Look at what we've already done," Michael replied, his gaze earnest, his touch grounding. "We're creating a masterpiece, one day at a time. And this..." He gestured to the serene lake, to Vivienne's sketches, "this is just another stroke on the canvas."

Vivienne, sensing the depth of the moment, gave us space, flipping through her portfolio with practiced patience. "Your love story deserves nothing less than magic," she finally said. "And I'm here to weave that into every element of your day."

"Thank you," I murmured, gratitude swelling within me. This woman understood the sacredness of our bond, the importance of personal touches that echoed the whispers of our hearts.

"Let's walk the grounds," Michael suggested, leading us along the water's edge. "I can see our guests here, laughing, crying, celebrating. And when night falls, those twinkling lights will not only illuminate our wedding but the start of our forever."

"Forever," I repeated, letting the word roll over my tongue like a promise. It tasted like redemption, like the sweetest vow to break free from the chains of our former selves and step into a love that was unbreakable, unwavering.

"Forever," Michael agreed, and together we walked under the vast sky, dreaming of a wedding that wasn't just an event, but a milestone marking our rebirth under the watchful eyes of the stars.

The tender resonance of the planner's words lingered as Michael and I ambled back towards the main hall, our hands entwined like vines reaching for the same sun. The air was rich with the scent of wildflowers and imminent promises. Every detail of our wedding felt like a petal slowly unfurling, revealing the heart of what we hoped to become.

"Do you like it, Elena?" Michael's voice was a soft murmur against the hum of nature, "Are you happy with this?"

A smile tugged at my lips, a silent nod my only reply. But before the vision could take deeper root, the sharp trill of my phone cut through the stillness, an unwelcome intrusion.

"Sorry, let me just—" I fumbled in the folds of my dress, fishing out the device. The screen flashed an unknown number, but intuition urged me to answer. "Hello?"

"Ms. Callahan?" The voice on the other end was smooth, practiced in the art of persuasion. "I'm calling from Global Arts Investments. We've been following the remarkable success of your gallery."

My heart skipped, then thundered with a mix of fear and exhilaration. Was this another twist in my ever-changing fate?

"Uh, thank you," I managed, shooting a glance at Michael, who raised an eyebrow in silent question. "How can I help you?"

"We believe your concept has tremendous potential for expansion," the investor continued, his tone honeyed yet insistent. "We're proposing to turn your local treasure into a global franchise."

The words hung in the air, heavy with implications. A global franchise. My mind whirled, images of pristine galleries bearing my name, blossoming across continents, each exhibit a testament to my newfound ambition. But beneath the glossy veneer, a twinge of dread crept in, whispering of art commodified, of soulful spaces turned sterile.

"Michael, they want to—" I began to tell him, covering the phone with my hand and whispering.

"Turn your passion into an empire?" He squeezed my hand gently, his gaze searching mine. "It's an incredible opportunity, Elena, but remember what you're building. It's not just walls and canvases; it's a sanctuary for artists, a place where creativity breathes."

I bit my lip, tasting the tang of responsibility, the weight of choices that could alter the very essence of my dream. "Yes, it's... it's a lot to consider. Can I give you an answer after my wedding? I need time to think."

"Of course, Ms. Callahan," the investor replied, though I sensed his impatience even through the digital divide. "We'll await your decision. Enjoy your special day."

The call ended, but the echo of opportunity and doubt resonated within me. I looked up at Michael, my anchor in the storm of change, seeking solace in the cerulean depths of his eyes.

"Whatever you choose," he said, his voice a soft caress against the tumult of my thoughts, "I'll be here, supporting you, loving you. Your dreams are mine too, Elena."

"Thank you," I whispered, leaning into his chest, feeling the steady beat of his heart. In that moment, under the canopy of impending dusk, the lure of success battled with the sanctity of authenticity. And as the first star blinked to life above us, I knew my true north would always be the love that grounded me, the art that set me free, one brushstroke at a time.

The phone rested cold and indifferent on the marble countertop, its silence then louder than the proposal it had delivered moments before. My fingers hovered above it, a ballet of hesitation. Expansion or singularity? Global recognition or the intimacy of the unique? I was entangled in a net of possibilities, each thread pulling with the promise of dreams I'd whispered into the night so many years ago.

"Think about it after the wedding," I murmured to myself, an incantation to ward off the seduction of immediate answers. The words were a fragile dam against the flood of ambition and fear. I needed space—space to breathe, to dream, to be.

"Are you alright?" Michael's voice cut through my reverie, his hand warm on my shoulder. His touch was grounding, a reminder of the tangible, true world around me, not just the shadowy maze of the future.

"Of course," I lied, offering a smile that didn't quite reach my eyes. "Just the usual pre-wedding jitters."

"Let's focus on the here and now," he suggested, and I nodded, grateful for the diversion.

We dove into the minutiae of the day, the delicate dance of decisions that would shape the moment we became one. Linens, flowers, the soft glow of lanterns by the lake—all puzzle pieces of a picture we painted together. We talked about the seating arrangements, the menu, the music that would lace through the evening air like whispers of love long past and promises yet fulfilled.

"Remember, no peonies," I reminded him gently, laughter bubbling up within me. "They're beautiful, but they make Aunt Clara's allergies go wild."

"Right, no peonies," he echoed, scribbling a note, though his eyes danced with mischief. "And the band knows not to play any songs by The Exes."

"God, can you imagine?" I chuckled, shaking my head at the absurdity. "My wedding march led by Alex's crooning about lost love."

"Speaking of which," Michael said, his tone shifting subtly, "you've been amazing, dealing with... everything. With Alex, with the gallery. You're strong, Elena, stronger than you know." After a few more threats, I had to report Alex. Had to. He shouldn't have come this far.

"Sometimes, I don't feel so strong," I confessed, the vulnerability in my voice as naked as my skin beneath the sheets. "I feel like I'm one step away from tumbling back into old habits, into the darkness that craves the numbness of a bottle, the oblivion of a pill."

"Hey," he soothed, cupping my face in his hands, "you're not alone. Not anymore. Whatever comes, whatever tries to tempt you away from yourself, I'll be here. We'll fight it together. And you," he continued, his gaze fierce and tender all at once, "will walk down that aisle free from the ghosts that haunt you."

"Promise me," I whispered, daring to believe in the strength of us.

"Always," he vowed, sealing it with a kiss that tasted like forever.

The conversation lingered between us, a sacred covenant, as we finalized the last of the plans. And when we stood by the lakeside, where soon our vows would mingle with the rustling leaves and lapping water, I felt a surge of clarity. This was my life—not an investor's dream, not an ex-lover's chase, but mine, molded by my choices, my love, my art.

"Under the stars," I said, gazing up at the canvas of the night sky, "that's where we'll begin anew."

"Under the stars," Michael agreed, his arm around me promising more than just a dance. It promised a lifetime of shared moments, of challenges faced and joys embraced, of two souls charting a course through the uncertain, beautiful journey of life.

The chords of a potential first-dance song reverberated through the room, a local band's rendition of "At Last" filling the space with soulful promise. My pen hovered over the guest list, the names blurring together as I tried to envision each face in the crowd, witnessing the moment Michael and I would become one.

"Too cliché?" Michael's voice cut through my focus, his blue eyes searching mine for a hint of disapproval.

I shook my head, a smile tugging at my lips. "It's timeless, not cliché. But it's also Etta James'—we need something that's ours."

"Right," he said, scribbling a note on the pad before us. "We'll keep looking." His dedication to even the smallest details, a reflection of his love, tethered me to the present, grounding my whirlwind thoughts.

"Let's talk about who we are now, who we want at our sides. This isn't just about filling seats." My finger traced the names, each one sparking a memory, a connection, a reason they were part of our story. The list was shorter than most would expect, but richer in its intention.

"Quality over quantity," Michael agreed, and there it was again—that understanding, that shared value that made this all feel like destiny.

"Exactly." I leaned back, the weight of decisions momentarily lifting as I allowed myself to simply be with him, in our cocoon of wedding plans and whispered dreams.

The lull in our conversation was a necessary respite, a chance to breathe and remember why we were doing all of this.

It wasn't about the perfect flowers or the right band—it was about us, our love, and the life we were building.

"Have you thought about the honeymoon?" I asked, breaking the silence. The question hung in the air, fragrant with the scent of possibility.

"Actually, I have," Michael replied, his gaze holding mine captive. "What do you say to Bali? Just you and me, an ocean away from everything, starting our forever on a canvas of white sand and turquoise waters."

Bali—a word that sounded like a prayer, an incantation that promised peace and a respite from the relentless march of reality. My heart leaped at the thought, at the image of us entwined beneath foreign stars, our bodies speaking the language of new beginnings.

"God, yes," I breathed out, feeling the last remnants of my old life—the addiction, the pain, the struggle—slip further away with the prospect of such paradise. "Yes, let's lose ourselves in Bali."

"Then it's settled." Michael's hand found mine across the table, his touch igniting a fire that no distance or time could ever extinguish.

"Settled," I echoed, my voice steady despite the storm of emotions within me. And in that simple exchange, I felt the power of our bond, a force that had carried me through the darkest of nights into the promise of a dawn filled with hope.

As the band packed up, their notes still lingering in the room, I realized that the music of our lives was just beginning—

a melody composed of love, resilience, and the courage to dream beyond the confines of the past. And with Michael by my side, I was ready to dance to its rhythm, whatever the tempo may be.

The key felt heavy in my palm, a metallic whisper promising change. I gazed at the polished silver, its edges catching the afternoon sun as it streamed through the open doorway of our future home—a grand edifice nestled in the heart of suburbia, yet exuding the opulence of an urban palace.

"Welcome to the beginning of everything," Michael said, his voice resonant with emotion and carrying the weight of dreams yet to be unfurled.

I stepped over the threshold, my heels clicking against the marble floor that sprawled before us like a blank canvas waiting for the brushstrokes of our life together. The air was fragrant with possibility, each room a testament to Michael's thoughtfulness, from the soaring ceilings that offered space for aspirations to soar to the expansive windows that bathed us in light, dismissing any shadows of my former self-doubt.

"Michael, this is... it's more than I ever imagined," I whispered, my words barely rising above the echo of our presence in the empty house.

"Only the best for you, for us," he replied, wrapping an arm around me, his warmth seeping into my skin, a balm soothing the scars left by years of battling demons that once threatened to consume me.

We wandered through the halls, our footsteps a duet accompanying the silent symphony of a future we were composing together. Each room sparked visions of laughter and love; the kitchen where we'd cook meals infused with affection, the living room where we'd unravel the day's events entwined on the couch, and the bedroom where desire would know no bounds, where whispers and moans would mingle with the silk of sheets and the sanctity of our union.

"Imagine," Michael breathed into my ear as we entered what would be the nursery, "a crib right here, the soft lullabies filling the air, our baby's eyes reflecting the universe of our love."

Tears brimmed at the corners of my eyes, not from sorrow but from overwhelming gratitude, a tide washing over the barren shores of the life I once knew. Here, amidst the echoes of a joyous future, I could almost hear the faint giggles of our child, feel the tiny fingers grasping mine, a connection so pure it seemed to cleanse away the vestiges of addiction's cruel grasp.

"Michael, I can't believe this will be our reality." My voice trembled, a leaf caught in the gentle gust of change. "You've given me more than a home; you've given me a sanctuary, a place where the ghosts of my past can't touch me."

He turned to face me, his blue eyes a mirror to the sky outside, limitless and bright. "Elena, you've fought for every step forward, for every breath of freedom from the chains that once held you. This house, our home, it's not just brick and mortar—

it's a symbol of your strength, of the beauty you've brought into my life."

Our kiss was a seal on the promise of tomorrow, a fusion of souls entwining in the dance of what's to come. We walked hand in hand through the garden, already picturing summer barbecues and autumn leaves crunching underfoot, the seasons of our lives unfolding in harmony with the natural world.

As the sun dipped below the horizon, painting the sky in hues of passion and serenity, we stood at the edge of our new domain, the key glinting one last time before disappearing into my pocket.

"Let's build something beautiful here, Michael. Let's craft a legacy of love, strong enough to withstand any storm."

His smile was my anchor, his reply the wind in my sails. "Together, Elena. Always together."

And in the quiet hush of dusk, with the first stars blinking into existence above us, I knew that the true journey had only just begun.

Chapter Twenty-Three

As the sun began to set, I stood on the edge of the lake, my heart pounding with excitement. The fading light painted the water with soft hues as I took in a deep breath, filled with anticipation. Adorned in a stunning Dior gown, I felt like something out of a fairytale - a reflection of the dreams that had carried me through my toughest moments.

"Beautiful," Michael murmured, his voice a thread woven into the tapestry of the evening. He stood there, under the blossoming night sky, a silhouette of strength and promise.

The bond between us drew taut, a connection charged with every shared confession, every tender touch, every battle fought side by side.

"Michael," I whispered, my voice barely rising above the gentle lapping of the lake against the shore. "This moment... it's ours, isn't it? Our beginning."

He stepped closer, our shadows merging on the soft grass. "Ours, Elena. And tonight, we vow to each other under these stars—witnesses to our love, eternal and unyielding."

The officiant's words swirled around us, but they were mere echoes against the profound truth that resonated within my soul. As I gazed into Michael's intense blue eyes, I saw the reflection of my own transformation—a woman who had conquered her addictions, her fears, and now stood ready to merge her path with another.

"Michael," I began, my hands trembling as I took his. "You are the harbor in my tempest, the calm in my chaos. With you, I found the courage to face my demons, to seek pleasure not in the emptiness of the past, but in the fullness of your embrace."

"Your love," I continued, my voice growing stronger, "is my redemption. And I vow to honor it, to nurture it, to be the sanctuary you have been for me. In this life, we've chosen, I pledge my heart, my body, my soul—to grow, to heal, to thrive—with you, for you, because of you."

As I spoke, I laid bare the scars of my past, the insecurities that once shackled me, now transformed into the very reasons I stood so fiercely before him. Michael listened, his expression a canvas of empathy and adoration, etching my vows into the core of his being.

Then it was his turn, his voice steady and sure. "Elena, you are the melody that gives rhythm to my life, the artist who painted colors over the gray shadows of my solitude. Your journey, marked by resilience, has inspired my own. You taught me that true strength lies in vulnerability, in the willingness to share one's soul completely."

"Tonight," he said, the stars catching the sheen of emotion in his gaze, "I vow not only to cherish and respect you but to stand beside you as an equal, a partner. To support your dreams, to soothe your fears, and to celebrate your triumphs. My love for you is boundless, as infinite as the universe under which we make these promises."

"From this day forward," Michael concluded, his thumbs tracing circles over the backs of my hands, "I commit to building a life with you grounded in authenticity, brimming with passion, and filled with the kind of love that—even in the face of adversity—will never falter."

The officiant pronounced us husband and wife, but those words were merely a formality. The true union had occurred long before, in the quiet moments and the tumultuous ones, culminating in this sacred exchange. When Michael's lips met mine, it was a seal not just of our vows but of every hope, every dream, and every silent prayer that had led us here.

Our kiss was a conflagration, igniting the night, burning away the remnants of who I once was and forging who I would become. As we parted, breathless and elated, the world around us erupted in applause, but all I could hear was the thunderous beating of our two hearts, now forever entwined.

Our bodies melded in the sanctity of our first dance, the soft sway of our intertwined figures undulating like sea grass in a gentle current. The notes of our chosen song wrapped around us, a private cocoon in the midst of our guests' awed silence. Michael's hand at the small of my back was both a tether and an encouragement, guiding me into the rhythm of our future as husband and wife.

"Every movement with you feels like a testament," I whispered against the lapel of his impeccable tuxedo, savoring the scent of his cologne mixed with the fresh outdoor air that had blessed our vows.

"Every step is a step toward forever, Elena," he replied, his voice a low thrum that resonated through my very core.

The fabric of my wedding gown, that symbol of my transformation, rustled with each turn, each dip. It caressed my skin like a second layer, a manifestation of the life I'd stitched together from the shreds of my past — the addiction that once threatened to unravel me, the love I'd feared would always elude me.

"Remember when we first met?" I asked, gazing up into his intense blue eyes that held stories yet to be told. "I was so entangled in my own web of fears."

"Ah, but look at you now," Michael said, twirling me out and then back into the safety of his arms. "You've taken those fears and turned them into strength. Just like this dance, love — it's a journey through shadows and light."

I let out a soft chuckle, feeling the warmth of his breath as he leaned in closer. "This dance... it's a metaphor, isn't it? For life, for us."

"Exactly," he affirmed. "For the days you'll wake up feeling invincible, and for the nights the old demons come whispering. For every time we fall out of step, only to find our rhythm again. That's what this dance is about."

"Through sickness and health..." I mused aloud, recalling the words we had just spoken under the stars.

"Through darkness and dawn," he added, sealing the promise as his fingers traced patterns along my spine, mirroring the constellations above.

Our conversation flowed like the wine that had been poured generously throughout the evening — rich, deep, intoxicating. We spoke of dreams and doubts, of the pain of withdrawal that still clawed at my insides on the hardest days, and the determination that fueled my sobriety. We shared whispers of the raw pleasure we found in each other's arms, the vulnerability that came with such intimacy, and the trust that made it all possible.

"Michael," I breathed out, feeling the weight of the moment press upon us. "With you, I am whole. Not because you complete me but because you inspire me to complete myself."

He held me tighter, and the stars seemed to swirl directly above us. "And I vow to be your partner in that completion, every day, until the end of time."

as indeed the dance of a lifetime — a dance of redemption and rebirth, a dance of unity and unyielding love. And as the music faded, I knew this was only the beginning of our eternal waltz beneath the stars.

As the song reached its end, our lips met in a kiss that was both a delicate brush and a fierce claiming. The applause that erupted around us was a distant sound compared to the symphony of emotions that played within our embrace. Our dance was indeed the dance of a lifetime — a dance of redemption and rebirth, a dance of unity and unyielding love. And as the music faded, I knew this was only the beginning of our eternal waltz beneath the stars.

In the quiet that followed, enveloped in Michael's arms, a sense of profound gratitude washed over me. Here I was, pregnant, standing on the brink of a future I had never dared to dream of. A single lottery ticket had rerouted the course of my life, transforming me from a woman ensnared by her past into someone empowered by love and burgeoning with possibilities.

As Michael and I stood together, surrounded by the warm glow of our wedding, I couldn't help but marvel at the journey that had led us here. Every challenge, every fear, and every triumph had been a step toward this moment of utter contentment and joy. The future stretched out before us, a blank canvas teeming with potential, waiting for us to fill it with our dreams and adventures.

In Michael's gaze, I saw not just the man I loved but a promise of endless possibilities — a life of shared happiness, challenges met hand in hand, and love that would grow and evolve with us. The realization that all of this sprung from a moment of luck, a single lottery ticket, was both humbling and exhilarating. As I leaned into Michael, feeling the life we had created together stir within me, I knew that no matter what the future held, we would face it together, our love a beacon guiding us through the unknown.

This was not just the start of a new chapter; it was the beginning of a new book entirely, one where every page was ours to write, filled with the love and the life we would build together.

To be continued...